UNSER KAMPF

UNSER KAMPF

OUR STRUGGLE

STEPHEN W. ADAMS

UNSER KAMPF
OUR STRUGGLE

iUniverse books may be ordered through booksellers or by contacting:

iUniverse
1663 Liberty Drive
Bloomington, IN 47403
www.iuniverse.com
844-349-9409

ISBN: 978-1-6632-3281-6 (sc)
ISBN: 978-1-6632-3282-3 (e)

Library of Congress Control Number: 2021924540

Print information available on the last page.

iUniverse rev. date: 12/03/2021

An Invitation to the Reader

Dear Reader,

My name is Fritz.

It has not been easy for any of us living in Germany during and after World War I. Now, in 1925, it takes extra courage for those of who, at our young age, are trying to make a place for ourselves in the world to deal with all the uncertainty and dangers of being in a nation that needs a strong leader.

One of us will act as narrator when needed. We want you to feel like you are a friend here with us who is involved in every part of our story, so you can ask yourself if your environment in the 2020s is so different from ours in the 1920s as we tell you of our struggle—or *unser kampf.*

We want to help you have all the hope and courage you need to recognize what is going on around you, so you can work with each challenge you have in your life. Know that *you are not alone—ever!*

It is simple enough that anybody can do it, but it is not easy!

We welcome you into our lives, our world, and unser kampf.

Trina, Sigi, Val, and Fritz

Internet Searches

As you read, you will find words and names that you may not be familiar with. Here is a list of suggested internet searches. Each one will lead you to more information on the historical event or item you are reading about.

1. Freicorp
2. Sturm Arbteilung
3. Brownshirts
4. Victoria Motorcycles Germany 1901
5. Hitler timeline
6. Treaty of Versailles
7. Hitler's bankers
8. German industrialists supporting Hitler
9. Heinrich Bruning
10. Paul von Hindenburg
11. Reichsmark
12. The beer hall putsch of 1923
13. Germany and its approaches map 1938
14. Fractional reserve banking

CHAPTER 1

"Hello!" Fritz quickly took a step back as a pretty little girl, maybe seventeen years old, ducked a little as she hurried under his arm through the doorway he had just opened to the recreation room. He was still leaning forward, holding the door—now with a pleasantly surprised look on his face, watching her.

"Hi," she said, looking back at him with a smile. Her brown hair, with its dancing red highlights, looked almost electric in its shining as it flowed down to her shoulders and against her blue dress.

She turned away just as quickly, and with her arms full of attendance rolls, went on about her business with great intent.

She must have been ready to open it herself, from the other side, he thought, following her with his eyes until she disappeared around the corner and down the hallway. *She is young but pretty. Four years younger than me is not too many. I will have to watch for her next time I am here.*

The solid wood door Fritz was holding open matched the other doors and highlights of wood in the hallways and other rooms of the new building. This church is one of the finest in Neidenberg, in southern East Prussia, and a great accomplishment for the members of its congregation. With the Great War ending just six years earlier, it had taken a great deal of sacrifice and work, during times of less than plenty, to complete such a major project. It helped to bring peace and stability to the people in the area. It was mainly used to learn about Christ on Sunday but also to teach children and to unify the congregation through activities on other days—like today, Wednesday.

The church is located on the east side of Neidenberg on the highway going east to Willenberg. Neidenberg is a town of approximately thirty thousand people. With all the traffic passing through on the highways and the railroad, plus the residents, there are better opportunities for trade and work here than can be found in the more rural surrounding areas.

Fritz looked into the recreation room but did not see Val—only the children of the Lutheran congregation and their teachers. All were playing a game that the children were having fun with. He closed the door and continued through the chapel to the other side of the building where more class-sized rooms were. *Maybe he is in one of those,* he thought.

Val loved to donate some of his time to the church during the week, to help keep the building clean.

"Hey, Fritz, what are you doing here?" Val asked, closing a classroom door.

"I came to see if you want to take a ride to Willenberg and back. When will you be through here?"

"I just finished." Val picked up the dustpan and broom. "Help me put this stuff away, and we can go." Fritz picked up the dust cloth and can of trash, and they started for the storage closet.

As they walked out into the beautiful, clear June day, Fritz said, "What a great day for a motorcycle ride. Were you able to clear away the problems caused by the bad gas you got a few days ago?"

"I think so." Val reached for his dust mask and goggles that were hanging on his handlebars. "This ride should let me know."

Val is not quite the mechanic that Fritz is, but together they are able to keep their motorcycles in good running condition.

The years since the Great War were hard years for Germany. The Treaty of Versailles and the war-reparations debt choked the economy so much that many people faced starvation. In these first few postwar years, the government was so ineffective and unemployment was so high that discouraged veterans and others were often drunk and disorderly and became a real threat to the peace and safety of everyone in Germany.

With a recently stabilized currency and the hard work of a few dedicated politicians, the resilient people soon regained confidence in the economy. There was more work, the outlook for the future was brighter, and most of the people were more at ease.

During these years of recovery, Fritz, twenty-one, and Val, nineteen, were working at their apprenticeships in careers that would support their future families. Fritz, an engraver of stones, mostly tombstones, is six months from finishing his, and Val has one year to go. Val works for the supplier of the stones for Neidenberg Memorial Stone, where Fritz works.

Nearing his physical prime, Fritz is six feet two and weighed two hundred twenty-five pounds. He has brown hair, blue eyes, large hands, and a body made straight and strong from working on his family's farm and in his chosen profession with stone.

Val is six feet tall and 198 pounds, with brown hair and brown eyes. He is straight and strong and had a fun-loving look and way about him that makes him easy to get to know.

They have been friends for three years but live on opposite sides of Neidenberg. Still living at home, they were each able to save enough money to buy their used motorcycles.

"I still think we could make a fortune from our dust mask idea," Fritz said, pulling his on. "Aren't you glad I thought of it?"

"What do you mean you thought of it? It was my idea!" Val said.

"But whose sweater did we use?"

"It was your sweater, but it was my knife."

They had nearly this same conversation many times before. They both seemed to enjoy it, because it reminded them of their friendship, which grew just a little stronger each time. Both know that is the real reason for it. They smiled at each other and sometimes shook their heads, always amused by it.

The masks were made from a six-inch section of sleeve cut from an old knit sweater, pulled up over their noses and mouths to block the dust and keep the bugs from stinging their faces. The black zigzag pattern, which made a band around the arm on the white sweater, now made them look like they each had a row of big black teeth all the way around their heads when the masks were on. With goggles to protect their eyes and their soft hats on backward to help them stay on in the wind, they were ready to go.

"There's got to be a way to make some money from this," Fritz said as he adjusted his goggles.

Val started his motorcycle first.

"It sounds good," Fritz said. "Let's see if you can keep up." With a quick kick on the starter, his motor came to life.

It was good to feel the power of the engine pulling on their hands and arms as the speed quickly picked up. First gear is strongest, and there is always the urge to try just a little more power. If the front wheel came off the ground from too much power when they were not ready for it, they could be in big trouble. The bikes were not made for that kind of treatment. They last much longer if they are rolled and not flown.

Val's engine performed well on the quick trip to Neidenberg. It took eighteen minutes. That was just over sixty kilometers per hour. With the turns, plus watching for potholes and sometimes a rock or branch in the road, that was quick time, almost a record.

These demands on their attention did not leave much time for talking. Both bikes showed a few things that needed work but nothing serious or expensive.

The ride back was at a much easier pace. They talked about the repairs to be done and decided to work on the bikes at their own homes rather than working together as they had done so many times in the past. Talking was easier with the dust masks down under their chins, but they still had their goggles on. Talk turned to some of their hunting trips together and nights spent sleeping in the forest. They both loved living in this place, around people who were so friendly they almost seemed like family.

They were now nearing the church.

"I know there are things going on in the world that I do not understand, and there are people who are not happy in our country," said Fritz, sounding serious. "I just hope that …

Wow! Who are the two girls walking back there? I saw one of them at the church earlier."

"They go to our church and live on the road that goes to the right just ahead of them. Hey, be careful. I don't think they would want you to fall off your bike for them!" Val chuckled at Fritz getting wobbly trying to look back at the girls. Even with Fritz being a good rider, it was more dangerous because they were on a curve in the road. "Come on, eyes back on the road ahead and finish what you were saying about the unhappy people in our country."

"Right, I just hope now that things have been getting better over the last few years, our country can keep building on the economic recovery that has begun. There are many people who are happy that the stress and distraction of war are now gone and who want to settle back into normal family life. You and I are fortunate to have jobs that we can build a future on."

"I have thought about that, too, but I am not sure I want to drive a stone-delivery truck for the rest of my li—"

Val stopped talking when three men in brown shirts, riding in an open-top car that was not from around here, passed in the same direction as the girls. As Val and Fritz looked at each other, they knew they had to turn around and watch the car until it was past the girls and out of sight.

What are we doing? This could be dangerous, thought Val, sure that Fritz was thinking the same thing.

Without saying another word, they rode slowly back until they were part-way around the curve. As soon as they could see the car and the girls again, they stopped on the side of the road, took their goggles off, and pulled their masks down. The car was slowing, and when it came to the girls, it began driving beside them, slowly enough so they could talk. The two men who were passengers were leaning over their rolled-down windows, trying to talk to the girls.

"Maybe they know the men," Val said, hoping for the best.

Fritz and Val could see that the girls seemed to be getting more uneasy with each step they took. They kept getting closer together to provide some comfort and security until their shoulders were touching as they walked. Suddenly, after a quick look at each other, they ran into the woods as fast as they could. Like hunting predators responding to the challenge of escaping prey they had been taunting, the men quickly pulled off the road, jumped out of the car, and ran after them.

"Go! Go! We go now!" Fritz shouted. "Put your mask up! Come on! Now!" And his motorcycle blasted off toward the car.

Val had known something was going to happen but was not sure what. Now that it was happening and Fritz was shouting, his tailpipe roaring right in Val's face, Val had a little trouble getting his bike under him and his mask up at the same time. Soon, he was off like a two-wheeled rocket.

5

Val watched as his friend up ahead neared the place where the girls and men had gone into the woods. He could see smoke from Fritz's back tire as it skidded off the edge of the highway pavement, then the dust from the dirt it stirred up as its skidding plowed through. Fritz jumped off in a run, with the bike still rolling. It came to a stop at the edge of the woods and dropped on its side at about the same time he disappeared into the tree line.

Just as Fritz was disappearing, Val stopped his bike near the car. The adrenaline pumping through his body made his fingers tingle and his ears ring. As he ran by the car, he saw a pistol and a rifle on the back seat. He stopped only long enough to grab the pistol and throw the rifle into the woods. By now, Val was talking to himself through clenched teeth from the stress. He was moving quickly, nodding his head up and down to emphasize his level-headed earnestness as he tried to convince himself to control the effect of the adrenaline. As he ran into the woods at the same point as Fritz, he checked to make sure the pistol was loaded and ready to fire.

Two of the men had caught the girls in a small clearing and were roughly taking them along the path that led deeper into the woods, while the third followed. All three men had a menacing laugh and used rough talk as they walked.

When Fritz came running into view in the clearing, the men did not react, likely unconcerned about one man. Fritz picked up speed and yelling as loudly as he could and growling like a bear on the attack as he ran right at them. They were so surprised by this noisy, wildman with a mask that they stopped in their tracks and watched. Their mouths and eyes continued to widen for the few seconds it took Fritz to get to them. He did not have a plan of attack but was acting on instinct. Running at nearly full speed, he hit the third man in the middle of his chest with all the power he could put into his large, working man's right hand. The man flew about four feet and was out cold when he landed, barely missing the second man, who jumped aside, released the girl he was holding, and raised his hands to defend himself.

The girls screamed. The one who had been in the second man's grip moved quickly away while he was stunned. The one the first man was holding intensified her struggle to get free. It took all his focus to keep his hold on her.

Fritz began to spin around from his initial impact with the third man, nearly losing his balance. But he is a natural athlete and solved two problems with one action. As his left leg swung around to catch his weight, he took out the second man, kicking him square in the ribs. The kick sent the man to the ground with broken ribs and caused the second girl to give a small scream and cover her mouth to stifle it.

By this time, the attitude of the first man had changed—not so smug as before. In fact, he was so surprised that he could not move—that is, until Fritz, having sufficiently regained his balance and momentum, put all his strength behind his left hand as it collided with the man's face, right next to his nose. This blow knocked him out before he hit the ground, leaving the first girl free.

Only three seconds behind Fritz, Val missed all of it except the state of shock everyone was in when he appeared.

As soon as the girls realized they were free, they started running again. Energized by terror, they went deeper into the woods. They knew where they were even if the others did not. In a few seconds, they were near enough to their home that their excited voices brought the family dog out to investigate.

"Ahlf! Oh, Ahlf!" The girls greeted the shepherd at the same time, sinking to their knees with their arms around his neck, with a great feeling of relief. With Ahlf close by, they felt safe enough to catch their breath.

He was soon loose from their hugging and began running around them in his alert excitement, barking and running from one to the other, licking their faces and still barking as if to say, "Wow, what just happened? Something exciting I'll bet. What was it? If it is a game, I want to play too." They patted him to settle him down, feeling sure the men would not come any closer to a big dog that excited.

After catching her breath, the second girl asked, "Who were those men who chased us?"

"I've never seen them before ... or the two men with masks who saved us!" said the first girl. "I had no idea there are such men living around here. I think we should not tell anyone about what happened until we understand things better. What do you think?"

"OK.

As the girls disappeared into the woods, Val got to the downed men. He stopped and squatted in front of the one sitting on the ground holding his ribs, pointed the gun in his face, and said in a purposely deepened voice, "Tell your friends, when they wake up, that if you ever come around here bothering our children again, it could be even more dangerous for you than this. We all may have been heroes while fighting in the Great War, but actions like this make you an enemy around here!"

It occurred to Val that with their masks up and their caps on, the men could see only their eyes, which meant the men would not be able to identify them. He then realized that was probably what Fritz had been thinking from the beginning. Saying "our children" and "being heroes together," along with the power and aggressiveness of Fritz, Val intended to have them think they had been attacked by older men and fellow veterans.

With the girls safely away in the direction of their nearby home, it was a good time to leave. Watching for a possible surprise from the three men, Val held on to the back of Fritz's shirt and walked backward toward the road, with the gun raised, until they were out of sight. Then they hurried out of the woods to where the motorcycles waited.

"Watch the path for a few seconds," Val whispered to an exhausted and shaken Fritz. Quickly he checked the car and found two more pistols in a box, with more ammunition for all the pistols and the rifle he had already taken. They hid the ammo and firearms under some branches and leaves just inside the woods, then went to their motorcycles.

Nothing was said while they picked up their bikes and quickly checked them out. With a finger to his lips, Fritz signaled for his friend to be quiet and started pushing his down the highway. Val did the same. Their pumping adrenaline made the job easy. They ran, soon rounding the curve, and stopped to catch their breath. Only then did they pull their masks down. Fritz realized he was still shaking from the experience. He showed his hand to Val. Val held his hand out, and they saw it shaking too. They looked at each other and saw each other's eyes so wide they were mostly white. Whether from wonder or fright, the look they saw on the other's face made them realize the danger they had just encountered.

"This is the first time I have acted so aggressively toward anyone before!" Fritz admitted breathlessly. "I respect our veterans, but this time

I think they are wrong." Fritz's voice grew stronger, though he was still shaking.

They started up the motorcycles as quietly as possible and continued toward Neidenberg, hoping the men in the woods would not connect the sound of motorcycles with the two masked men.

After riding quietly for a for about three minutes, Fritz took a deep breath and said, "Now you can tell me more about those girls. What is the name of the one in blue?"

Her name is Siglinde," Val said, "but we call her Sigi. She lives about four hundred meters through the woods … in the direction they were running. The other girl is her sister, Trina. On the little farm their family has, there are some chickens, a cow, and a pig. They grow a nice garden, plus corn and hay for their own use and for trade. If you want to know more, you will have to come to some of our church meetings or activities and ask her yourself." He showed his funnyman smile.

There was no more talking as they rode to Val's house. Each knew that the other was trying to collect his thoughts and calm his nerves and maybe think of what they should do next.

After stopping in front of Val's house, Fritz said, "We will not tell anyone about the incident with the three men today. We should not even talk about it ourselves, because someone might overhear us. It is possible that someone might come looking for us, seeking revenge … even years into the future."

"We need to go back in a couple of days and move those guns to a better place," Val suggested.

I will come over on Saturday, and we can hide these too." Fritz pulled off his mask and handed it to Val. "The girls did not see our faces and may not know who was behind the masks. The best way to protect them and us is to keep everything a secret. Will you shake on this?"

"I think it is a good idea." Val put out his hand.

Chapter 2

Fritz was proud to work at the biggest and oldest producer of grave-marking memorial stones in East Prussia in 1925. He has already become one of Neidenberg Memorial Stone's finest engravers during his three and a half years of apprenticeship. In another six months, he can look forward to a change in responsibilities, an increase in pay, and added respect—possibly even envy—from his friends and coworkers. He has also been noticed by and become friendly with Eldrick Kemp, current owner since his father's retirement two years ago.

The business was started in 1882 by Eldrick's father, who soon brought his teen-age son into it and began teaching him. Together, they grew it steadily until the war. When he returned from the army, Eldrick helped his father bring it to the success they were now seeing. The building is fifty meters long and thirty meters wide. The warehouse/shop section has three engraving stations and a storage area for keeping stones that were waiting to be worked.

Jochem, a thirty-one-year-old Jew with nine years' experience, has the carving station nearest the front. Urs, Herr Kemp's second son, sixteen years old and in his first year of apprenticeship, has the job of keeping the warehouse clean and the machinery lubricated. His carving station is also near the front, where he is near the journeyman Jochem, who has the main responsibility of teaching him. Urs is a strong young man and learns quickly.

Fritz's station is nearer the loading dock, where he can receive deliveries and manage their storage. A reception and showroom area and Herr Kemp's office are in the front section of the building. Erna has been secretary, receptionist, and bookkeeper for four years. Just over a year ago,

Herr Kemp's oldest son, Bernhard, and his wife opened a second store in Koenigsberg, about eighty kilometers to the north. Bernhard is good at this work but seems to be looking for something better.

Herr Kemp was an *oberstleutnant* (lieutenant-colonel) in the Great War. He is now nearly fifty-five years old and walks with a limp. He is one of those who now think that the politicians had failed the military and the German people in how they conducted the war and ended it with the Treaty of Versailles. Along with most of his fellow officers, he thinks there needs to be a change in the government, but none of them had a good idea for a solution. While looking for someone he could support politically, he is keeping current with political and military news through newspapers and his army friends. Fritz thinks of him as one of his best sources of political information and current events.

"We should be getting some stones delivered today."

Fritz turned around to see Herr Kemp coming and turned off his engraving machine so they could talk.

"I hope Val is the driver," Fritz said. "I have not seen him recently. I want to talk to him about visiting the Lutheran church where he goes. I saw a girl there a few weeks ago that I would like to know more about."

"I'm glad to hear that. You are going to be twenty-two in a couple of months, and you should be finding a nice girl soon." He is wearing his big fatherly smile. "You are a good worker and a fine young man, and I think you will do well with a family."

"Whoa, wait a minute." Fritz raised his hand like he was trying to stop a runaway horse. "You are talking like you would have me married by the middle of next week. I have not even talked to her, except to say hello."

"Maybe not, but in the past few years, I have come to have full confidence in you." Herr Kemp was still wearing the big smile and patted Fritz on the shoulder. "When you finish your apprenticeship in five or six months, you should be able to get a small place and start your own life. I, for one, would like to see you happy."

"Thank you, Herr Kemp. I think having a good family is important for the happiness of everyone in it. I will do my best to make mine that way. I think it is the best way to build a strong community ... and even a nation."

"Those are big thoughts for a young man, but not too big for someone who is ready to start his own family and become part of the world around him. I have come to know something of your family and have a lot of respect for them. Your parents are good people and have done a good job raising their children."

"Papa reads to us from the Bible at night and has taught us to believe in Jesus. By what he says and how he lives, we know that he does. His example to his family makes it easier for us to understand Christ's teachings. Last night, Papa was reading from the seventh chapter of Matthew, where it says, 'If ye then, being evil, know how to give good gifts to your children, how much more shall your Father which is in heaven give good things to them that ask Him?' This shows that God is not an indescribable thing but is a *Him*, who can be talked to whenever we need something or just feel alone. I am trying to memorize that verse because learning amazing things like that are exciting to me! Papa said that Martin Luther believed in Jesus too but had little patience with some people, like the Jews, who seemed to refuse to believe. I think that everyone would want to believe."

"Well, Fritz, maybe people like your father and you can continue to help others to believe by the way you live. I think the world needs more good people to learn from.

"Here comes another fine young man." Herr Kemp motioned to the truck backing up to the loading dock. "Val has never worked for me, but Konstantin Deforest, who is his boss, talks about him in a positive way. Hi. Have you been busy today, Val?" Herr Kemp is always interested in the activity of others in the monument business around his area.

"Hello, Herr Kemp. Not many deliveries today, but we have enough stones to prepare and polish to keep us busy for about two weeks," Val said, getting out of the truck. He closed its door and walked back to the ladder that went up to the loading dock. "Some of them will be coming here in a few days. Business is up right now in the area we service."

"Good. I am glad the other guys are doing OK too. It is good that you came. Your friend here has something he wants to talk to you about." Herr Kemp was pointing a thumb back over his shoulder at Fritz as he started toward his office. "It is something important!"

Val looked worried. "What did he mean? Has he heard any—?"

"No, no," Fritz interrupted. "We were talking about Jesus and families, but it all started when I told him I wanted to ask you how I can meet the girl in blue … *Sigi*. From there, *Papa Kemp* got excited and started sounding like he would have me married next week!"

Val grinned, chuckling. "Married! Wow, you have not even been on many dates, have you?"

They carefully picked up the first stone from the truck and started into the building.

"Go ahead, laugh. If I had been trying to keep up with you, things would be different, I know. I have not met anyone I could get interested in."

They put the stone in the storage area and went back to the truck to get the other. Fritz punched Val in the shoulder to punctuate his intention. "I want to have a good family, and that takes the right girl."

"I know what you mean, Fritz, but how do you know which one is the right one? My mother told me that you should start by finding someone who likes you. She also said you still do not get to know each other well for four years or more *after* you are married. Then you can believe that you made the right choice!"

The second stone was much bigger and heavier, and they had to pay more attention to carrying it the five meters to its storage place. There was not much time for talking.

Once they placed the stone, Fritz said, "I think the place to start is with a girl who wants the same kind of family that I do." He was speaking in the quiet, matter-of-fact tone he used whenever he was saying something he wanted people to listen to. "I think there is another way to know, and I think it is from God. When I have a tough decision to make, I pray for guidance. If I feel confusion or unsure, then I know it is wrong. If I feel peaceful and confident, and my mind is clear, then I know it is right. This has worked many times for me, but I am still learning to read my feelings without trying to follow my own wants too much. I believe God loves us and wants to help us with everything we do in our life, and this is how He talks to us. That is why nobody should feel he is alone. It may sound simple, but it is not always easy. With practice, it gets easier.

"In a country functioning as poorly as ours has over the last ten or fifteen years, it is comforting to know that God is always there for us when we need more personal peace. All men have the right to make their own choices if they do not interfere too much with His purposes. He is always in control."

"I like that idea," Val agreed. "This world will not last if it is dependent on man's poor wisdom."

As they walked back to the truck, Fritz's hand was on Val's shoulder, who was walking slightly bent over, with a stressed look on his face and his arms hanging straight at his sides.

"What are you doing?" asked Fritz.

"My arms feel like they have been stretched," said Val, looking very much like a gorilla.

Urs and Jochem were watching them, smiling and shaking their heads. Fritz could not help but laugh himself.

"If you want to meet this girl," said Val, returning to the lighter subject, "you should come to the church this Saturday night. At six, we are having a potluck dinner and a movie! My family is planning to be there, and friends are invited! Ooh-ooooh-ooh," Val painfully moaned, returning to his gorilla posture and lumbering into his truck.

"I'll see you there," Fritz said, shaking his head at his younger, funnyman buddy.

When Fritz got to the church, Val and his family were already there. The large recreation room was still being transformed into a buffet dining hall. Three serving tables along one side were magically growing more food as people came in. There were enough tables with chairs to seat one hundred fifty people.

Frau Adlar brought a casserole and some brownies and was busy organizing the food on the serving tables. Val and his dad were helping set up the last of the tables and chairs. Younger children were running around playing or helping to set the tables. In the years they have known each other, Fritz has visited there, but not enough to know anybody well. Tonight, he was in time to help with the chairs. Val introduced him to some of the people, who seemed happy to meet him and make him feel welcome.

The children were excited about the movie and especially the cartoons they would see tonight after dinner.

"I do not see Sigi here," said Fritz, looking a little worried. "I had such a quick look at her that I might not recognize her if she is not in that same blue dress that I saw her in then."

"Don't worry, good buddy. I am sure she will be here. Her family always comes to activities like this." Val patted his friend on the shoulder like he was reassuring an impatient child.

Fritz responded with a quick shrug, too busy looking for Sigi to do more. After five more minutes, he nudged Val. "Is that her who just came in with some other people, probably her family?"

"You are a little nervous, aren't you?" Val looked at his friend with an amused smile, assuring him that it is her. He immediately started toward her.

Fritz put his hand on Val's arm and said, "Wait. Let me watch her for ten more minutes so I feel that I know her a little."

"OK, Romeo, whatever you like. She is not going anywhere for a while."

Sigi has on a yellow and a white dress outfit that she probably made, which makes her look like a little girl.

"Do you know how old she is?" Fritz had a worried look on his face.

"I think she is about seventeen, but I can ask Mom. She has known Sigi since she was a kid." Val went to find his mother.

Fritz continued to watch, trying not to look like he was staring, hoping all the time to convince himself that she was eighteen rather than the fifteen that she looked now. Her long brown hair with the red highlights added a deeper, more mature tone to her appearance. The warm smile and pretty face, along with her confident manner, gave additional hope. She appeared to be liked by all the other girls and was even comfortable talking to the older ladies.

Val was back and happy to report, "Mom told me she is nearer nineteen than seventeen."

A feeling of relief and a look of hope came over Fritz. "Thank you! You have been a great help. I'm sure I can take it from here."

All the preparations were done by six, and a few minutes later, one of the men got everybody's attention and welcomed them all. After thanking those who brought food and helped in other ways, he invited another man to ask a blessing on the food. When the prayer ended, the kids all knew it was time to eat, and those who could help themselves headed for the serving tables.

Fritz was sitting with Val and his family. His mom and dad took the two littlest of their children to get their plates filled. Val's six-year-old brother, Kyler, wanted Fritz to go with him. Over the many times Fritz had been to Val's home, Kyler took a special liking to him, and they have become good buddies. By the time Fritz and Kyler got to the tables, Sigi was there with her six-year-old brother, Warin.

"Hi, my name is Fritz, and you probably know Kyler here."

"Warin!" Kyler grabbed two handfuls of Warin's shirt in an excited greeting as they started chattering and playing.

"I am here with my friend Val, which is how Kyler and I got to be buddies," Fritz explained.

"I am Siglinde, but everybody calls me Sigi."

All four of them started filling their plates.

"Fritz is short for Friedrich. I live on the northeast side of town. I got to know Val at work."

"Have I seen you before?"

"Yes. We sort of met a few weeks ago … at that door over there. I was looking for Val and happened to open the door in time for you to come scooting through with your arms full of attendance rolls. I am sure I helped you avoid an accident by getting the door out of your way in time."

"I remember that," Sigi said, nodding.

Her pretty smile seemed warm to Fritz, making him feel welcomed by her.

She continued, "I was hurrying to get home to some other things I had to do. I did not get everything done that I had planned that day.

"It all worked out well enough," she said. She turned away with a solemn look and a slight coolness to pick up some carrots. Fritz understood she was not ready to share that day's distress with anyone, especially someone she did not know.

Kyler and Warin were trying to decide if they wanted macaroni and cheese with ham or roast beef with potatoes and gravy. They had already decided that best friends should eat the same food, which was why everything else on their plates matched.

"Why not take a little of both?" suggested Sigi.

The boys liked Warin's big sister's idea.

"Can I go eat with Warin?" Kyler looked up at Fritz hopefully.

"Do you think that would be OK, Sigi?" Fritz asked.

"Yes, there is plenty of room. You can come too if you like."

"I'd like that, but I came with Val and his family, and I should eat with them; besides, Kyler needs to ask his mom. When I pick up my dessert, I can come over and check on Kyler and sit with you then. How would that be?"

Kyler was already heading for his mom.

"That would be nice."

The boys were happy with Mom's answer and were soon heading for Warin's family. With a good-bye smile for Fritz, Sigi was too.

"How did it go?" asked Val as Fritz sat down.

"She is very nice."

"I already knew that!" Val said, impatiently shaking him by the shoulder. "How did *you* do?"

"Sitting with her family is Kyler's idea, but she invited me to come too. I told her I would come over to check on Kyler when I get my dessert, and I could sit with her then. You sound like you have less confidence in me than Herr Kemp does."

"Wow, that is great! Do you think it's time for dessert?" Val did not try to hide his excitement as he talked through a tight grin, showing clenched teeth with big, impatient eyes.

"You are more excited than I am! Calm down. Go get your food. I just sat down with my food, and I plan to eat it." Fritz began cutting his roast beef. "There will be plenty of time to talk to her tonight."

"I am excited *for you!* And I hope there is!" Val stood up. "I am just rooting for you, that's all." He left to get his food.

"You have him stirred up. What is it all about?" inquired Herr Adlar, amused by his son's intensity.

"A few days ago, I told Val I would like to meet Sigi, and he suggested I come here with you tonight. Like my boss, Herr Kemp, he is sounding like he would have me married in two weeks or so."

"She is a fine girl," said Frau Adlar, smiling as she began to understand what she had seen in the actions of Val and Fritz. "It just seems to make people happy to see two good young people get together."

"See what I mean? Everybody is talking like there should be a marriage soon! Before talking to her tonight, I had only seen her long enough to say hi. That does not mean I am ready to spend my life with her," Fritz teased, with a smile of understanding. "It is helpful to hear good things from people who know her. It will take time to learn what her values are and her attitude toward families. I can be patient."

Fritz had not eaten much of his dinner when Val returned with a plate of food.

"You still here? No dessert yet? Sometimes I think I should worry about you," said Val, sitting down with his dinner. "That's OK. As long as I am here for you, you need not fear." Again, Val gently patted Fritz's shoulder like a patient parent comforting a lovesick son.

The two six-year-olds soon finished their dinners and were heading for the dessert table. Sigi assigned herself the job of chaperoning them. She hurried to get to them before they caused any problems.

They did not know if they should take the apple pie or the cherry cobbler. How could they decide until they tasted them both, they reasoned? Sigi was just in time to stop two forks from landing in the cobbler.

"That is not the way to do this. You must choose *before* you taste. You should take some apple pie, Kyler, and you should take some cobbler, Warin, and when you get back to the table, you can share with each other."

Fritz's attention had been drawn by the two boys heading for the dessert table. When he saw them having trouble trying to decide, he got up to see if he could help. Seeing Sigi on her way, he slowed a little and got there in time to hear her advice to them. The boys agreed with her and were soon on their way back to their table.

"Another good idea from big sister, it looks like." Fritz's smile was one of approval and respect. "I think it is time for dessert." He looked over the brownies and picked one. "Have you had any of these? Can I get you something?"

"I was just finishing my dinner, but I can take a piece of pie back with me. Are you coming over to our table now?"

She has such a pretty smile, he thought as he saw another one.

"If the invitation is still open, I would like to." Fritz smiled, pointing to a piece of pie. "How about this one?"

"That one looks good. Of course it is open. Come on." She took her pie from him and motioned for him to follow.

"Mom, Dad, this is Fritz, a friend of Val Adlar. I met him at the food table when he brought Kyler to get his food and I had Warin."

"Hello, Fritz," said Sigi's father. "I am Leon Backman, and this is my wife, Elke. You have met Sigi; this is Trina, fifteen, nearly sixteen; and Klaus, eleven. You know Warin, six, and little Lora is two. Will you join us?"

"Thank you, sir, I would like to. My name is Fritz Abbot, and I am a good buddy of Kyler's."

Kyler got a big smile and acted a little embarrassed. Everybody else laughed.

"So, you are here with Val and his family. How do you know them? Are you related?"

"No, sir, we are not related. I met Val three and a half years ago at work. The company he works for delivers stone to Neidenberg Memorial Stone, where I work as an apprentice engraver. My apprenticeship will be finished in five months. Val is usually the driver for our supplier of stones, and very often, we unload them together."

"We have known Val's family almost ten years; they are good people. Do you live around here? Are we going to see you at church on Sunday? Did you just come for the food?" Herr Backman had a fun-loving smile on his face.

"I live northwest of town with my parents and family. I might come to church on Sunday. The food is very good!" Fritz smiled. "But the real reason I am here tonight is to meet Sigi."

Sigi suddenly had a surprised look on her face and was a little embarrassed. But her mother was smiling, and her dad now had a look of new understanding. Trina put her hand to her mouth to cover a smiley-faced, "Oh."

"You thought it was an accident, right?" Fritz smiled at her. "About three weeks ago, I came here looking for Val and was almost run over by a girl in a hurry as I opened that door over there. I thought my first impression was worth following up on, and I wanted to learn more about her. Val suggested I come here tonight. I did not come here to embarrass or worry anybody. Those are the best answers to your questions, sir."

Herr Backman was almost laughing. "I didn't mean to fire so many questions at you, but you have answered them well."

Kyler and Warin finished their desserts and were getting fidgety. Frau Backman told them, "You two can go and play, but come back here when the cartoons start." Kyler looked at Fritz, who nodded, and the boys were off to find more of their friends.

"Maybe after the cartoons, some of the children will be asleep and a little quieter for the movie," Trina said. She had to quickly move her arm from the back of her chair when two little girls ran by.

Some people were starting to pick up dishes and other things on the tables to get ready for the cartoons. The children began to pick their spots to sit on the floor in front of the screen. Fritz helped Herr Backman and Sigi take dishes to the kitchen for washing, while Trina took some things to the trash.

"The cartoons were fun! The kids enjoyed them, and so did I," Fritz said with a childlike wonder on his face and in his voice.

Sigi's warm smile shined again upon this young man who was willing to have some fun at his own expense.

The movie was not on long before something went wrong. Nearly half an hour was spent trying to fix it while people visited with one another. Fritz spent the time getting to know Sigi and her family.

One of the congregation leaders suggested that everybody sing some songs. The children started things off by singing some songs they had learned in Sunday school. When they sang some activity songs, some of the adults recognized them and joined in the fun too. When they started singing popular songs of the day, it was not long before people of all ages were dancing to the ones they liked and having a good time. Fritz started to become uneasy; he did not think of himself as a good dancer. Sure enough, when one of Sigi's favorite polka songs began to be sung, her face lit up, and she wanted to dance. She pulled him by the hand to get him to stand up.

"Oh no," Fritz said as he looked around at the dancers, then into her face and saw her delight. She was hopping around in front of him in an imitation polka step, holding onto his shirt, trying to get him to dance.

"Come on, Fritz—look how much fun it is!"

It doesn't look very hard, he thought, then took a deep breath and relented. "OK, let's try it."

Off they went, slowly at first, while he made sure his feet knew what to do. While concentrating on his feet and not running into somebody at the same time, he caught a glimpse of Sigi smiling and giggling and having a lot of fun. He almost tripped over his feet and hers. But she just laughed. They made it around the floor one and a half times before the song ended.

"That was more fun than I thought it would be," he confessed, realizing he was slightly out of breath.

"That was wonderful!" Sigi said, still catching hers. "Let's do it again!"

The next song was a polka too.

Just when Fritz was beginning to relax and have some fun, and believe he could do this, Val went breezing by with Trina, saying, "Hi, guys!" both wearing their smiley, this-is-great-fun faces.

"Showoffs," said Fritz, with an understanding smile to Sigi.

After a few more songs, a decision was made by one of the church leaders to pick up all the tables and chairs and try the movie another time. With everybody working together, the large room was cleaned up very quickly. Fritz made sure he stayed close to Sigi.

When there was a break in activity, he said to her quietly, "This has been fun tonight. Can I see you again?"

She looked right at him and answered warmly, "Yes, I would like that."

"I could pick you up Saturday ... around noon ... for a motorcycle ride and a picnic lunch by the river, if you like?"

She agreed, and they smiled good-bye.

Fritz had not paid much attention to Val since meeting Sigi at the dessert table. When he came to where Val and his family were standing, they were talking to other people. As soon as they noticed him, he started to apologize for being impolite by being away so long, but Frau Adlar stopped him.

"No need to apologize, Fritz. It is fun to watch because we knew what was going on. We are rooting for you. How did it go?"

"I am going to see her again on Saturday, and we will go for a motorcycle ride and picnic along the river. Her family is nice too."

"Great!" Val slapped him on the back. "Glad to hear it."

Chapter 3

At work on Monday, Herr Kemp was interested in how the meeting with the girl had gone on Saturday. "What happened? Did you like what you learned?"

"Yes, she is nice, and her family is friendly. I felt comfortable around them," Fritz said matter-of-factly, almost casually. He was busy with a stone that he and Val had unloaded on his last delivery.

"That bad, huh? Sounds like you are not interested in seeing her again then?"

"I *am* interested. I will see her on Saturday. But we have not started planning the wedding yet … if that is what you're wondering." Fritz smiled and turned off his machine.

Herr Kemp could see he had the young man's attention. He continued, "There are some good men in our government who are working very hard to see this new democratic system work, and their effort is what we are benefiting from now."

"What does this have to do with me, Herr Kemp?" asked Fritz, wondering where this lecture was going.

"There is one fairly new politician named Adolph Hitler, a young man who has caught the attention of a lot of important people in Berlin and Munich. He seems to have the ability to talk to people in any size group and get them excited about what he is saying. His Nazi Party—it is short for National Socialist Party—has also been able to organize thousands of veterans and other discontented men to become *freikorps*—soldiers for hire—for the party's own small army. They originally were organized to keep disruptions down at Nazi party rallies—a security detail—but they have also been used to enforce his demands when needed.

"This man got so bold as to burst into a meeting of businessmen and government leaders in Munich with some of his troops! He declared that a revolution had begun, and a new government would be announced in the morning. He took three of the most senior men in the Bavarian government into a back room and *forcefully persuaded* them to tell the crowd they supported the Nazis in this revolution.

"There was great excitement and support for this man Hitler at the meeting. Here was finally someone who said the things these businessmen wanted to hear. It sounds like this man is going to get Germany's industrial strength of the past working again and get the government organized to manage things well. At that moment, you could say that he had control of Bavaria, our largest state. Like a young lion that had a full-grown wildebeest by the throat, Bavaria was at his mercy. This feat by itself shows far more organizational skill, political sense, and persuasive ability than we have seen in all of Germany since the war! He has impressed the leaders of the army, banking, and industry in such a way that they are beginning to support him for political office!"

"You said 'was *at his mercy*' and he '*had control.*' What went wrong?" asked Fritz, trying to listen between the lines.

"Herr Hitler's mistake that night was to get distracted by another event he had going on that night, just enough to ease his hold and let the prize get away. His revolution lasted only a few hours. The three elected leaders and their government soon arrested him and put him in prison, because of his radical actions. He could have been shot or kept in prison for life, but because some in his party were in control of his trial, he was released in about nine months. Hopefully, that served as a clear message to other troublemakers that if someone as persuasive as Hitler can be put in prison, they could too, and for much longer.

"There is still a lot of squabbling going on in our government. I hope that it all gets settled soon, so we can keep this current growth going. If more good people get involved, we could be a great country again!"

"I know you keep well informed, Herr Kemp, and you sound very sure of what you are saying. I want my family to have a safe future, with opportunities for learning, growth, and freedom!" Fritz said, smiling and feeling encouraged. "Thanks for the hope you give me."

"I do think we are on our way to better times," declared the boss, and with a little wave, he walked over to Jochem's station to see how his project was progressing.

Saturday is so far away, thought Fritz, surprising himself with the thought. He turned his machine on again. He could not remember looking forward to seeing a girl this much before. He really was feeling a little bit nervous. This was unusual. *This time it is different!*

Thursday, Val delivered another stone. This time, Urs was working around the loading dock and helped Val bring in the granite block. A small statue of an angel came with it.

They talked about the new soccer fields that the government was building just north of town. "It will be good to have a nice, flat green lawn to play on," said Val, illustrating with a sweep of his arms.

"No more rocks and gopher holes and weeds, like on the field we have been using," agreed Urs, shaking his head side to side at the bad memory.

"There is also a park being built in Osterode, with soccer fields and a swimming pool. It will be worth the ride to go try it out!" Val comically demonstrated his diving technique.

"I wonder how high the diving board will be," said Urs, looking way up and pointing with a look of awe on his face.

As he listened, Fritz thought, *Maybe Herr Kemp is right; maybe things are getting better!*

Saturday morning, Fritz was up early enough to have plenty of time to take care of his responsibilities around their small farm and do his personal errands. He also spent some time getting his motorcycle ready for the day's ride. Finally, he felt prepared for his part in the plans for the day. The ride over to the Backman home was less than five kilometers and went by quickly. As he rode, he let his thoughts wander. *These are the last days of June. Spring has been mild this year, not too windy or too hot. Today is clear and warm, just right for spending a few hours at the river with someone I like to be around.*

Fritz got there about fifteen minutes before noon. He was greeted by Ahlf, the Backmans' medium-sized German shepherd. Ahlf was more excited than usual by this stranger, probably because he arrived on a noisy motorcycle. Warin came running after him, yelling, "Ahlf, be quiet! Stop barking! It's Fritz! We already knew he was coming today!"

Fritz stopped his engine; he was not too concerned about Ahlf because his tail was wagging. When six-year-old Warin finally caught up to him, his tail stopped wagging. He turned his body in front of Warin to stop him from getting any closer to this stranger and started growling at Fritz. Warin yelled again for Ahlf to be quiet and slapped him on the back.

"Hi, Fritz! Ahlf will not hurt you. Why didn't Kyler come with you?" Ahlf began to settle down when Warin sounded friendly toward the stranger. When he gave one final growl, Warin slapped his back again and said, "Stop, Ahlf," which was enough to start his tail wagging again.

"Sorry, Warin. Maybe I can bring him next time … Ahlf sure seems to like you."

"Ahlf is my friend. His name means Noble Wolf. We play together!"

The barking of Ahlf let the rest of the family know that Fritz was there.

Trina waved from the kitchen window, where she was cleaning some vegetables from the garden. "Hi, Fritz!"

Klaus waved from the barn door, where he was feeding the cow. "Hi, Fritz!"

Sigi came out of the barn with a basket of eggs she had gathered and a pail of milk. "The cow's name is Clothilda."

"Clothilda!" Fritz almost laughed. "That name means *the famous battle maid,* doesn't it?" Fritz was already having a wonderful time. He stood still, cautiously letting Ahlf, now warming up to him, sniff his boots and pant legs. He extended the back of his hand to be sniffed and then petted the protective dog's head.

Sigi laughed too. "And that is why she has that name. It took nearly thirty minutes to get this much milk from her; it should have taken only five." Sigi's patience was worn thin. "She's one of the reasons I'm running a little late with the things I wanted to get done before we go. I still need to get cleaned up and change my clothes."

"I know I am early, so I would like to help you with chores if I can. No need to change—long pants like those you have on are good for riding a motorcycle." He went with her to feed the chickens.

"The chores are done now. I just need to get cleaned up. Would you like to come in?" She opened the door to the house.

"I think I need to get better acquainted with Ahlf here so there will not be so much commotion the next time I come. Warin can show me how."

"OK, I will be out soon," said Sigi as she disappeared into the house.

"Warin, does Ahlf have a toy he likes to play with?"

"Yes, he likes to chase a stick if I throw it."

"Good. Will you show me?"

Out of the corner of his eye, Fritz noticed Trina smiling through the window and Klaus from the barn; both have an increased interest suddenly.

"There's one over here that we've used before. Watch this!" Warin ran and picked up the stick. "Here, Ahlf! Here, Ahlf!" He had Ahlf's full tail-wagging attention. "Go get it!" He threw it as far as he could down the long driveway. Ahlf ran so fast that the stick was still moving when he picked it up.

"Wow, Warin. He's really fast." Ahlf brought the stick back and put it in Warin's hand. "See if you can throw it a little farther this time."

Warin got a look of concentration on his face and threw it again. It went about the same distance, and Ahlf brought it back to Warin.

"That was a good throw. Can I try it?"

Warin handed the stick to Fritz, and Ahlf watched it carefully as Fritz made a practice throwing motion once.

"Here, Ahlf! Go get it." Fritz threw the stick, and Ahlf turned his head to watch it fly down the driveway. The dog saw it land but made no indication he was going to get it. "What's wrong? Why doesn't he get the stick?"

Now Trina had her hand over her mouth. smothering a laugh, and Klaus had a big grin across his face.

Sigi came out carrying a picnic basket, wearing long pants and a bright spring-colored blouse. She had one of those controlled smiles on her face too.

Fritz looked at the stick laying in the driveway, then at Ahlf, who was also looking at it. He looked at Warin, saw the childish innocence staring back at him, and started to ask, "Why won't he g—"

Warin interrupted and pointed at the stick. "Go get it, Ahlf!" Ahlf was off again as fast as any time before. He brought the stick back and put it in Warin's open hand again. "Me and Ahlf play this all the time, and I throw it a lot of times, until sometimes I get tired, and then we quit, but I didn't say he would chase it for you!" Warin, with the stick in his hand and Ahlf right behind him, watching it very closely again, went running around the corner of the house.

"Ahlf won't get the stick for anybody but Warin," Sigi explained, still smiling. "They came into our family at the same time, six years ago. As near as we can tell, they might have been born on the same day. A friend of our family gave us Ahlf a few weeks after Warin was born, and they have been friends ever since. Val tried everything he could think of for almost thirty minutes one day, but nothing worked. After about twenty minutes, we were all laughing so hard at him that we begged him to stop. Now every time somebody new tries, we remember Val and can't help laughing again."

"You have known Val for a long time, haven't you?"

"Yes, nine or ten years. He is like a big brother to me."

"It is hard for me to look at you and understand why any guy would not wonder if he could be more than your big brother."

"That is nice, thank you. It is easy for you to say what you think, isn't it? I like that."

"Life's easier if you try to keep things simple." Fritz smiled back at her and motioned to the motorcycle. "Have you ridden on one of these?"

"Yes, a couple of short rides with Val." She looked at it skeptically.

"The look on your face shows me you probably did not make friends with it." Fritz smiled at her. "Really, it is fun. It might take some getting used to, but I think you will like it. All you have to do is sit back here and hold on around my waist." He swung his leg over, pulled the bike upright, and kicked the starter. The motor started up, and he sat down on the seat.

At the noise of the motor, Sigi stepped back.

"Come on, it's OK." Fritz patted the seat and pointed to the footrest. "Put one foot on this peg and the other foot on the other side. I'll hold the basket."

She came closer with the same look on her face.

"I will hold it steady while you get on." He put the handle of the basket over the handlebars so he could use both hands. New riders usually caused a lot of wobbling when they got on.

She felt awkward as she sat down. He checked her feet to see that they were safe.

"There, now just hold on to me, and we are ready to go. Are you OK?"

"I think so." She sounded uncertain.

He put the basket on his arm and started down the driveway. The place on the river where he planned to stop was only four kilometers away, so there was no need to hurry. After about two kilometers, he could feel her begin to relax. "How are you doing back there? We are halfway there!"

"I'm doing fine; this is kind of fun!" She sounded more relaxed.

Railroad tracks and the road ran side by side along the river through the hills that separated East Prussia from Poland on the south. Being the end of June, this forested area was thick with foliage.

Everything is so green and fresh—just the way God meant it to be. Whoa, I need to see how she thinks before I say something like that. This day could affect my future!

Fritz slowed down as they came to the path that led to the place near the water that he had in mind. When he stopped, Sigi climbed off and reclaimed the basket. She turned to look around while he moved the motorcycle farther off the road.

He came to her, took the basket again, and said, "This way." He looked back, motioned for to her to follow, and started down a lightly used path toward the river, about twenty meters away. When he came to a small clearing next to the river, he turned back toward her and with a sweep of his arm said, "Here we are."

"It is nice here," she said, taking the basket back from him as she walked by and headed for a flatter grassy area by a large rock. "How's this?" she asked, smiling at Fritz and holding the basket like she was ready to put it down.

"This is a good spot." He nodded. "I like it here. The moving river is kind of reassuring to me that things are going along as they should. It is clear … and tastes good and clean. I like how I feel when I am here. I can walk up the hills into the woods and feel the same kind of thing. Let's walk down along the river and look around before we eat, OK?"

"I like it here too," she said. "Even an occasional car going by doesn't change the peacefulness. It was a good idea to wear the pants and the heavier farm shoes for walking through the rocks and the bushes."

Fritz reached back for her hand to help steady her as they walked. She looked down at his hand and hesitated, then without lifting her head, moved her eyes up to see in his face what he might be thinking. *He is not even looking at me!*

He was checking ahead to find the best way over the rocks and between the bushes.

Well, there can't be much of a problem brewing there. She took his hand with an innocent smile when he looked back around. She was glad for the help, feeling bad for thinking wrong of him. *It must be the pants and the shoes!*

A few minutes farther, and he stopped and let go of her hand, then climbed up on a rock and sat facing the river. "Here, this big rock is where Val and I came one day so he could teach me to fish." Fritz pretended to be casting a fishing line into the river. "The pool there, where the water is calm, is where he said he had such great success one day. He was excited to show me his secret place and impress me with all the fish he could catch here. We were probably here for three hours that day, and he did not catch a thing! I felt slightly embarrassed for him. But he just grinned and shrugged his shoulders, and we went home.

"I have come here a lot of times since then, sometimes to be among the trees and other plants when they are green and fresh and growing like today, and sometimes when the leaves are in their autumn colors and ready to fall. I usually end up wondering how it happens. On a summer day, it's nice to come here to listen to the birds and the water."

Looking warmly at Sigi, Fritz jumped off the rock. "It's a long ride just to come here to take a nap, but it's worth it! What do you like to do?" He took her hand again and started back to where the picnic basket is.

"I like the farm we live on," she said. "I like the animals. I get so I think of them as friends. That makes it hard when we must take one of them for food. When you grow older, you understand that is one of the ways God has planned for us to have food. Some people in the world cannot grow food in their ground and have to live by hunting … or trading. I am glad we can grow fruits and vegetables. It's fun to put a seed in the ground and watch it grow into something we can eat."

"You know I'm an engraver, mostly of headstones, right? Have you thought of what kind of work you might like to do if you left the farm?"

They sat down on the grass by the basket.

"I work two days a week at a furniture store in town as a secretary. You might say it is like the apprenticeships you and Val are doing. I make phone calls, write letters, keep financial books, and file important papers. In another year or two, I'll be ready to work full-time for any business in town."

"Do you like doing that kind of work?"

"Yes, I think so. I'm good at it, so it's getting easier, and farm work can be really hard sometimes." Sigi's face exaggerated the hard work.

She unfolded the large cloth that had covered the food and spread it out on the grass. Then she started to lay out the food from the basket on it.

"I know how much work *our* little farm can be at times," Fritz said, nodding his head. "I think the work you do throughout your life should be something you like."

"I like to sew. I make most of my own clothes!" She pulled at her shirt and put on a modeling smile. "Plus, I make some for my brothers and sisters. My mother has made things for other people and been paid for it. Maybe I could do that too."

"Going by the things have seen you wear, I think you could!" Fritz has been watching what she is bringing out of the basket. He realized he is quite hungry. "This food looks really good! It looks like someone in your family likes to cook." He leaned against the big rock with an approving smile.

"Mother started teaching us when we were young. By the time we were nine or ten, Trina and I were able to fix dinner for the family."

The lunch Sigi brought included fried chicken, rolls, and rhubarb pie from dinner the night before, plus fresh carrots from the garden and a bottle of water.

"My family always asks a blessing on the food before we eat. I do when I eat lunch at work too. I would like to now also," Fritz said, looking for understanding and hoping for approval in her face, or surprise or discomfort from something she was not familiar with.

"Yes, of course! Not many people take time for that or even think of it. It is a good habit to get into."

There is that warm, pretty smile again. She passed that test, he thought happily. He finished the prayer and reached for the chicken. "Did you cook this?"

"I cooked the chicken and the rolls; Trina made the pie, and Warin pulled the carrots. It sounds like a family project, but it was not all done today."

"This is good. Thank you for bringing it." *I don't mean to be keeping a scorecard, but she can cook too!* he thought, trying to keep his happiness in check. He was glad she could not hear his thoughts.

"I have never liked eating fish much," he said, "which makes fishing seem like such a waste of time to me. On the other hand, I have spent a lot of time here. I have thrown so many rocks into the water that I probably could have built a small dam and made another small pool like the one I showed you earlier."

Fritz threw another rock into the river and took a bite of a roll. "One rock does not make a difference to the water flow ... like one person usually does not make a difference to the world and the things that happen in it. Why then do I keep thinking that there must be something I can do to improve or help the world to be a better place? What can I do for the world, or our nation, or a few people, or even one person? Many times, I have walked along here, or sat and thrown stones, and wondered what it might be. Have you ever had thoughts like that?"

"Maybe not as much as you have, but I do feel that I have something to contribute to life. It might be in my own little family, but I feel like there is a purpose for me being here in this world. Is that what you mean?" Sigi studied his face for a response.

"Yes, I think it is. What makes us feel like that?" With a drink of water, he finished his chicken and roll and then picked up a carrot.

"Have you ever held a really young child, maybe a newborn, and looked into his face and tried to imagine his future and the kind of person he might be as an adult?" She watched him smile as he nodded in recognition. "How about imagining his past and where he came from? Has he been inside his mommy all these years, holding his breath, waiting for his time to come out? Looking into a baby's eyes, I have seen a real individual—not just a piece of his mother but a real, independent intelligence that must have come from someplace beyond my understanding. I believe that someplace is where God is! There is so much that I do not understand beyond that. But I believe we are supposed to try to understand; otherwise, why were we given the Bible with the things it talks about?"

"I have always liked to hear my dad read from the Bible at night." He smiled at the warm feeling he had during some of those times. "In all the years he has read and studied it, he has come to understand many of the things it talks about. One of the things that he says must be really important is for us to pray, because Jesus did so many times, and even showed us a pattern in the Lord's Prayer. This is how we can ask God to help us in our lives. Many people say they do not need to pray—"

"Like who?" interrupted Sigi.

"I do not know. Like a war-hardened soldier?" answered Fritz, blushing and suddenly unsure. Then he finished his thought. "But when the time comes that death is staring him in the face, he suddenly thinks it might be a good idea! That is a little bit funny to me."

"Why are we talking about these things?" asked Sigi, who could not remember going out with a boy and talking about God. But as soon as she asked it, she realized she was not sure she was ready for the answer yet.

"Because they are important to me, and I want to know what you think," Fritz said, bold and vulnerable at the same time. He pointed across the river, where there were five squirrels on the other bank running around, chasing one another like they were playing tag. "Is there anything that you would like to ask me about?"

Sigi took a breath and decided to take his guilelessness at face value, to meet it with a genuineness of her own. "Not that I planned any questions, but tell me about your family. How many brothers and sisters do you have?"

Fritz quickly finished a piece of the pie that Trina had made, then suggested they walk along the river to help their food settle before they got back on the motorcycle. While helping Sigi put things back in the basket, he began to answer her question. "I have two brothers and two sisters. One sister, Kreszenz, is twenty-four, married, and has one son, almost two years old. They live in Osterode. Her husband's name is Amal Deemer. He's a very good automobile mechanic, and that is the kind of work he does. I am next oldest, then Archie, who is seventeen. Dieter is fourteen, and Hanne is eleven. Hanne has been the princess of our house from the time she was born. Since Kresie got married four years ago, and we boys got interested in different things, Hanne does not get the same attention that she used to. She is taking it well, though, and growing up into her own kind of person. Let's walk in the other direction this time."

They finished with the basket and stood up.

"What about your folks. You do not go to Val's and my church. Are they still ..."

"Oh yes, everyone survived the war, thank God. We all go to some church often, except Dad, who is religious. He just does not think that what he hears from the leaders of the different churches he has visited fits with what he reads in the Bible. I trust his judgment. I believe like he does ... as far as I understand it. We are both looking for more answers from God or one of His teachers. Meanwhile, we live in this world and must deal with it the best way we can. Would you like to meet my family?" Fritz suddenly had the thought that this might be a little early for that to happen. *She hardly knows me yet!*

"Sure, I would," Sigi said, "but it might be better to wait. I want to get to know you first."

"Yes, I thought of that just as I finished asking," he said, somewhat sheepishly.

"I do not know what kind of fish can be caught in this stream." Fritz laughed a little as he so obviously changed the subject. "That shows how uninterested I am in fishing. The only thing I like about fishing is that it gives a reason for being out here and clearing my thoughts, as if nothing else in the world is important. Maybe that is why I usually do not bother to bring a pole. Do I sound like too much of a daydreamer to you?"

"That might be a fair word to describe you, especially when you are here, except for what you think about. Your thoughts are on things that are important in how you guide your life; I do not think they are a waste of time."

"I just had an idea! At work, Val and Urs, one of the guys I work with, were talking as they unloaded a stone. I heard them say something about a park being built where there will be two new soccer fields. I have not seen these fields he talked about, but I am curious. Would you like to ride over there and look with me?"

"Do you mean now, in my pants and boots?" Sigi was a little embarrassed to think that someone she knew might recognize her.

"Sure, I think you look fine. There will probably not be anything going on at a park that is not open yet, and there should not be anybody working there on Saturday. It will give you more time on the motorcycle to help you get used to it." He started toward the picnic basket, reaching his hand back for her.

She took his hand just before it was out of reach. "These rocks are not easy to walk on gracefully."

"Oh, no, they are not designed for dancing, are they?" His smile was apologetic for not thinking about her needing his help. "Come on, I'll race you back!" Pretending to run, he pulled on her hand until he saw the look of surprise and fear cross her face. "Here," he said calmly, holding her hand steady as she looked down at her feet and, quickly stepping, got them steady under her again. When she looked up at him, showing her relief, he gave her a short *gotcha* kiss.

She did not pull away.

"Hey, that is not fair! I was not looking!" This time it was a coy, warm, pretty smile.

CHAPTER 4

When Fritz and Sigi got to Neidenberg, and to the intersection with the east-west road from Willenberg, Fritz turned left, which took them past the beer hall. He pointed to a parked car he thought he recognized, especially when he saw four men, two whom he did not know, getting into it. He asked Sigi if she knew who they were. When she said no, he became very curious and decided to follow them.

Fritz drove a little farther down the road to turn around, to prevent the men noticing them. They were all walking unsteadily because of their drinking, which meant they were not paying much attention to what was going on around them.

The men all wore brown shirts with a badge on the front and red armbands that displayed a white spot with a black X in it. They looked like adults trying to be part of a neighborhood boys' club, but there was something dark about these men. They seemed to be in a good mood, laughing and talking loudly.

Fritz and Sigi were too far away to hear what they were saying. Fritz was sure this was the same car used by those men who had stopped Sigi and Trina. If it was the same car, and some of them were the same men, then it might be a good idea to follow them to see if they were up to some trouble. When their car pulled out onto the road, Fritz and Sigi followed from as far back as they could, keeping them in sight.

"Are you sure we should be doing this?" Sigi sounded worried. "What if these guys are dangerous?"

"We will be OK if we stay far enough away from them. That car could never catch my motorcycle anyway."

The car continued through town and past the church on the road toward Willenberg. Slightly over two kilometers outside of town, Fritz slowed down as they came to the curve where he and Val had watched three men follow two girls into the woods four weeks earlier. He now knew it was the same car, because there it was again, stopped at the same place, and again, the men were going into the woods. This time, the men were laughing and talking loudly, as they had been doing in town. There were so many coincidences with last time that Fritz just had to try to find out what they were talking about.

Sigi recognized the coincidences with her experience as well and was getting more nervous and frightened by the minute. "Can't we just go on home and forget about these guys? I'm getting scared."

"We could do that," Fritz agreed, "but if these men mean any trouble around here, it will be good to know about it before it happens, so we can help someone be safe from it. If there is someone in that group who lives around here, we should find out who it is and try to talk him out of it."

"Those are good ideas. I am just scared, that's all."

"Sometimes scared is a good way to be, but these guys are not armed. If we stay out of sight, we will be all right. We need to go closer if we are going to hear what they are saying. OK?"

"Yes, I will be all right," she conceded, trying to smile.

They drove up nearer the car as quietly as possible, then turned off the motorcycle and pushed it into the woods where it would be out of sight. They carefully moved toward the men, whose voices they could now easily hear because they were talking so loudly. When they could see the men and hear what they were saying, they stopped and listened.

Two of the men were telling the other two that they brought the girls this far when the mystery men appeared. As Sigi watched, her interest suddenly picked up. They then described the encounter they had with a wildman and a gunman who were both wearing masks. The first man said, "That is why Hall here now has a nose that looks off to the left!"

The second man said, "And that is why Jarvis there has pains in his chest when he takes a deep breath. A kick in the ribs nearly caved in his chest that day!"

One of the men listening said, "You guys are crazy." Sigi gasped as the man whose voice she recognized continued, "There are no wild men around here!"

"What's wrong?" Fritz whispered.

"The man who was just talking is my uncle Ben!" she said, clearly surprised.

"I, for one, want to meet that wild man again. I think he would make a good recruit. The gunman must be good also." Hall had a wise, all-knowing look on his face, even with the crooked nose.

"How do you know? You were asleep when he got here. I want to find those girls again and bring them back in here, like before." Jarvis's smile was masterful, confident, and menacing.

"Come on, we should move back. I think we've heard enough," whispered Fritz. After moving a short distance back toward the motorcycle, he stopped and, with an intent look on his face, added, "Wait right here, and be as quiet as you can. He pulled her down into a squatting position and said, "I have an idea." He disappeared in the direction of the car.

The men kept talking loudly enough that Sigi could still hear them, but she could not understand what they were saying, and she could not see them. *What does Fritz have in mind?* she thought as the minutes went by. *I have not known him long, but I have confidence in him and believe he knows what he is doing.*

Listening to the men let her know she was still a safe distance away as the time seemed to go more slowly. *As long as I can hear how far away they are, I can stay here and wait for Fritz. I am close to hom—*

Her thoughts were interrupted by a tremendous explosion, startling her to her knees and hands, in a crouch, to be as invisible as possible. The men stopped talking for about two seconds. Then they realized that the sound came from the direction of their car and began talking again, then yelling and cursing. She could hear them crashing through the woods, bouncing off trees and bumping into branches and bushes on their drunken way back to their car. She was concerned about Fritz and had to do her best to remember her confidence in him to believe he was OK.

Suddenly, there were gunshots, five or six of them. She thought, *What could be going on now?* She knew the men were not wearing guns, so how could they be shooting? Then she realized Fritz did not have a gun either.

There is nothing I can do but get into greater danger if I try to investigate the shooting. Fritz is the only one who knows where I am, so I should stay here until he comes. Soon, she heard a car start up and take off, probably as fast as it could. *The men will be gone now, and I must know what happened to Fritz!* She waited another two minutes and started moving on her hands and knees carefully toward the explosion. She heard some noise, and her heart skipped a beat. *Someone is coming through the woods!* She crouched down again, to keep from being seen, and looked in the direction of the noise. It was Fritz, trotting toward her and laughing!

When he got to her, Sigi said, "What do you mean by trotting through here, laughing like you are having a really good time?" She sat back on her feet, her knees still on the ground, with a look of impatience, confusion, and anger on her face.

He held out his hand to help her up, still laughing some.

She stood up and, pounding on his chest, said, "I have been here listening to drunk men and what sounds like a war going on—wondering who is doing the shooting when nobody is wearing a gun; what that explosion was; how much danger is there really; should I try to find you; if you are even still alive; and you come casually trotting up, laughing, like you're winning some really fun game."

He put his arms around her to calm her and to stop the pounding.

"Everything is OK now. They are gone. This has not been fair to you, has it?"

"No, it hasn't."

He noticed she was shaking from the ordeal. "No, but it certainly was funny!"

She started pounding again. "No, it was not funny. I have not had any fun here."

"Oh, I think I know what will help. Let me tell you what happened after I left you here. Come sit down and lean against this tree.

"When I left, I hurried to their car and looked in. I found a cigarette lighter, some guns, ammunition, and a can of gas they probably kept in case they ran out. I hid the guns in the woods under a log and some branches and leaves. I took the top off the gas can and poured all of it in a line in the dirt five feet from the car between the woods and the car, so that the flames would hide the car when the men came running out. I put the gas can on the line of gas I poured out, with the top off, and lit the gas in the dirt. This made a huge wall of fire. When the gas can exploded, and they came running out of the woods, all they could see was fire. They must have thought their car was gone! They were so excited—and drunk—that they looked like a bunch of clowns, all running back and forth and in circles and into each other, yelling and throwing dirt on the fire to put it out, but they were getting nowhere for all their effort."

Sigi was starting to relax and chuckle at the men but even more at Fritz's exaggerated demonstrations.

"When I went back into the woods to hide and wait for them to come and check out the noise, I picked up a pistol and rifle where I hid them. When they got to the wall of fire and could not see their car, I could not help laughing as quietly as I could at them. I thought they could use some help finding their car, so I started firing both guns into the woods above their heads. It was like shaking a beehive; all four of the bees suddenly doubled their speed—but were still not getting anywhere!" Sigi was laughing, and Fritz was having a good time.

"Finally, one of them got around the end of the fire and found the car. His yelling soon brought his friends to it. When they left, the last man in the car was hanging on, with one hand on the car and one on the door and his foot dragging, desperately trying to get in. He finally did get into the car, with the help of his friend pulling him by the shirt. The last I saw of them, they were all looking back, through eyes wide open, still trying to figure out the war zone they just escaped from."

Sigi felt much better now, from almost too much laughing.

"It was sure funny; I wish you could have seen it. I thought you might be worrying, so I hid the guns again and hurried back as soon as I could." Fritz sat down on the ground near her and watched her face for a reaction.

"I am glad you did, because after what I heard through the trees, I was afraid of what I might find out there. You sure make dating interesting. In the past three hours or so, you have taken me to a beautiful, peaceful spot on the river, where we talked about some wonderful eternal things, and you shared a beautiful side of you in your thoughts and feelings. Then you bring me here, to a spot that already has some bad memories for me, following some bad men, and take me through some of the most awful fears and worries that I can remember having. This is one date I will remember for a long time."

"You have had some of the good and some of the bad of being with me today, in large servings it sounds like! I hope the good outweighs the bad." He pushed some leaves around on the ground with a stick and then looked at her for the verdict.

She smiled and gave him a kiss on the cheek. "Oh, I think the good wins out, but please try to take it a little easier, OK?"

"I will try. I promise. I hope you do not think I am breaking that promise, but I think this is a beautiful place too, and it should not hold bad memories for anyone. Can you tell me about those bad memories you mentioned? Maybe I can help them be better." He hoped she had enough confidence in him to do that.

"Oh, I don't know what you can do; they will get better in time. I am resigned to waiting and hoping."

"I understand that you do not know me well enough to know that I can help, but you do not know that I ca not either. Does it help that I would like to try?" He was making a pile of leaves with his stick.

"You have a real interest in this, don't you?"

"I have a real interest in you, and this is important to you."

"OK, I will tell you about it just to see what you would do or what you think of it." She made it sound like a test. She took a more official posture as she prepared to give the test.

"The two girls the men talked about bringing into the woods were me and a friend from church. We were on our way to my house, which is through the woods over there. You know that because you were there today. We were so scared that all my friend could do was cry. I was starting to cry, out of fear and desperation, and I could not think of what to do except pray. The next thing I knew, some masked stranger came running out of the trees, yelling and growling and making a lot of noise, and knocked all three of the very surprised men down in one or two seconds. When another masked man came running toward us with a gun in his hand, we ran to my house.

"Now you see what I mean when I say that I have had two bad experiences in this same place in about a month. That is why I do not like this spot and why I am suspicious of men now." Sigi paused, then asked,

"What do you think of my story?" Sigi looked at him as if she was daring him to try to pass the test.

"Have you talked to anyone else about this?" Fritz asked.

"No, we did not think it was anybody else's business, so we agreed to keep it to ourselves."

"We did the same thing." He stood up quickly with a smile on his face and held out his hand to help her up. "I want to show you something."

"What did you say?"

"Come on. It will be better to show you."

As she took his hand and stood up, she could not understand why he looked happy and excited as he led her a short distance through the trees. He stopped and said, "Here we are. Do you see anything unusual?" Sigi looked around and shook her head no, wondering what was going on with all that she had been through with him today. "Good, you are not supposed to see anything." He bent down, brushed away some leaves and dirt, and opened a buried box. "Do you recognize this?" He pulled on one of the dust masks he and Val had hidden.

Sigi gasped a long, surprised gasp, put her hand over her open mouth, and stepped back as she realized she was looking at the wild man who had saved them that day. It only took a moment to know what to do now. She ran the three steps to Fritz and gave him the biggest, warmest hug she could.

"Wow! I could get to like this!" He took off his mask and dropped it into the box, then put his cheek down against the soft, shiny hair of the girl pressed against his chest and put his arms around her to accept her hug.

"It was you!" Sigi said, beginning to cry. "The masked wildman that day was you, wasn't it? Or wasn't you, or he, or—oh, these weeks of keeping the secret of those men, not knowing who they were, worrying if they came back what I would do. And wondering who the masked men were. Do they live around here? And if so, are they good men or as crazy as they acted? Who could I trust? You met my sister Trina at the dinner at church and then earlier today at my home. You must know she was the one with me that day! She has had a hard time too. We wonder if we will ever feel safe again."

All the tension and pressure and relief were now coming out in soft sobs as she held tightly to the one person who knew and understood and who she knew could protect her from men and events in her world that she did not understand. She held onto Fritz for a few minutes until she began to relax and catch her breath. With one more deep breath, she exhaled, in little jerks, because of the releasing tension. A she turned to the side just enough to let her knees start to bend, she looked again into the box to confirm that Fritz really was the crazy wildman and that she no longer had to worry about any danger from them. She relaxed her hold on Fritz and began to sit down.

"Whoa, just a minute there." He held on a little tighter to steady her.

"Oh, thank you, but I would like to sit down."

"OK, one second please." He playfully picked her up, carried her to a nearby tree, and, with his foot, pushed some leaves up into a pile by the tree. "A soft seat with a backrest, fit for a queen."

"How considerate of you, sir; this is very nice." She settled against the tree. "I need to just sit and think for a while about what's happened today."

"It has been an unusual day, hasn't it?" He lay down next to her, relaxing with his hands behind his head.

"This day has given me so much to think about that if days like this happened very often, I would not be able to keep up." She smiled at him, shaking her head. "Who are these men in the brown shirts, and why do they think they can cause trouble for people like they do?"

"Herr Kemp, the man I work for, keeps up with events in our country, and he tells me of an impressive but new politician named Adolf Hitler. He has some radical ideas about politics, the Treaty of Versailles, the men who signed it for Germany being traitors, the Aryan race being so superior that all others should be honored to serve it, and the Jews being our greatest enemy. This man Hitler is such a powerful speaker, and he offers such a variety of ideas that he can get people excited and win their support almost every time he speaks. There are many bankers and industrialists who give him money in hopes that, when he comes to power, he will cause business to become strong again. With that money, he can hire some of the very rough men off the streets and veterans who cannot find work and organize them into a sort of military outfit commonly called the Brownshirts. That is who these men are! Originally, they were needed to keep the protesters quiet at his Nazi Party rallies, but sometimes they get too rough and think they can do whatever they like.

"In the last couple of years, our economy has been steadily improving, and the government has been able to keep troublemakers in check, but there is still so much bickering among politicians that our country is not strong. I am interested in this stuff, because someday I expect to raise a family, and I want to do that in a peaceful country where they can get an education and a good job. The government is setting up some great programs to help individuals and families be more successful. That should help keep the peace. I do not like to think we will keep having trouble with these Brownshirt guys or others like them. They sure are a problem now!

"Did you say your uncle was one of the men we saw today? Will you tell me about him? Is he a troublemaker?"

"I do not think he is, but he has had trouble finding a good job. Like so many others, he worries about taking care of his family." She tried to sound hopeful while feeling worried about the kind of men he was with today.

"Maybe men like your uncle can help keep them from bothering people sometimes." Fritz tried to be encouraging. "How is your sister doing after the experience with the men? Is she able to keep your secret? Do you think she will be happier if she knows who the masked wildmen are?"

"Yes, I think she needs to know about you. And the other guy, who is he?" Sigi suddenly became interested in who was with Fritz that day. In her mind, she went through some of the young men she could think of that he might know, maybe from his work or some of his friends from the other side of town where he lives. There was nobody she knew, or had even seen, who was likely to do something like that. "I cannot think of who it might be."

"I have told you about me being one of them, but I promised the other guy I would not tell anybody. I have to ask him if he is ready to talk about it. If he says yes, maybe we can plan another picnic for the four of us, where he can decide if he wants to tell Trina about his part in this. He might say no because he does not even want you to know who he is. I have to honor my promise to him that much. I will come to your house next week, probably Thursday, and let you know what he said. For now, let's get you home so you can get some rest."

On their way back to the motorcycle, they stopped by the box Fritz had taken the mask from.

"We took these guns from the men's car that first time we saw them bring you two in here so they would not be used against us, but also in case we needed them." He closed the box and covered it and the rifles again. "The way the economy is improving, it is less likely every day that we will need them. I wish they could stay here and waste away like everything else on the forest floor."

"This part of the woods *is* nice, isn't it?" Sigi looked up at the bright green tops of the tall trees where the sun was still shining on them from its place lower in the sky. "It is much better than it was when we came in! I think Trina will feel a burden taken off her when she learns about you, just like I did. It should make her much happier."

CHAPTER 5

Val came with another delivery on Tuesday. Fritz was waiting to help him unload as he backed up to the loading dock and got out of his truck. "Hey, Fritz, I thought you might come over and tell me about your date last Saturday. I want to hear how it went."

They walked into the bed of the truck to get one of the stones. "It went really well! She's a great girl."

"She does not date much," Val said. "I think the guys see her as being too independent, too strong. She knows what she thinks, and they are not comfortable around her. It sounds like you did not have any trouble talking with her." Together they picked up the first stone and took it into the warehouse. "Where did you go? What did you do?"

"We went to that place by the river where you were going to show me how to fish. At that big rock, remember? We talked for a while, then ate the picnic lunch that she brought on the smaller grassy area." Fritz grabbed the dolly on the way to get the next stone, because this one was bigger than the first.

"A picnic lunch. This story sounds good so far," said Urs, who was listening from his workstation.

"I asked her what she liked to do and what she thought about different things and ideas. She really is smart." They loaded the second stone on the dolly and moved it into the warehouse.

"You didn't finish about the picnic lunch," Urs reminded Fritz, because he loved to eat. "What was in the lunch?"

"It was all good food, and I took care of it all. Shall I save you some next time?" With a smile on his face, Fritz teased Urs, then said to his friend, "Val, I will come over after work tonight, and we can talk more about it. Is between four thirty and five OK?"

Val nodded his head about the time and said to Urs, "I will tell you what was in the lunch on my next trip, Urs, if Fritz doesn't."

Urs was exaggeratedly mimicking Val back as he got into his truck. Jochem and Fritz were laughing.

Fritz hurried to Val's house after work, hoping that he would not interrupt the Adlars' dinner.

"Hi, Fritz!" squealed Kyler, excited to see his big buddy again. Alf, who is always ready to join in anything exciting or fun, began barking and bouncing with his front feet as soon as Kyler squealed, trying to be part of the action. "Did you come to see Val? Are you going to stay for dinner?'

"Hi, kid. Yes, I came to ask Val something. Is he home?" He picked Kyler up and held him under his arm like a sack of potatoes while he punched him playfully with the other hand.

"No, he's not here yet. We have some new baby chicks. Wanna see 'em?"

"Sure. Lead the way." He put Kyler down, who hit the ground running toward the chicken coop behind the barn. Fritz caught up with him, grabbed the back of his pants and lifted him off the ground. They both laughed at Kyler still running through the air. Alf was running and barking and bouncing along with them to add to the fun.

"Here they are, in their own little pen so nothing can hurt them."

"Wow, how many are there? One, two … three …" Fritz bent over to get a better look.

"There are seven! Here are the rest, under the straw!" Kyler showed him where to look.

"Do you have names for them?" Fritz heard Val's motorcycle come into the driveway and stop.

"No. What shall we name them? How about Lulu for that one? Azzo for that one? Kathe for her?"

"How will you remember their names and which one is which?" Fritz was sure he had stumped Kyler.

"Oh, that's OK. If I can't remember their names tomorrow, I'll give them new ones." Kyler flashed a confident, I-know-what-I'm-doing smile.

"Oh, I see. That should work just fine!" Fritz stood up, recognizing the reasoning of a practiced mind. "It sounds like Val came home. I think I will go find him."

When Fritz walked around the corner of the barn, Val was coming out of the house. "Hey. I should have known Kyler would have you out here someplace! Have you been here long?"

"No, Kyler came running up when I stopped, and we had to go see the baby chicks. I do not know how soon you will be having dinner; do you have time to ride to the new soccer fields so I can tell you more about my time with Sigi on Saturday?"

"You make it sound like this could be interesting, but with dinner soon and some things I need to do around here, I do not have much time. We can walk out along the fence between our field and the neighbor's if you want to be away from people." Val got a curious look on his face as he wondered exactly what this was going to be about.

They walked between the house and the barn and past the chicken coop to the field.

"After our lunch at the river, we decided to go look at the soccer fields. Driving through town, we saw the same car that the three men were in that followed the girls that day." Fritz started the story as a suspense thriller and ended it as a high jinks comedy. Val was soon laughing and enjoying it as much as if he had been there.

"Here is the part that I have to ask you about. After the men left, Sigi and I talked some more. She was so scared and upset, I decided to tell her about my part in that first experience with the men. When I showed her one of the masks, she began crying and holding onto me, shaking with relief to have the fear and stress lifted from her. I did not tell her about you, because of the promise you and I made that day. She said she could not think of who the masked man with the gun could be, so I think your secret is still safe. Do you think it might be a good idea to tell Trina about your part in this—to help relieve some of her anxiety too? Sigi said she would not tell her about me being one of the men. How well do you know Trina? Do you think she can keep our secret?" Fritz listened closely for a reply.

"I have known her for a long time. She is not as strong as Sigi, but I have heard no talk about the incident with the men from anybody at all, not at church or around town. I think neither of the girls has told anybody, which means it will probably stay that way. I am sure we can continue to keep it if we all know the full story. If it will help her, then I think we should tell her. We will probably all feel better."

"Tomorrow after work, I will go to Sigi's and tell her what you said. Maybe we can think of a way to get all four of us together on Saturday to talk about this. Will that work for you?"

"Sure, but I need to know what time and how long we will be gone, so I can take care of my duties around here that day. Are you talking about a double date with me and Trina? I have not done anything like that with her! This will be different—like a date with my sister!" Val was starting to sound a bit worried.

"Just think of it as a picnic lunch, not a date. Imagine how she will feel; she will not know who will be there. I will not tell Sigi either, so you can see the look on her face when she sees you and realizes that it was you in the mask with the gun. And all Trina will know is that I am bringing a friend and that Sigi and I want to tell you both about a funny experience we had on our date last Saturday. This should be good for all of us." Fritz looked pleased with himself for the plan he had come up with so quickly.

The late afternoon was turning into evening, and both have responsibilities around their family farms. They talked more about the positive results their plan should have and got more excited about Saturday as they walked back to the house.

Wednesday after work, Fritz rode to Sigi's to tell her about the plan for Saturday. She said, "Come back tomorrow after work. I should know by then if we can both come."

When Sigi asked Trina to come with her on a picnic lunch with someone neither of the girls knew, she was not interested. She was skeptical of all men, like Sigi was before Fritz showed her the mask.

Sigi said, "But I know Fritz, and I trust him completely. This other fellow is a good friend of his. With that, plus what Fritz has told me about him, I am sure I can trust him too. When we tell you about our funny experience last Saturday, I think you will feel the same kind of relief and peace that I felt when it happened. I trust Fritz in a way that you can't understand until you have heard our story."

"Well, Sigi, you have never asked me to do anything so irrational as this, but I've never seen you as sure and excited about something either. You are usually a level-headed thinker who does not take chances like this, which could be one of those terrifying, traumatic experiences like we just had a few weeks ago." Trina was trying to understand why she was being asked to do something that sounded so impossible for her sister to ask her to even consider.

"I would feel the same way you do if you were talking to me this way. I know the story that we want to tell you, and I know something about these two guys that makes me sure that this is something you will want to hear about. Please understand that I believe this is in your best interest. Besides, it should be fun."

"Well, OK—not that I'm convinced this is a good idea but because I can see that you are. Your excitement is making me curious. I am curious about your story and about your guy Fritz. I think you really like him." Trina was happy for her sister and the enthusiasm she had for him.

"I think I like him too! Good, I am glad you are coming! We will each need to make a small picnic lunch, like a sandwich for us and one for them, and some veggies and a drink or whatever you like. They will be at our house at eleven thirty on Saturday. Be sure to wear pants because we will be riding on their motorcycles!"

"Motorcycles? I've never ridden on one before." Trina almost sounded scared. "Except for that time Val had his at a church activity. Remember? Our funnyman friend did not make me want to ride on one again soon!"

Sigi did remember because it was her first ride too. *Val does have a motorcycle!* she thought. *Could he be Fritz's mystery friend? No, he could not be the masked gunman in the woods that day ... not the Val I know! He is too much of a clown and not aggressive enough.*

"I was really worried the first time Fritz asked me to ride with him too, but it was all right, and after a short time, I even started to like it. We'll see them on Saturday."

Fritz was at Sigi's as soon after work on Thursday as he could be. Ahlf came running and barking, doing his job of letting everybody know that a stranger on a motorcycle was there. Klaus yelled at Ahlf from the barn,

"Stop, Ahlf! Stop!" Hi, Fritz. Sigi is in the house. You might have to knock on the door."

Ahlf's tail was wagging now that he heard friendly talk from someone in the family to this outsider.

"Thanks, Klaus. I think I will talk to Ahlf here for a few minutes, so that he can get to know me better.

"You and I need to be friends, Ahlf, because I plan on coming here a lot. You may not chase a stick that I throw, but you can try to be friendlier."

When Fritz got off his motorcycle and started toward the house, Ahlf ran ahead and barked again. Sigi came out and said, "Ahlf, stop! Be quiet! You might as well get used to Fritz, because you will probably be seeing him many times now." She walked by Ahlf and, with a glad-to-see-you smile, went over to Fritz, who was waiting for her so he would not bother Ahlf's protective nature. "Hi." She took his hand.

"Hi. Ahlf will take some time to trust me, but that's the way it should be."

"I trust you. That is why I could ask my sister to go on a picnic with someone who neither one of us knows, because he's a friend of yours and you trust him." She squeezed his hand.

They turned and walked toward the back of the farm so they could talk without being overheard.

"So, did she say she would go?" Fritz wanted to be sure.

"Yes, we will be ready at eleven thirty Saturday. We'll have picnic lunches with us and pants for the motorcycles."

"Please tell Trina that if either of you recognize my friend, you need to try not to be too surprised or disappointed or anything like that, and just be patient until we tell our story. The purpose of this whole plan is to help her be free of the burden of the bad experience you both had, just as you were relieved when I told you. We will try to not make finding out all this stuff another traumatic experience for her."

Fritz really is thinking of Trina, isn't he! Sigi looked at him thoughtfully.

"I told my friend I would let him know about the time on Saturday. I should go now to see him. It's nice to see you again." Fritz gave her a little kiss. "We'll see you on Saturday, a little before noon."

Riding to Val's house gave Fritz time to think about Saturday and get ideas on how to tell the story. It came to him that it would be better for

Sigi to tell it than for him, because Trina knew her better and trusted her to tell the truth more than she would him, whom she did not know well.

Val came from around the corner of the house where he had been chopping wood. "I heard your engine as you were coming up the road. How's it running?"

"It runs good—all ready for Saturday! The girls will be ready at eleven thirty. If I meet you here at that same time, it will give them time for whatever final things they want to take care of before we get there at noon. We will take them to the place where the incident with the men happened, so we can do a better job of telling the story of the second one. That is where we will have our picnic. On the way over here, I had the idea that Sigi should do the telling. Trina will be more comfortable with that, I think. Will getting home around three be OK in your day on Saturday?"

"I think it will. I will have to check with Mom and Dad, but I think it will work. We don't have as many children in our family as some do, so we have to cooperate closely to make sure everything gets done that needs to be done."

"OK, I'll see you Saturday. Shall I come at about ten to see if you need help finishing up something?" Fritz knew that even a little help on a farm could make a big difference.

Val was glad to accept the offer.

At ten minutes after ten Saturday morning, Fritz turned in at Val's, who was working with his dad unloading some hay and chickenfeed from a truck and putting it into the barn. "It looks like I haven't missed all the work." He parked his bike out of the way in the driveway.

"Val told me of your plans; we are glad to have your help," said Herr Adlar.

"I'm happy to be here; just tell me what you want me to do."

"It might be best if you work with Val; he knows what needs to be done. I'll go and take care of some other things." Herr Adlar offered him his pitchfork with a nod of appreciation and went out of the barn.

At eleven thirty, the work was caught up, and the boys went to get cleaned up. "We got more done this morning than we expected to. I think

Dad will be happy with our work." Val was happy he could go on this picnic without feeling bad about leaving something undone.

"I like your dad. He is a good man to work for."

When Fritz and Val rode up the driveway to their house on Saturday, Sigi and Trina were sitting in some chairs on the front porch. They immediately recognized Val, but their reactions were very different. Sigi took a deep breath of surprise through a big, happy smile, with her hands together over her nose and mouth. Val saw her surprise and, with a funnyman shrug of his shoulders, smiled back.

Trina looked over at Fritz to see again the guy who has her sister so excited. "There is Fritz, but the other guy is Val. We have known him for years. Is he my mystery date whom you did not know about?" She sounded disappointed.

"This is great! You'll understand when you hear our story." Sigi was very happy and very surprised to see Val was the friend Fritz would not tell her about. She knew him as someone who was already a friend she could count on and felt happy that the funny guy she knew came through so bravely in that first incident with the attackers.

The boys got off their bikes and walked up to where the surprised girls were waiting.

"There seems to be something going on here that I don't understand. Will someone please fill me in?" Trina felt that she had been tricked and taken advantage of and had no idea why her sister would do this to her.

"Yes, we will," Fritz reassured her. "That is what this whole thing is about today, to explain to you something that has been so much fun for us that we are sure it will be for you too. Please be patient with us for a few hours while we do this in the best way we could think of."

Fritz seemed so hopeful and gentle that Trina felt no threat from him. Val, her friend from church, however, was always friendly and good to her, even when they teased each other. She felt she was around three people she could trust, which made her very curious about the story they wanted to tell her.

"How could any funny story be so good that it made all three of you, usually normal, good people, so anxious to tell me about?

Fritz and Val both shrugged a little, and Sigi just smiled.

"It looks like the only way I will find out is to go with you until I hear it and hopefully understand." Trina was beginning to believe in their sincerity.

The three of them sounded like a cheering section at a game when a point was scored.

"Good!" said Sigi, standing up.

"Yes!" said Val, thrusting his hands into the air like goal posts.

"Great!" said Fritz with a wide grin. "OK, let's go," he said, turning toward the motorcycles.

"Have you ever ridden on a motorcycle?" Val asked Trina.

"Only with you … that day after the church activity." She was still not sure it was safe.

"Oh … yes. Now I remember. Sorry about that. Do you remember how to get on?"

"Not really."

"Then we will watch Sigi get on with Fritz."

After only one day of riding, Sigi got on so easily that it looked like there was nothing to it. Trina looked at Val. "That was so quick that I really didn't learn anything."

"That's because it's so easy. Come on." They walked over to his bike. "Wait while I get it started."

He pulled it upright, lifted the kickstand with his foot, and jumped on the starter. When the engine came loudly to life, Trina stepped back. Pointing to the footrest, Val said, "Put your left foot here … and your right foot on the peg on the other side." She came to the bike, handed him the lunch basket, and holding onto his shoulders, settled onto the seat. "Put your arms around my waist to hold on." He put the lunch on the gas tank in front of him, looked over at Fritz and Sigi, and said, "Last one there has to fix lunch!" He started down the driveway just quickly enough to get a little scream from Trina and to make sure she had a good hold on him.

Fritz and Sigi were watching them and laughing.

"Stop that!" Trina said loudly as she hit him on the shoulder.

He pulled quickly on the throttle, which made the bike lunge forward, causing another scream and a tighter hold from Trina. "You'd better be nice to me," he said playfully.

"If we have far to go, this could be a long ride for her," Sigi said to Fritz, wondering if she should worry about her sister.

"I will make you a deal, Val. I will be nice to you if you will be nice to me, OK?"

"OK, at least until it gets to be boring." He looked back at her with a teasing smile.

"Well, at least that's a start." She smiled at him and gave him one last poke in the ribs.

"I think they are going to do just fine. Do not worry about her while she is with Val; he will take good care of her." Fritz knew there was more to his friend than the funny man that most people saw.

"I hope she will let him. She will need to adjust her opinion of him like I have since he rode up with you. What a surprise that was!"

"Most people know him as a clown. I also know Val as a good man who can be counted on when he needs to be."

The girls did not know where they were going for their picnic. They were both surprised when Val turned off the road and drove just into the trees at the same spot where they had run in on the day of their incident with the three men. Sigi soon understood the reason for being there, but Trina thought of this as another hard piece of a puzzle that she was trusting her friends to help her understand. As soon as Trina was off the motorcycle, she went to Sigi and quietly asked her, "What is this about? Why are we here? These guys do not know what happened to us here, or they would not have brought us here. Do you know what's going on?"

Sigi's smile began before her sister started asking her first question, because she saw the puzzled look on her face as she came up to her. "Yes, I do know. I did not know we were coming here for our picnic, but I understand why, and you will too when you hear our story. Do not worry. I am happy to have all of us here. You will see why soon enough."

Trina saw the peace on her sister's face and heard the confidence in her voice.

"Fritz, is this the place where we will tell them our story? I do not think she can take much more of this." Sigi smiled a compassionate smile and put her hand on her sister's face. "I am sorry this has been hard for you."

"Yes, this is the place, and now is the time. We need to go this way a short distance to set up our picnic." Fritz led them to the tree that Sigi had sat by and leaned against when he brought her there to rest after showing her the mask.

As they arranged their lunch and sat on the ground, Fritz began by saying, "Sigi, I think you are the best one to tell the story, because Trina knows you better than me. Tell her about the day of our picnic by the river. Start from when we left the river. Tell everything you can remember, up to when you sat down by this tree. Val and I will help you from there. But first, before you start, I want to tell you two that when Sigi and I were on our picnic, we asked a blessing on our food. This would be a good time to do that, OK?"

"I like that idea," Val said with an approving smile. "It is good to be thankful and to remember where our blessings come from."

"Good," Trina agreed, surprised at the gentle, religious side of her sister's new friend.

In his prayer, Fritz expressed gratitude for the food and asked a blessing on it, then asked for a blessing of understanding among this group of friends during their discussion.

"Thanks, Fritz. That was a good idea." Sigi patted his hand. "But I thought you would …" She had assumed that Fritz would do the telling, because he did such a good job the day it happened. "Never mind. It does make sense for me to tell it."

The others started to eat while Sigi began telling the story of following the black car with the four brown-shirted men to this very place.

As the story went on, Sigi became more animated, acting out the suspense of the danger the men presented, what they heard them talking about, the terror of the explosion and the shooting, and the fear of not knowing what she would find afterward.

Trina could feel what Sigi was describing. She felt Sigi's anger at Fritz for laughing as he came through the woods. It brought "That's not fair" from Trina and a short laugh from Val. The big eyes of the men driving away made everybody laugh.

"After telling me about the men's eyes and the fear on their faces, he asked me what it was about this place that seemed to bother me. He convinced me that he wanted to know, because he was interested in me and trying to help. I told him the story of the men we saw that day, how they grabbed us and were taking us deeper into the woods, and the wild men that saved us. He asked if we had told anybody else. Have you told anybody else, Trina?"

She shook her head, saying, "No, because we agreed not to tell anybody. Why have you broken that trust? Why do these guys need to know about it? There have been a lot of strange things about coming here with you guys today, -but this is the worst! I am ready to go home!" She stood up and started walking in the direction of their home, a short distance through the woods.

Sigi jumped up and ran to get in front of Trina. Putting her hands on Trina's shoulders firmly enough to stop her in her tracks, she said loudly, "Wait a minute, sister. I did not betray your trust! I told Fritz about *my* experience that day, with a friend. Your name was not mentioned! The reason for the strange things you just talked about is because it has been very awkward for us to find what we thought was the best way to tell you the story. If I were in your place, I would be upset too, but I know the rest of the story, and I know it is something you need to hear." Releasing her hands from Trina's shoulders, Sigi said, "You and I have always had faith and trust in each other. Now is an important time for you to rely on those and listen to what we have to say."

"Well, again, I can see that you are so absolutely positive about this, and"—she turned to look back at the guys—"I trust you and Val. And Fritz seems like a good enough guy. Maybe I should at least listen. Please try to keep the traumatic stuff down to a minimum." The girls walked, each with an arm around the other, back to where the boys were still sitting at the picnic. They both knew that Sigi was the one to talk to her sister, and she did not need their help. Trina looked at them and said, "Sorry, guys. This has not been easy," as they sat down.

They both smiled back at her, nodding their heads in forgiveness and understanding.

Sigi continued, "When Fritz felt sure that day that you and I had not told anyone, he looked happy and seemed excited. I thought, *What is wrong with this guy? Doesn't he understand the stress we've been under?* He said, 'Come over here. I want to show you something.' He helped me up, and we walked through the woods."

Fritz helped Sigi up and said to Val, "You need to bring Trina, so we can all see what Sigi saw that day."

Val helped Trina up, saying, "You are probably thinking, *This better be good*, huh?"

"That's right! It's been a great story so far, but I would like to know how much of it you knew about before today." She was still not sure how he fit into all of this.

Fritz stopped, and Sigi had an excited smile on her face. "When Sigi and I got here, I asked her if she saw anything. Do *you* see anything unusual, Trina?"

"No, there's nothing but the natural forest."

"Good. That is all you are supposed to see."

Fritz and Val moved some leaves and dirt on the ground and opened the box buried there. They each took something out of the box and pulled them over their heads. When they turned around, Trina saw the two masks that she had seen that horrible day. She looked into the box and saw the pistols and ammunition and said, "How did you find this stuff? How did you know it was here?"

Sigi, Fritz, and Val looked at one another and almost started laughing.

"Trina, *they* buried it here!" Sigi said to her puzzled sister. "These are the two wild men that saved us that day! That is why I did not have to tell Fritz the story of the first day we were here with the three bad men! He knew about it, because he was the one that knocked the three men down, and Val was the one with the gun!"

"No, I don't think so. You guys are not the kind who would do something like that." Trina just could not make it all fit together in her mind.

Val quickly reached into the box, grabbed a pistol and a magazine of ammunition, loaded the pistol, fired it into the air, unloaded it, and put it back into the box in about five seconds. His quick, sure movement and the shot made Trina jump back one step and put her hands to her face. "Both of us have handled guns for years. Tarzan here was acting out of the urgency of the moment and a natural desire to save you both from harm. It was something we *had* to act on, and there was not much time to plan. I am glad it turned out as well as it did!"

Still, Trina looked disbelieving. "But … how?"

"We had taken a ride to Willenberg. When we passed you on our way back, then we passed those men in the car, it did not feel right. We thought we should see if they were going to go on by you. We turned around and came back to the curve where we could watch. When the men jumped out of the car and chased you into the woods, he"—Val pointed his thumb at Fritz—"started yelling, 'Go, go, let's go!' taking off as fast as he could."

Trina's hand again went up to her mouth, opened in surprise as she began to understand that this could be true.

"When I ran by their car, I picked up a pistol out of the seat. The masks are something we use to protect us from the dust and bugs on our motorcycles." They both pulled the masks off. "They are made from the sleeves of an old sweater," Val said, almost apologetically, as he was suddenly the funny man again, looking hopefully for a positive reaction from Trina.

Fritz and Sigi laughed at their friend's ability to change so quickly from hero to funny man to try to ease Trina's confusion and stress.

Trina looked over her hand at Sigi, who had a happy, reassuring look and was excitedly nodding her head up and down. Tears started to well up in Trina's eyes as she gave Sigi a hug. She then gave each of the guys a hug and a kiss on the cheek. "Thank you, thank you, thank you! What a relief from stress and fear and uncertainty and suspicion of every man I see. I have wondered who I could say that to! Now to find out you were one of them, Val? The guy we all know as *the funnyman*. I am really proud of you."

"I need to say thank you too, Val, because I did not know you were the second wildman until you rode up with Fritz today." Sigi gave him a hug and a kiss on the cheek. "Thank you, thank you."

"Is it a relief, Trina, to know that there are more than just the two of you who know about your incident with those awful men?" Fritz said as he and Val put the masks back in the box and covered it again.

Trina was nodding her head up and down and looking at Val somewhat shyly and with a new heroic respect for her funnyman who showed so much courage when she and Sigi needed him.

"You two now know that the two wild men *do* live close by, but there is no need to worry about them being a threat to you. Plus, they can help you feel safer in the future from the men who are known by their brown shirts. Val and I also now know there are more than the two of us who have concerns about those men, and we can also share ideas with them."

They all started back to their picnic spot.

"I want to tell you why I think it is so important that we have not told anybody else about our experiences. The first reason is now we can all feel the security of knowing that there are others we can trust and talk to. That alone reduces the stress we feel from our past experiences and the fear of future ones. Another reason is that I agree with Herr Kemp and many others that these Brownshirts could be even more of a problem as their Nazi Party leader, Adolf Hitler, gains more political power, especially if he tries using his forceful methods again to reach his goals."

Fritz went on with what he was saying. "Hitler is a powerful speaker who can win people quickly to his way of thinking. His financial supporters have made it possible for his party to have an organization throughout our country that can grow into a replacement for our current government."

Val jumped in. "These men in brown shirts could develop into an army to carry out Hitler's orders, and there would be little anybody could do about it." There was concern in his voice.

"Our government has been able to keep things from getting out of control for now, but it is weak because of the constant bickering and lack of leadership. The financial burdens and restrictions of the war are so great that it just cannot seem to get its feet under it again. If our economic growth even stutters, our once-great country will be available to the first strong leader who comes along."

Fritz continued. "It is a good thing for us that most of the political activities happen in Berlin and Munich. They are a long way from us here in East Prussia. At our ages, we need to be aware of what is happening in all of Germany, because we will be starting families soon, and I for one want to have a chance to do that in peace—and in a country where there is hope and opportunity. I think that we have a responsibility to ourselves and to our unborn children to do all that we can to oppose this man. With what we have seen from these Brownshirt men, we know they have extraordinarily little care for people. From what Herr Kemp tells me, Herr Hitler writes in his book about the Jews being so evil as to call them 'an enemy to Germany.' It makes me think this man sounds unbelievably dangerous!"

The four sat in silence for a moment or two.

"I do not really know what we can do," said Fritz, looking to see what else was in the lunch box, "just the four of us, but I know we have prevented those few men from causing some of the harm they had in mind. We must do it as secretly as possible to keep from attracting too much attention or action ourselves. That is why I was so interested in whether or not any of us had talked to anybody else about our experiences."

Everyone ate in silence for a minute or two, mulling over Fritz's words.

"What do you think about what I said?" he finally asked. "Can you see the reasoning behind my ideas? Can you see yourself involved in this kind of activity? If we do nothing, will we be happy with a life where we are told everything we can or cannot do? If Hitler can call the Jews an enemy to Germany, who will he name next? Will it be the Catholics? Will it be the older ones, because he sees them as not productive enough? How much fear and death can he cause if he gets enough of our angry, unemployed veterans and others to follow him?"

His three friends finished their lunch while Fritz talked, leaving some of his.

"Are you saying that the four of us become a resistance group *by ourselves*?" Trina could not believe she was even asking this question.

"Resistance group sounds too militaristic for me; I think more like a protect-our- freedom-and-safety group of friends." Fritz believed in what he was saying to them. "Would you have been happier if we had not happened by at the right time, and those men had their way with you?"

"No, of course not!" The appearance of being greatly insulted showed in her face and gestures.

"I am sorry I had to ask that question, but if we had not recognized a problem and acted on it, things could be quite different today. Somebody had to do something, and we did it! A funnyman and a stone engraver *did it*! This kind of action is not in our training or our experience, but it is in our nature as men, and it is in your nature as caring human beings. If you can imagine how badly things might have gone for you, you can imagine what we might be able to save somebody else from. We did not have to help you, and we do not have to help anybody else, but what if we can? What is our life worth to us, or anybody else, if we do not even try?"

Sigi and Trina were picking up after the lunch, except for Fritz's part.

"What if there is shooting? Would we have to shoot back?" Sigi cringed at the thought.

"I do not like the idea of shooting anybody, but if somebody is trying to kill me or someone I love or should protect, yes, I would shoot back!" Val responded. "If an innocent person is having someone else force their dangerous or evil intentions on them, I could shoot the one doing the forcing. The pistol in my hand at that first incident was loaded and ready to fire! I am glad Tarzan here made that unnecessary."

"The thing that makes that a tough question is this: what if someone you know happens to be part of the group doing the shooting?" Fritz's question did not get a quick answer. Sigi looked down, visibly upset, and then at Trina, with tears in her eyes. There was one more part of the story she has not told. Fritz continued, "The reason I say that is ... and I know this was not clear in our story, but Sigi's uncle was one of the men in the second group. The other three were regaling him with the story of the first incident."

"Uncle Ben," said Sigi to her sister.

Trina looked quickly at Sigi. "Are you sure?"

"I thought I recognized him, but I didn't have a good line of sight. When I heard his voice, I was sure!"

"As time goes on, we *all* might find someone we know has joined the Brownshirts or started supporting Hitler. I think what Val said is a good way to handle that too."

"We have talked about some things that will take time to think about ... before we decide how we each feel. If all goes well, we will not need to talk about any of it again, or even think about it. That would really be nice. For now, we need to hope for the best, look to the future, and plan the rest of our lives. We should stop doing anything about the Brownshirts for a while if we do not hear about any trouble caused by them. But we must continue our agreement not to tell anybody else about our actions against them. We do not know how dangerous they might be." Fritz had been taking bites of his lunch when he could.

"I, for one, can agree with everything that Fritz has just said," injected Val, looking at the two girls. "I would add to that my belief that God could not approve of the actions of these men or anybody else who would force their will on somebody and take away that person's right to make their own decisions. That is one of the most important gifts that He has given us. I think that is one of the reasons we have been successful in our encounters with them. If we are careful and prayerful, I think He will continue to protect us in doing what's right."

Sigi picked up the rest of the lunch accessories and put them in the baskets. "I like what both of you guys have been saying," she said, thoughtfully nodding her head. "It is a little scary, but I can agree with and support you both. And I do feel an additional strength knowing there are four of us now."

Trina added, "It is a relief to know Sigi and I are not alone in this secret we shared." Her relief and understanding plainly showed in her whole demeanor now. "The power displayed by *the two masked madmen* was a worry, because they could show up again at any time. I thought they might live close by, but I did not know them and was not sure it would be safe to be outside alone around here anymore. Now that I know who you are, I realize that instead of being an added mysterious threat, you are a protection from the growing problem of the Brownshirts that started this whole thing. I like what I have heard from all of you today. I too can agree with and support our little army of four. In some strange way, it almost seems like we are talking about a larger than reality game of chess that is played with people and nations instead of chess pieces on a board."

Fritz was quickly downing water from the bottle the girls brought.

Val said, "I have wondered how many of our military and political leaders think of war and politics as some kind of ultimate game." He paused to look into the eyes of his friends. "One where the winners receive honor, respect, glory, riches, power—and the losers pay with the loss of those very same things, plus their freedom and lives, as do their families and friends."

Fritz responded, "I do not think about a game, but I do think freedom and lives are too much to lose!" His group of friends knew Fritz was speaking out of love. "That is why we have to do what we can … and hope that others will do the same."

They all started back to the motorcycles.

"You know what?" Trina said. "This part of the woods does not hold the fear for me that it did just a little earlier today." She looked at her friends. "Thanks, guys, for giving me the woods back."

Trina saw Val in a whole new way. No longer was he just the funny boy who was not to be taken seriously. He is now someone she respects for what he and Fritz had done for them and who could respond strongly to protect her when she needed it. These are new ideas that she will have to get used to. She had a lot to think about as she rode home with her head resting on his shoulder.

The rest of that summer went by very pleasantly for the four friends.

Trina and Val now have more in common than just being friends at church. With their shared religious background and their respect for each other, they were careful not to ruin a good friendship by getting recklessly involved in a physical way. With Trina just having turned sixteen, and Val nearly nineteen, they realized they could still end up married to somebody else, which would be ruined if they were not careful now.

Sigi and Fritz have the same kind of growing interest in each other as Trina and Val and the same commonsense approach to trying to do this approach-to-marriage thing right. They shared the same long-term goal of raising a happy family and felt sure that it could best be done from a foundation of honesty and integrity with their eternal values, which they talked about often.

There is a great strength to be shared among friends who respect, support, encourage, and try to help one another be the best person they can be. As they found from the experiences they shared, personal burdens can be greatly relieved by caring friends.

CHAPTER 6

It was early November, and Val was making a delivery. When he stepped out of his truck, Fritz welcomed his friend with an elaborate flourish, bowing at the waist and offering a sweeping gesture appropriate for royalty. "My liege!" greeted Fritz. "Your humble stone man, at your service."

Climbing up the ladder onto the loading dock, Val responded with "Thank you, my good man." Gently touching the top of Fritz's bowed head, he turned back to nobody there and said, "Jester, give this poor guy a sucker."

With that, Fritz stood up quickly, saying, "Oh yeah? Sucker, huh?" And a playful scuffle began.

"Get him, Val!" cried Urs, cheering him on.

"Do not let him get away with that, Fritz!" shouted Jochem, taking Fritz's side. "Bite his ear!"

"He can't do that! It's not fair!" Urs protested, throwing a wadded-up piece of paper at Jochem.

"All's fair in love and war, my boy—and this looks to me like both of those things at the same time." Jochem ducked another piece of paper.

Herr Kemp came through the door from the front section of the building. "Whoa, what's going on out here? You two had better settle down before somebody really does get hurt with all the stuff there is out here to trip over. Fritz, come into my office."

Fritz and Val looked at each other, puzzled. Fritz shrugged his shoulders and walked toward the door Herr Kemp had just closed behind him. As he passed Urs, he motioned to Val and said, "I leave him in your capable hands." Urs acknowledged with a sort of military salute and went to help Val unload.

Fritz opened the door to Herr Kemp's office and peeked in.

"Come in, come in. I have something to talk to you about."

He took the chair in front of Herr Kemp's desk. There always seemed to be too many papers, too many books, and not enough organization in there, even on the bookshelves. Fritz had been in the office many times, usually to talk about work—and sometimes politics—but this time, he did not know what they would be talking about.

"You have been seeing a girl for some months now, haven't you?"

"Yes, sir. She is a very nice girl." Fritz could not help but smile.

"By the look on your face, I can guess that you think there is a future there for you. Am I right?"

"I certainly like to think so. I am getting surer all the time, but that is as far as it goes for now. We do not have any definite plans, if that is what you mean." Fritz was wondering when the conversation would turn back to work.

"Definite plans or not, it sounds promising! I'm glad to hear it!"

From the changing expression on the boss's face, it looked to Fritz like any second now, Herr Kemp was going to start on his real reason for bringing him in there.

Herr Kemp began, "The economy has been improving for some years now, and our business has been growing, both here and in Koenigsberg, where Bernhard has the second store. He needs help! I have been trying to find the best way to take care of his needs and ours too."

"Yes, sir? How can I help?"

"I'm glad you asked! Fritz, you are about to complete your apprenticeship with me. You have become a good engraver and a reliable worker in all other areas of work in this business."

"Thank you, Herr Kemp."

"What do you think of going to Koenigsberg to help Bernhard?"

Fritz was taken by surprise. Koenigsberg was a good 140 kilometers away. It would change everything. Still, it might be an important opportunity. "Your son is a good man. I consider him a friend. I would like to work with him again, but a move like that ... I would d need to plan it very carefully, sir."

"In what way? What's to plan, son?"

The main thing was how could he make sure Sigi was safe from so far away? How could he keep himself in the forefront of her mind? He answered, "Well, I do not make enough to rent an apartment, and I would not want to live with Bernhard and his family—that would not be fair to him. And it would be a long ride back here on a motorcycle to see the girl I told you about. It might take some time to plan it properly." Fritz was plainly uneasy about the idea.

Herr Kemp peered at him under his thick eyebrows. "I was a young man like you once, so I have already thought about those things. I tried to think as if I *were* you, and here is what I came up with. After your apprenticeship, you are entitled to an increase in salary, which still would not be enough for a young man to start his family on, mind you."

"Yes, sir, that's why—"

"I'm not finished."

"Sorry, sir."

"My family has a small farm near Koenigsberg that nobody has lived on for years."

"Yes, sir?"

"I've got a proposition for you. If you will go live there and work with Bernhard at the plant for ten years, I will give you the farm … without you having to make any payments for purchase or rent for ten years. After ten years, I will give you full ownership of the farm. Plus, you will receive the full amount of your increased salary.

"Sir?"

"That way, I would not have to worry about it again. You would have a place to live, and Bernhard would have a good worker, and that would be good for my business! What do you think of that idea?"

Fritz knew not to look a gift horse in the mouth. "It does sound like a good opportunity. With due respect, sir, may I look at the farm before I give you my answer?" Fritz was afraid to get excited. It sounded almost too good.

"Sure! I will give you directions, and you write them down; then you can go whenever you like. I will call Bernhard, so he knows when to expect you. If you go on Saturday, he will be able to show you around both the business and the farm. Shall I tell him you will be there this weekend?" Herr Kemp thought his plan was fantastic and was ready to help.

"If that is good for him, I am sure it will work for me. I will not say anything to anybody about this until I am sure I understand it all. It looks like you are happy with the plan, but it is new to me. I will need to take some time to get my thoughts around it. It sounds great, though. Thank you, sir." Fritz felt overwhelmed at what he had heard. "I am sure you thought about this carefully before you told me, and I have confidence in your judgment. Because of those two things, I will act as if it is a done deal while I gather more information." He stood to shake Herr Kemp's hand and leave. "Thank you again, sir." He closed the office door, gave Erna, the receptionist, a little wave, and went through the door into the warehouse. Thoughts of his conversation with Herr Kemp were already crowding together.

"What was that about?" Urs was of course curious, and Jochem was listening too.

"No problem. It was all good. I will tell you about it later." Fritz had a happy but puzzled look as he tried to sort this out in his head. *By tomorrow, I will have some questions for Herr Kemp that will help me understand what he is offering me. Until then, I hope I am right about what I think I heard!*

That night was a restless one for Fritz. With all the questions buzzing in his head, he did not get much sleep. *If it is true that I will have my own farm in ten years, then I will have a place to start a family. What will Sigi say when I tell her that? If I ask her to marry me, what will she say? How much work and money will it take to get it into good, livable condition? I will have to take her to see it as soon as I can. When will Herr Kemp want me to move?* There were so many questions.

It was so exciting that he wanted to tell Sigi about it right away.

Tomorrow is Friday. That means the next day, Saturday, is when I go to see what he is talking about. I cannot make it come any faster by staying up all night. I need to go to sleep!

Friday morning is going by very slowly. It feels like it is taking forever for Herr Kemp to call me into his office.

"Fritz, Herr Kemp wants you in the office," Erna yelled through door to the shop that she was holding open just wide enough to poke her head through.

Finally! I will know soon if I am going to Koenigsberg tomorrow, Fritz thought as he went into the office, and before he could even sit down, Herr Kemp was speaking.

"I talked to Bernhard yesterday, and it will be OK for you to go there tomorrow as we planned. Will that be good for you?"

"I am sure it will. When I told you I would not tell anybody about this, I was so excited that I forgot that I need to tell my dad and mother, so I can be cleared from my farm responsibilities tomorrow. I have some questions for you that will clear things in my mind. Do you have time to answer them now?

"Yes, ask me whatever you like." Herr Kemp was pleased with the gratitude and humility of this fine young man.

"When do you want me to move up there?"

"Your apprenticeship officially ends in December. You should be ready to start work with Bernhard the first of January. When you look at the farm, try to estimate how much work it will take to get it ready to live in; then we can arrange for you to have the time off here that you need. Bernhard will help you with supplies as much as he can."

Fritz felt that Herr Kemp was being very generous. He continued with his points of clarification. "Would you please explain the payment arrangements for the farm again? I am not sure I heard you right." Fritz wanted to believe what he remembered from yesterday, but it seemed too generous. What was the catch?

"OK, the farm has belonged to my family for a long time, but nobody has lived there for many years now. If you will go and work with Bernhard for ten years, I will consider that payment enough for the farm, and I will give it to you at the end of that time. You will make no payments for it." Herr Kemp had a large, amused smile, because his young friend looked like he was hearing the plan for the first time.

The offer seemed so out of this world that Fritz could hardly believe his ears. But there it was, the same offer. He took a deep breath and let it out before saying anything. "I plan to leave at about six in the morning if Dad and the others at home can cover for me. I think they will. Thank you again, sir. I am looking forward to tomorrow." Fritz was almost shaking his head at this opportunity and hoping it was as real as it sounded.

The morning had gone slowly while he was waiting to talk to Herr Kemp; he only now realized it was not even ten o'clock. He found he had to concentrate on his work more than usual to keep from being distracted by the questions in his mind about how Sigi was going to respond when she heard about all of this.

Urs and Jochem started asking questions as soon as he came out of Herr Kemp's office. All Fritz said was "I do not know what to tell you, because I am not sure I understand it well enough yet. When I have more answers and am sure about things, I will tell you."

When Fritz got home after work, his excitement gave him more energy than usual as he took care of his chores that day. His dad had noticed the difference and asked what it was about. The others had finished their chores by now and were in the house getting ready for dinner. Fritz and his dad were both in the barn finishing up. Fritz put a little more hay in the cow's feeder.

"You know that my apprenticeship will be finished the end of December. Herr Kemp has offered me an opportunity that I think is really good, and I need to go to Koenigsberg tomorrow to check things out. I told him I have to ask you if you can cover for me."

"Your help on Saturday is important to us. Will you tell me about this opportunity?"

As Fritz explained, his father listened carefully, nodding his head in understanding.

"We'll talk about it at dinner tonight so everybody knows why they'll be asked to do extra chores tomorrow. We do not need to talk about Sigi or the farm yet—just the job improvement and your need to look things over. Later, when we are all in bed, I will tell Mom the rest of it."

"Thanks, Dad. I do not like to put a burden on anybody, but I think I need to take a good look at this, and tomorrow will be the best time for at least a week. If I go ahead with Herr Kemp's plan, the next two months will be busy." They left the barn and walked to the house. "It is a little scary to think how important this one decision is in my life, because of all of the things and people that it will affect. I think sometimes people make the wrong decision when a great opportunity comes along just because it seems too big for them. If this is as good as it looks, I do not want to let it get away."

The ride to Koenigsberg took less than two and a half hours. The weather was not cold yet, but he was glad to have the wool face protector he recently made.

It was after eight thirty when Fritz knocked on Bernhard's door. It is a nice home near the shop, which had opened just over a year before. Frieda, Bernhard's wife, opened the door.

"Hi, Fritz! Its good to see you again!" She took his arm and hand to bring him in. "Come in, come in. You haven't been here since you helped us move, have you?"

"No, I have not. It is good to see you too—and *Liesl*. Hi, Liesl. Do you remember me?" The Kemps' toddler was acting shy and unsure about Fritz from her seat at the breakfast table. "A year is a long time to remember when you are only three, isn't it?"

"Hi, Fritz! How are you doing?" Bernhard came in from the kitchen carrying a baby. "You have not met Hagan here. He is two months old."

"Hagan, hi there. What a good-looking little guy. What a good-looking family you have here, Bernhard! The move up here has been good for you, hasn't it?"

"Yes, business is steadily improving. Come on, you must be hungry. Let's go sit in the kitchen." Bernhard led the way.

Bernard's house was fairly new. There are two large bedrooms, a living room with a cozy fireplace for a cool evening, and a kitchen and dining area. The table looked like they had just finished breakfast.

Frieda was already pouring him some orange juice as she asked, "Can I get you some eggs, ham, coffee, a biscuit and jam? By the time the eggs are done, I can have the rest set out for you."

"That's good of you to offer. I do not want to eat everything you have—or has business been so good as that? I was so excited about making this trip that I got up before breakfast to take care of some chores around the farm before I left, and I have not slowed down until now." Fritz could feel himself beginning to relax after his ride.

"Eat then, please!" said Bernhard, as hospitable as his wife. "I think one of the reasons business is picking up is so many people are moving into the city to get a job now that the economy has been improving. There are more people who have more money to spend on our stones."

Baby Hagan started fussing, so Bernhard got up to walk around, patting him to help him settle down. "Dad worries that all this money from foreign investors will result in too much control of our government being purchased with it."

"This is a great-looking breakfast, Frieda; thank you very much."

"You are welcome. I'm happy to have a friend from Neidenberg visiting us."

"I do not understand everything your dad tells me about politics, but when I do understand, I always agree with him. That makes it easy to trust him on other things. Have you seen much activity from the Nazi Party around here?" Fritz cut a bite-size piece from the ham on his plate.

"They try to have meetings to explain their party's ideas, but they are not getting much attention. I see some men in brown shirts that have red armbands with a white circle and a black cross, but I do not know of any problems from them. I know Dad does not trust them!"

The baby was settling down with the movement and patting from Bernhard.

"He sure doesn't. He sees the support Hitler is getting from the military and some financially powerful people and thinks he could be a powerful political figure in time. Of course, the stronger Hitler gets, the more unpredictable the Brownshirt guys will get. That is what worries me! With the economy doing well, the best thing we can do is contribute to its growth by working at the service we provide! That is why I am here, to learn what your plans are and see what I can do to help the most. What do you have in mind for me to be doing in the business?

"We are getting more people who are interested in iron crosses for grave markers. When these are made with a shiny kind of decoration at the center, they can be beautiful, and they cost less than a standing stone memorial. In the interest of business, we provide them with what they want, and everybody is happy. This additional business is one of the reasons we need your help."

Hagan fell asleep in his dad's arms. Frieda took him and put him in his crib.

"Frieda has been working very hard up in the front of the business with bookkeeping, being secretary and receptionist, plus helping customers." Bernhard sat down in a chair at the kitchen table with Fritz. "When I leave what I am doing to help her, our production suffers. Dad thinks you are the best one to bring up here to help us. We already have the equipment to do everything. We just need a good man to help with the workload. I know about your stone experience, but I do not remember if you have done any welding."

"I have done some welding on our family farm but not a lot."

"I am sure you can do everything I need after I show you a few things. Along with the welding, there will be some metal bending and shaping and painting and polishing," said Bernard, his arms and hands waving as he demonstrated some of the work.

"It sounds like something I would like to do, once I understand just how you want the iron crosses made. Together, we can probably grow the business even more." Fritz was feeling better about this whole move idea and what the future could hold for him here.

After a pause of two or three seconds in the conversation, Bernhard suddenly had a fatherly look about him and a different tone in his voice. "So, Fritz, you are about twenty-one, aren't you?"

"I turned twenty-two this past month."

"Do you have a special girl, or are you open to suggestions?" Bernhard's fatherly look now took on a playful, slightly scheming smile.

"I met a great girl a few months ago whom I like a lot; that is why your dad's talk of a house being part of the deal caught my interest. You were not counting on introducing me to someone around here, were you?" Fritz looked at both for a reaction.

"We did not know for sure where you stood in the favorite girl/marriage process, so we thought of some who might suit you, all in looking out for our favorite employee, of course!" Frieda laughed softly as she sat down at the table with them.

"You two are just too good to me! Your dad did not say anything about a wife being part of the deal." He was shaking his head no. "I can hardly wait to find out what else you have thought of for me. I think I have the future wife part under control, thank you!"

Fritz was nearly finished with his breakfast. "Getting back to the house and farm, I saw the business when I was here before, and I am sure you now have that set up the way you want for the new direction it will go. I would like to see the house and what it will take to get it ready to live in."

"It has been a year or so since we have seen it," said Frieda, now with Liesl on her lap, picking small pieces off a biscuit from the table and eating them. "It is a nice house in a beautiful setting in a wooded area. There is a small stream that cuts through a corner of the property. It will take some repair to the roof and some places on the walls where the plaster has come off. With the right person, or *couple*, it can be a pretty home again."

Bernhard took on a distant, thoughtful look. "I do not know for sure how long it has been since someone has lived there. It sits on about ten acres, which are more suitable for pasture than for farming, because the land is not all flat enough to water easily. It is just over fifteen kilometers out of town. When we came here to work, we had a chance to get this house, so we decided not to live on the farm. We should go on out there so you can see it for yourself."

"Do you know that your dad has told me that if I work with you for ten years, he will give me the farm?" Fritz was nervous about what Bernhard's answer would be.

"Yes, he told me he was going to do that."

"And it is OK with you?" Fritz was watching Bernhard closely to see his expression.

"Sure. Nobody in the family wants it, probably because most of them are like me, not really the farm-type people. I like it right here in our city house, closer to work. With putting most of our savings on this house when we moved in, and both of us working at the business, we will own it in three more years."

"I am glad to hear that. I just had to make sure we are all thinking of this deal with the house in the same way. Nobody wants to have problems due to disagreements later. Thanks, Bernhard, for making it clear. Well, I am ready to look at it now, if you are." Fritz finished his orange juice and nodded a thank you to Frieda.

"There are many things around here that need to be done, so I will stay with the kids." Frieda began clearing the table, with some help from Liesl.

It took less than thirty minutes to get to the farm from Bernhard's home. The first thing Fritz could see of the ten-acre square property was a split-rail fence, which was nearly hidden by weeds as it ran along the road. There was a break where the driveway went back toward the house.

Fritz began making his assessments from the time they turned into the property. *The growth of weeds indicates there has been little traffic here for years.*

Bernhard stopped the car between the house and the barn, which stood facing each other about twenty-five meters apart.

Fritz got out of the car and went into the barn. *This barn is big enough to house stalls for the animals, plus equipment and a shop for the farm.* He looked the barn over while he walked to the back door, opening it to look around outside. *There may be some loose and missing boards, but it is built well, with a frame that is still solid enough to make it worth repairing.*

He came back through the barn and turned toward the well and water tower at the far end of the house, already beginning to plan some repairs. He said to Bernhard, who was watching and following, "It looks like this was a very nice place at one time, but after not being used for so long, I wonder how tight the water systems are."

"I remember visiting here as a kid, and it seemed really big and nice. There was a swing in that big tree in the backyard. The uncle and his family who lived here then live near Munich now."

There were some farm tools and equipment showing through the weeds in the yard. Fritz walked to the well, looked into it, and could see water only about two meters down. "Frieda said there is a stream nearby. Where does it cross the property?"

"It crosses in the upper-right corner for only about fifteen meters. Then it runs under the small bridge we drove over as we came down the road, before we turned into the driveway."

"Yes, I remember."

Fritz started toward the front door of the house, looking at the roof, the walls, the front porch, the large windows in each room, and the door as he went, still taking note of what needed repair.

There is no electrical connection from the street to the house. It must not have been readily available when the house was last lived in.

The house was twenty meters long and thirteen meters wide, making it one of the larger country homes in the region. When he opened the front door, Fritz was surprised. "Wow, there is a lot of room in here! It will be a long time before a young family will be crowded in this house!" He could see a living area to the right, a dining area in the middle, and a kitchen on the left. The wall that went from end to end in the center of the house divided the family living front half from the three bedrooms and bathrooms in the back half.

Fritz could not help being excited about the possibilities—and concerned at the same time, seeing the work that would be involved.

From the kitchen area, Bernhard said, "If water mechanisms in here do not work, you will have to rely on water from the well outside until they can be fixed."

Fritz walked through the hallway and opened the door to each bedroom and water closet to look in, then went out onto the porch. "On an engraver's salary, it will take time to get everything done, but I expect to be here for a long time!"

"The first thing to take care of will be the roof on the house. By the marks on the ceiling, there is a leak up there somewhere. The next will be the fireplace; a couple of the rocks are loose. After that, the water systems will need to be checked out."

Bernhard smiled in amusement as his friend and future employee continued thinking out loud.

By now, Fritz was sure that even with all that needed to be done, he and Sigi could manage. "The stream is just through the trees there, isn't it?" He motioned straight out the door as he walked out onto the back porch.

"Thanks, Bernhard, for showing me the house and property. I like what I see! Maybe we should go by the business on the way back to your house so I can see just what you want me to do." They closed the house and went to the car.

"There is a lot of work to do here." Bernhard looked around again. "It does not have to be done all at once, and that will make it easier to handle. Besides, you will know you are working on your own place!"

"That is right! I like that part!"

The stop at the business did not take long. Fritz understood quickly how Bernhard planned to work with the iron crosses. Both were sure it would not take long for him to be good at it, because of his natural, mechanical, and artistic abilities. It was still before noon as they got back to Bernhard's house. He opened the door and, seeing Frieda, said, "Hi there!"

"Hi! I thought you guys would be much later than this. Did you go to the farm *and* the shop?" Frieda sounded worried that there might have been a problem with something they saw or talked about, which would stop the move they were counting on.

"Yes, we went to both places. We are just fast, that's all!" Bernhard picked up Liesl, who had come running from the bedroom yelling, "Daddy, Daddy!" when she heard his voice.

"It seems like a quick trip to me." Frieda really wanted this move to happen.

"No. There are no major problems," Fritz answered with a calming voice. "Everything is just fine. I like the farm! I am anxious to get started on fixing it up. During our stop at the business, we agreed that I will be able to work right into the plan Bernhard has. It will be fun living around you two—I mean *four*—again. I will be ready to come here next week to get started, but I need to talk to Mom and Dad, and your dad, to work out the best way to do it. I have a lot to think about. I also want to talk to Sigi; she is the girl I said I like a lot when you asked me earlier if there is someone special. Her reaction is going to be important to me. There may be time to see her tonight."

"It sounds like you should be getting started then," Frieda suggested.

"Is there anything else that we need to talk about today, Bernhard?" Fritz started toward the door.

"I do not think so. You should easily get home before dark."

They all went toward the door. "Thank you, both, for today! Goodbye. Bye, Liesl." Fritz waved to her through the open door. She waved back and smiled but said nothing, still playing shy.

Bernhard walked out to the motorcycle with him. "I think I would have a hard time riding one of those as far as you are going."

Fritz turned the ignition on and kicked down on the start lever, and the engine fired right up. "You would have to get used to it. I do not have any trouble."

"I hope you have a good trip."

"See you soon." With a little wave, Fritz was on his way back to Neidenberg.

CHAPTER 7

The two-and-a-half-hour trip was taking much too long for Fritz because of his excitement to talk to Sigi. Finally, he is getting near her home. So many things are going through his mind. *How should I start the conversation? What should I say? What do I want to tell her first about the farm? This is a nice day to take a ride like this. The trees are tall and straight ... Whoa! ... Chuckhole!* He barely was able to avoid the chuckhole and almost recovered when—"Ho ... Now what? A duffel bag?" It took some fancy horsemanship to avoid the bag and keep the motorcycle upright, especially being on a curve and looking up at the trees. He figured somebody must have hit the chuckhole and jarred the bag off their car. He could not do much about the hole, but he could get the bag out of the road. He wheeled around, rode back to where the bag was, turned around again, and stopped on the side of the road near the bag, with his motorcycle heading toward Neidenberg again.

When he picked up the bag, it opened enough for him to see that there were military clothes inside. "Russian Army clothes!" he said with surprise. He quickly looked up and down the road and into the woods on either side. *What are Russians doing in this area? I never see them in military dress in public. The borders are so easy to cross that they could have many groups in this country gathering information or trying to stir up trouble. I need to get this out of sight. I might be able to use these things someday!* He carried the bag into the woods, laid it behind a log, and covered it with branches and leaves. *This will be good for now. Home is less than five kilometers from here; I can come and get this any time.*

After coming out of the woods, he had just reached his bike when a car he did not recognize came into view from around the curve in the direction of Koenigsberg, with four men in it that he had not seen before. All of them were looking anxiously at the sides of the road. *I must have passed those guys while I was thinking of Sigi or looking up at the trees.* He started up his motorcycle and gave them a friendly wave as they went by, then continued his ride to Sigi's. He soon passed the men in the car, who were still going slowly and looking around.

Ahlf began his welcoming bark as soon as Fritz turned into Sigi's driveway. The wide sweep of his stout tail was wagging the rest of his body. Everything from the tip of his tail to the tip of his nose swayed in rhythm.

"Hello, Ahlf! Who else is home now?" Ahlf was too busy soaking up the rubbing and patting from his newest friend to think of anything else. Fritz turned off his motorcycle and started toward the house. "Ahlf, where's Sigi? Is she in the house?" Ahlf walked right along beside Fritz, within easy reach of any more attention that might come his way.

Sigi opened the door just as Fritz and Ahlf got to it. "Hi." She gave him her big, welcoming smile, just like the ones he had been seeing over the past five months.

"Hi there. It is always good to have you smile at me. Are you busy now? I have had a good couple of days, and I want to tell you about them. I usually see someone outside when I come here. Is anybody else home?"

"Yes, Mom is inside with Lora. Dad and the others are at the church. Trina and the girls her age from our church are having a volleyball game with a team of girls from another church in town. They are a lot of fun to watch, and it is a good chance to get to know new people."

"That sounds like a good time."

"We can talk now if you want to help me with a few chores."

"Sure!" He took her hand as they started for the barn. "We have come to know a lot about each other in the last five months!"

"Yes …" Her answer sounded a little uncertain, like she suspected something was up.

"For example …" he started as they went through the barn door, and then he pulled her quickly around the end of the door, out of sight of the house. "I know that I love you." He bent down, took her in a big hug, lifted her off her feet, and began spinning around. She hung on to his neck, laughing happily as he kissed her and then kissed and nibbled at her neck to make her laugh even more while they spun, four, five, six times around, kissing, nibbling, laughing, with his warm and loving, masculine growl.

"I love you too, but we need to stop before we get dizzy and fall!" She was still laughing when the spinning stopped and he put her down. "I thought something was coming, and now I am sure. Maybe you should tell me about these last couple of good days you were talking about."

"Yes, yes," he said, with a big smile. "Back to business!"

Sigi looked at him curiously, smiling, then started checking the chicken nests for eggs.

"It all started when Herr Kemp called me into his office on Thursday to talk about my apprenticeship ending soon. Apparently, he has been thinking about this for some time. He wants me to go to Koenigsberg to work with Bernhard!"

She could see that Fritz could hardly contain his excitement.

"Business is improving up there, and he needs some help to expand even more."

"That could be expensive. Will you be earning enough to live on your own?"

"He told me that I would be getting a regular engraver's salary, which might be enough to make it." He stopped, smiling for effect, and then continued. "He also told me that I could live at a farm that has been in his family for a long time but has not had anybody living on it for years. I know it sounds like a lot of work to come home after all day at a full-time job, then have to fix up an old farm too."

"It sure does. You could wear yourself out that way."

"Herr Kemp said that if I would go and work with Bernhard for ten years, I could *have* the farm without ever making a single payment on it!"

Sigi suddenly stopped the chores and stood looking down past the eggs in her apron as she listened intently to what Fritz was saying. Stifling her excitement and surprise, she said, "How *bad* is the farm? That is what you need to find out!" She was always the common-sense realist.

"That is what I thought too. That is why I went to look at it today. I have seen it. It will take some work, but it can be done slowly … if we need to."

"If … *we* … need to?" she asked, as her look of surprise widened into hopeful questioning.

"Yes! It has a large house … with plenty of room for a family—on ten acres!"

"Room for a … *family?*" To hopeful questioning was now added a smile as she turned to look at him. With her head now straight up and her eyes wide open, he had her full attention while she stood holding six eggs in her apron.

"Yes, room for … *our* family! I want you to go with me as my wife. Will you marry me, Siglinde Backman?"

"Yes!" The eggs hit the ground as she put her hands to her mouth to contain a smiling gasp. "Yes." Again she ran the few steps to be in his arms, just like the day in the woods when she realized he was the masked wildman who saved her from the three men from the car. This time, she jumped high enough that when they caught each other, their faces were the same height, just right for the kiss she had for him. With her arms around his neck as he held her and her feet off the ground, she said, "I have been thinking for months now that I would love to go with you anywhere you go."

"Great! Wow, it feels good to have that question settled! It has been in my mind for a while, but until today, I did not know how to make it happen. Sorry about the eggs."

She looked down and saw the ground around them gooey with broken eggs. She gasped, laughing. He smiled and, with one more warm, loving kiss and a couple of smaller chasers, put her back down on the ground.

She just wanted him to hold her for a few more minutes while so many thoughts raced through her mind. *This is real. This man is going to be my husband. I know he can take care of me and my children. I am ready for this. I can already feel the peace and the love we can have together; I will do my best to make that happen!* "Oh, Fritz, I feel wonderful! I am so excited that I can hardly feel anything else." She began to loosen her hug. "We have so much to talk about!"

"All of that will come in time."

"You have had some time to think about the farm and what needs to be done; tell me what your ideas are." Sigi went back to checking the feed for the chickens.

"The first thing to do at the farm is to get the house ready to live in. The roof has a leak, and some repairs need to be done inside before it can be repainted. I plan to go there on Saturdays to take care of things like that. Can you go with me next week to see the place yourself?" He followed her to the hay to get some for the cow.

"I am looking forward to that. How would we go? On your motorcycle?"

"My dad will probably let me use the truck to take supplies for the repairs; we can go in that. I should look for a truck to buy for us, which would be enough for us until our family outgrows it in four or five years."

She put more hay into the feeder for Clothilda. "I'm excited to tell Mom and Dad that we are getting married." Sigi patted Clothilda's head when the dairy cow came to get some of the fresh hay. Clothilda responded by shaking her head to rid herself of this friendly gesture.

"This girl is just not the nice and friendly type," said Sigi. "Speaking of not friendly, did I tell you that my uncle Ben has been talking to my dad about joining the Brownshirts—for the extra money he could make? I know you do not like them, and why, so I wanted you to know."

"No, I do not like them! Maybe it is time to tell them you were one of the girls in the story they were telling him. I think they are dangerous, and I plan to keep doing what I can to disrupt them whenever I can. What do you think about your dad joining them?"

They came out of the barn and were met by Ahlf, who was wagging his tail and looking for some more rubbing and patting.

"Hi, Ahlf. It is too bad all people cannot be like you, boy—happy, friendly, eager for love and attention, and always ready to be nice to those who are nice to you."

They turned toward the wooded part of the back of the property to take more time walking and talking together.

The sun was getting lower in the sky, and the shadows of the trees were getting longer. "I agree with you, my husband-to-be ..." She realized she liked saying that, which showed in her happy smile and sparkling eyes as she looked up at him. "I do not like the idea of Dad—or Uncle Ben—joining them."

He gave her a quick kiss on her young, pretty, happy face with its simple beauty. He put his arm around her as she turned to look thoughtfully down at where she was walking.

"Maybe they do not know how bad some of those men are. Maybe Uncle Ben and the other man thought the story of the girls in the woods and the wild men was more beer and brag than truth."

"How can we find out?" Fritz realized that if Sigi's dad and uncle were among the Brownshirts, it would affect their marriage. He hoped she had an idea how it might be possible to change their minds about joining.

"Uncle Ben and Aunt Anina are coming over tonight. After dinner, they will probably be talking about the Brownshirts. If you stay for dinner, you will be here for their conversation."

"That is a good idea. But I have been up since three this morning and on this motorcycle for five hours, so I should get cleaned up and maybe rest a little. I also want to tell Mom and Dad what *we* have been talking about. I can be back at about six."

"That will be just fine, I am sure."

"If your dad is not home yet, we should check with your mom to see if she thinks it will be all right with the others." They started back toward the house. "I do not want to interrupt anything that is supposed to be private."

"I see what you mean."

Ahlf was with them again and, for the same reason, wagging and waiting for a friendly hand while they walked.

Frau Backman was in the living room doing some knitting. "There you are, Sigi! I see why you didn't come back to your knitting. How are you, Fritz?"

"I am doing well, except for being a little tired. I have been to Koenigsberg today. Herr Kemp wants me to go there to work with his son Bernhard in the new shop up there. My apprenticeship will be completed in December, which will mean an increase in pay. I am looking forward to the move; that is why I came here to see Sigi today." He looked at Sigi. "Would you like to continue, or shall I?"

Frau Backman sat listening, only half concealing her amusement at his rushing story. She knew what was coming.

"I will. Mom, the offer Herr Kemp has made to Fritz includes a raise to a normal salary and a farm that has been in his family for years but has been vacant and worrisome. There will be no payments for the farm. Then after ten years of working with Bernhard, Herr Kemp will give it to Fritz. He has asked me to go with him as his wife … and I have said yes!

Oh, Mom, I am so excited! This sounds wonderful to me!" Sigi knelt on the floor next to her mother's chair, watching the smile grow on her face.

"Dad and I thought this might happen as we watched you together over the past five months. Our big concern has been how you would be able to make it financially in the beginning. It sounds like that has been answered already. I am sure Dad will be happy for you too, like I am." She put her hands on Sigi's face and pulled her close to give her a kiss on the forehead. "When do you expect things to happen?"

"Fritz will begin repairs to the house next weekend. I will go with him to help and to do whatever I can to get the house ready for us. He needs to start work the first of January. If we are married in the middle of December, we will have time to get settled before he starts! We have not even talked about this yet, Mom! How does that sound to you, Fritz?" With a warm, respectful smile to her future husband, she waited for his response.

"That seems like a very good plan to me." He was pleased that things were going so smoothly. "We can think through the details in the next few weeks."

"Mom, there is something we want to ask you: is Uncle Ben coming over tonight?"

"Yes, he and Anina will be here for dinner."

"Will they be talking about Dad joining the Brownshirts?" Sigi went to stand by Fritz, holding his hand.

"Probably. Why? Is something wrong?"

"We have concerns about the kind of men some of them are. Do you think it will be OK for us to join the discussion?"

"I think it will. Why don't you stay for dinner?"

"That is what I asked him. With his trip today, he wants to get cleaned up and come back at six. I thought that is about when Uncle Ben will be here."

"I think they will be here before that. If so, your time for going home is running out."

"It might be. I will feel much better if I were cleaned up. I am sure I can get back by five thirty. I should let Mom and Dad know that the trip went well and that I will be here for a couple of hours before I come home. Thank you, Frau Backman."

Fritz began moving toward the door, with Sigi still holding his hand and walking with him. "I am looking forward to this discussion." He opened the door. "I will be back soon." They went out to his motorcycle. "Sigi, if you tell them about your part in the story, try to do it in a way that does not involve any of the rest of us. The less they know, the safer everybody is, OK? You should tell Trina what we have planned so she does not think we have betrayed her trust."

"OK, I am glad you will be here."

"I love you. I will be right back." After a quick kiss, he gave his starter a kick, and the bike's motor was ready to go.

When Fritz got home, his dad was coming from the garden, where he had been checking for any late produce to put in the root cellar for the winter.

"Hi, Dad! I have had a great day, and I want to tell you about it quickly before I go back over to Sigi's for a few hours. Was there any problem covering for me today around the farm?"

"No, we did OK. There was a little grumbling but no problems. You seem excited. What's it about?" He put the bucket of produce down as Fritz finished parking his bike.

"Bernhard and his family are nice and doing well. The business looks like it is growing, like they say." Fritz could feel his excitement growing again while talking with his dad. "The farm is about ten acres with a large house on it that can be very nice in time, after some repairs are made. I believe Sigi and I can get a good start in Koenigsberg with this opportunity. I have told her about it, and she is excited too. I have asked her to marry me, and she said yes. We think that a good time for us to be married would be in mid-December. By doing repairs to the house on Saturdays, I should have it ready by then."

"You *have* had an exciting day!" Herr Abbot smiled at his son's enthusiasm.

"I sure have; this is a great opportunity for us, and I am sure we can do it. Right now, I need to get cleaned up and go back to Sigi's to talk to her dad and uncle about the Brownshirts they are getting involved with."

"Are you considering joining them?" his dad asked in a puzzled tone.

"No, no. I do not trust them, and I think her dad and uncle do not really know what kind of men some of them are—or they would not be connected with them either. My purpose in going there tonight is to tell them what I know and see how they respond. I think it is important to discuss this with them as soon as possible before they get too involved." They started for the house.

"I will tell Mom about this if you want to hurry back to Sigi's."

"Thanks, Dad."

Fritz opened the door and went into the house first. "Hi, Mom! Hi, everybody!" He waved to his brothers and sister and walked over to his mom, took her hand, and said, "I have had a great day. Dad can tell you about it. I have got to get cleaned up."

The sun had just gone down, but it was not getting dark when Fritz turned into Sigi's driveway a few minutes before five thirty. *There is no visitor's car, so Uncle Ben and Aunt Anina must not be here.* Ahlf came wagging his whole self and barking his friendly bark to announce to the family that there was a visitor as he rolled to a stop.

Warin came running out the door. "Hi, Fritz! Are you going to marry Sigi?"

He turned off his motorcycle and got off just in time to grab Warin, pick him up, and tuck him under one arm so he could poke and tickle him. "I sure hope so, partner. I have not talked to your dad yet. What do you think of that?"

"I think it's great! I could use another older brother, one who is big enough to beat up bad guys with me."

Sigi came out in time to hear what Warin said. Fritz looked at her with a questioning expression and was relieved to see her shaking her head in a silent no, indicating that she had not told the family about him being the wildman.

"What bad guys are you talking about, tough guy?" He put Warin down and squatted in front of him, helping to straighten his clothes.

"The guys that Ahlf and I have to fight in the woods to save the good people in our house and our village. We can beat them, but they keep coming back."

"You and Ahlf need to keep beating them until they stop coming back. Then we can all be safe and happy. Can you do that?"

"You bet we can! We always win! Come on, Ahlf. Let's go get 'em!" Warin went around the corner of the house at full speed, with Ahlf right beside him, barking his support and looking up at his best friend.

Sigi took Fritz's hand as Warin disappeared. "He likes you. So does my whole family—except me; I *love* you!" She gave him a quick kiss.

"Hey, you two. Quit that. Come in here and tell us more about all this." Herr Backman was holding the house door he had just opened and smiling as he motioned them in.

They looked at each other, smiled, and hurried to the door. "Thank you, sir," Fritz said as they went in.

"Hi, Fritz." Frau Backman and Trina were in the kitchen, finishing up making dinner.

"I could go with you on your motorcycle to help on your house," Klaus volunteered.

"Wait a minute, Klaus. That is a long ride in a car; on a motorcycle, it would be a long, *hard* ride," Herr Backman reminded his excited young son.

"Good!" Fritz responded positively to Klaus. "Willing help is hard to find. There are many things that you could help with, but riding a motorcycle that far can make you very tired. It is like riding a horse with all the shaking and jiggling; you have to get used to it before you try to take a long ride, or you might get a lot of sore spots that last a long time."

"Come sit at the table where Mother and Trina can hear, and tell us more about the house and farm where you'll be living. Do I understand correctly that after ten years of working with his son, Herr Kemp will give you the farm?" Herr Backman asked in such a way that it was clear he could hardly believe it.

"That is what he told me when he first mentioned it to me. I could not believe it either. So, when I visited his son Bernhard today, I asked him about it, and he told me that is what his dad said he was going to do. From the beginning, this has been the most interesting part of the deal to me."

Warin must have made short work of the bad guys because he walked in the back door in a triumphant strut. "We beat 'em, Fritz. We put the last of 'em in jail, and Ahlf is watching 'em."

"That's great! We need more good men like you, and Ahlf's help too!"

Lora came over to Fritz, showing him her small stuffed doll and talking in her baby noises. "Hi, little lady. Who is this?"

She began explaining in her two-year-old chatter, probably telling him what they had been involved in that day as she pointed to the doll and raised it up so he could see and understand better. The rest of the family watched and listened with smiles and quiet chuckles, trying not to interrupt the conversation.

"Wow, that's quite a story. Do things like that happen often?" She watched and listened to him as he talked. When he finished, she continued to talk, this time with different gestures, because the story had obviously changed. One of her other toys must have been involved now, because she suddenly looked across the room to where they were and ran to get it but got distracted before she came back. "I think her story just ended."

Everybody laughed. It was all over their faces, the love they have for one another and the happiness they felt in being together as a family. Six-year-old Warin jumped up from where he had been playing and listening and ran over to hug his dad's arm to satisfy what he was feeling. Dad picked him up and was hugging him back when there was a knock on the door.

Klaus ran to the door and opened it. "Hi, Uncle Ben and Aunt Anina!"

Frau Backman got to the door in time to invite them in. "Come in, come in! We are talking to Fritz about a change in his work and the offer from Herr Kemp that involves moving to Koenigsberg and living on a farm that belongs to the Kemp family." She closed the door and began leading them toward the kitchen table. "Dinner is ready, so you might as well sit here."

Fritz stood up to welcome the new guests and to be introduced.

She continued talking excitedly. "This is Fritz Abbot. He has been seeing Sigi for about five months now and has just asked her to marry him. We are all excited and want them to tell us more about their plans. The girls and I will get dinner on, and we can all listen while we eat. Our family is about to grow!"

"It is nice to have you over," said Herr Backman. "I love my family. I would like it if we kept our dinner conversation on the subject of family and save the Brownshirts for after."

"I like that idea," Frau Backman said, bringing nods of agreement from all the adults.

The discussion ranged from family history to religion to farm life, education, and animals and ended with ideas for what use Fritz could put his new farm to. There was no shortage of suggestions. It was at that point that Frau Backman invited the ladies to help clean up the dinner. When four women worked together, it did not take long.

Soon she said, "I think we're finished in the kitchen, so we can move into the living room and be more comfortable."

"As you can tell by now, we are all happy with the opportunity and plans that Fritz and Sigi have," said Herr Backman as he, Uncle Ben, Aunt Anina took seats in the living room. Trina, Fritz, and Sigi brought chairs in from the kitchen table, Klaus and Warin sat on the floor, and Lora was playing by Trina.

"Can I get you a drink of water?" Frau Backman asked before she took a chair by her husband.

"No, thank you. That was a wonderful meal," Aunt Anina replied.

"Fritz asked if he could sit in on the discussion tonight. I told him it would probably be OK. Is it all right with you?" Frau Backman asked before she finished settling into her chair.

"I think so," Uncle Ben answered. "What is your interest in the Brownshirts?"

"They seem to be growing in number. I want to know more about them. Because you are wearing your shirt now, you must have good things you can tell us."

"One of the good things about being a Brownshirt is the extra money that it means for my family. This has been a great help for many of the men who have had a hard time finding work since the war."

"Are all of you full-time?" Fritz asked, trying to help the conversation flow well.

"Not all. Most are part-time. Our main purpose is to help keep order at meetings of the Nazi Party. Sometimes there is a person who disagrees with the speaker and begins shouting questions or insults at him and tries to disrupt the meeting. It is our job to ask him to be quiet and let the meeting continue. If he does not, we may have to remove him. Sometimes we have the job of distributing printed material about a belief or goal of the party. There is a variety of things that we might be asked to do."

Uncle Ben continued, "Most of us believe that Herr Hitler has the ability to lead our country out of the confusion and political inaction that now has it so crippled. It is true that right now our economy is steadily improving, but without strong leadership, that could crumble at any time." Uncle Ben seemed sincerely interested in helping Germany regain some of her earlier strength and respect.

"Somebody has to do something to get us more stable than we are, or we're just riding on luck, and that's not going to last forever." Herr Backman's good-natured smile was made a bit smaller with his concern. "I have not joined them yet, but I like the idea of supporting stability, along with the extra money that it will mean."

"I have seen some of the Brownshirt men going through town or coming out of the beer hall, but I do not know about any meetings that have been held around here. Is there some activity that I do not know about going on in this area?" Fritz looked at both men to see who wanted to answer.

Uncle Ben answered, "About the only things they stop for in Neidenberg are food and beer and to recruit a new member if there is a good prospect. That is why I am here tonight, to try to convince Leon to join us. I can talk to him, but I am not the one who makes the decision to let him in. That is for Jarvis to decide. He is the recruiter."

Sigi and Fritz looked at each other to see if the other recognized the name they just heard as the driver of the car and the leader of the first group of men, and one of the men telling the story to Uncle Ben in the woods that second time.

"This Jarvis sounds like an important man in the group. Does he do more than recruit?" Fritz was searching for more information while trying not to look like he was prying where he should not be.

"He is responsible for recruiting and paying in all of East Prussia." Uncle Ben made a large sweeping motion with both hands to help impress everybody with Jarvis, as much as he was himself. "He has an interview with each recruit and decides if he can join us. Also, once each month on the fourth Saturday, he brings our pay and distributes it. That is a full-time responsibility—and a big job with over one thousand men to deal with. Some of the men are easier to work with than others, because we come from so many different backgrounds. That is what Jarvis is for, to decide who will be useful to the group and who will not."

"Herr Backman, have you met Jarvis or any of the other men in the group?" Fritz asked.

"No, I haven't met him, but one day when Ben came over, he had a man with him who was a new member. Like Ben, he seemed like a nice enough fellow. I think he lives near here someplace."

"Is he the one who was with you when Jarvis and another man were telling the story about the girls in the woods?" Fritz asked.

"What story about girls in the woods?" Frau Backman had been sitting casually and listening until now, but she asked this question with a great deal of interest and a bit of a frown on her face.

"I haven't heard about this!" Aunt Anina added. "What is he talking about?" She looked at her husband.

"Sigi told me about it months ago on our first date!" Fritz began to explain with a look of surprise. "It was so long ago that I have heard it talked about by others who live around here. It sounds like there are some here who do not know the story."

"Sigi, where did you hear of such a story?" Uncle Ben was trying to act puzzled and unbelieving.

With an encouraging look from Fritz, Sigi asked, "Do you remember the day, about five months ago, when you were part of a group of four men in brown shirts who came out of the beer hall talking loudly after having some beers? You all got into a car and started down the road toward Willenberg?"

"Oh, yes, I think so."

"How many people inside the beer hall could have heard what you were talking about? How can I know which of them talked to others?"

Uncle Ben shifted uneasily in his chair. "I see what you mean."

"So, there is a story about girls. Maybe you should tell us," Herr Backman suggested.

"There is a story. I thought there was probably nothing to it, because you can hear most anything from a man who has been in a beer hall. I saw no purpose in repeating such a tale to anybody."

"Normally, that would be good logic, but if this story is true, it can tell us something about the kind of men there are in this group. If it is a story they made up, it still will show us how their minds work." Herr Backman still had traces of his good-natured smile, but he now wanted to know more about who these men really were.

Everybody seemed to have a growing interest in how this part of the conversation would turn out.

"OK, I will tell you the story as accurately as I can, and you can tell me if you think it was made up by men in their beer," said Uncle Ben, hoping it was not true. "After we left the beer hall, we had not gone far down the road when Jarvis stopped the car on the side of the road and said he would show us where the whole thing happened. The place we stopped is where they said they talked to two girls who were walking on the side of the road. Suddenly the girls ran into the woods. The fellows told me that all three of them ran after the girls and caught them. They then decided to take them a little deeper into the woods. I did not ask to what end, because I thought they were putting me on. Suddenly, they claimed, a masked man came running toward them, shouting and carrying on. They were so surprised that they did nothing, and before they knew it, this charging man had knocked two of them out and left Jarvis on the ground with broken ribs.

"Jarvis says he sat up, holding his side, and a second masked man ran up holding a pistol and pointed it in his face, saying, 'Do not come around here again!' Then the masked men apparently left. Now, does that sound like a beer-drinking story if you ever heard one?" Uncle Ben asked, shaking his head in disbelief. "What kind of crazy man would attack three others in brown shirts, who are probably hardened by war or by living on the tough streets of the city?"

Fritz looked at Sigi and Trina with a comical smile as he said, "That's a good question."

"That is an incredible story. It does sound like a beer hall story. Where did you say you stopped on the road?" Herr Backman asked with a jovial tone in his voice.

"Just through the woods from here." Uncle Ben motioned toward the road.

"You did not say what happened to the girls," Sigi pointed out.

"That's another odd thing. They told us that the girls ran deeper into the woods as soon as they could. You have to wonder why." Uncle Ben had a puzzled look on his face.

"It was because I lived so close by!"

There was sudden silence, except for Trina's gasp, as all eyes went to Sigi in total surprise.

"That's right! The girls they were telling you about that day were me and a friend of mine."

Trina's eyes were as big as they could get, her hands clenched tightly together in front of her mouth as she remembered the fear she felt that day.

"So it *was* real … and it was *you?*" Herr Backman had no trace of his good-natured smile as anger grew so clearly on his face. "This Jarvis fellow and two of his men took you and someone else into the woods?"

"They were very rough. If we stumbled, they dragged us. It was the most frightened I have ever been, and all we could do was cry and pray."

"Everything that concerns Sigi now concerns me; that is why I am here, to learn more about the Brownshirts," Fritz reminded everyone. "This incident happened five months ago. That means that the Backmans could be just over halfway to being grandparents, possibly by this Jarvis we have been talking about."

Trina jumped to her feet. "It wasn't just a friend with Sigi that day. I was the other girl!" She ran into her bedroom crying loudly when she realized more deeply how her life could have been changed that day.

Frau Backman held a handkerchief to her face, and her eyes showed the terror being played out in her imagination.

Aunt Anina was looking at her husband in horror and disbelief.

Herr Backman was now up and pacing the floor as his anger grew. "Ben and Anina, we were having a wonderful experience of love and peace and happiness in being part of a family that liked being together, just before you knocked on the door. In the short time we have talked about the Brownshirts, which has changed to imagining my sweet young daughters—both of them—running from the kind of men you want me to join. The money is simply not worth it! Nothing is!"

"Ben, I feel the same way Leon does; the money is simply not worth the damage that could be done to our family." Aunt Anina voiced the shock that was so plainly growing in the expression on her face and everyone else's as the story and comments unfolded.

Fritz looked at Sigi and motioned toward the bedroom where Trina had retreated and quietly said, "Maybe you can help." She nodded and started for the bedroom.

"As you agreed, Leon, it sounded to me like a story from someone's imagination. Except for showing how a couple of these men think, I tried to believe there was nothing to it. I really wanted to be a part of something I thought could be good for Germany—that paid me too. I can see now that the price is much too high; I will return my shirts and leave the group immediately! I would like to know who the two masked men were though." Uncle Ben shook his head with a puzzled smile on his face.

"With their masks on, the girls could not recognize them and could not think of anybody they knew who could do something like that." Fritz shrugged his shoulders while putting on an exaggerated puzzled smile to help lighten the feeling that was weighing on everybody.

Even Klaus could feel the tension leaving the room as Fritz tried to shift the conversation. Warin had gone from a sitting to a lying position during the conversation and was now sound asleep.

"Elke, do we have enough of the cake you made for each of us to have some?" Herr Backman wanted to finish the correction of atmosphere and spirit in his home. "I think we're through talking about Brownshirts in my home. I would like to give you another shirt to change into, Ben!"

"I would welcome that, Leon. Thank you."

"Cake is a good idea! I think there is enough. Maybe we can ask Fritz more questions about the farm." Frau Backman was eager to return to happier conversation.

CHAPTER 8

Early Monday morning, Herr Kemp called Fritz into his office. There were puzzled looks on the faces of Urs and Jochem again, just like last time that happened. With his little wave and a comical smile, they realized he was having fun keeping them guessing. When paper balls and other things started flying at him, he ran for the door! This time, Fritz was sure he knew what it was about.

Fritz could see that Erna noticed him come through the door from the shop in a hurry. He knew she was wondering what was going on. His walking on tiptoes, like he was trying to be quiet and sneak through, caused a very puzzled look to come to her face. When he put his finger across his lips and said, "Shhhhhh," to the closed door he just came through, her look changed, and more things started flying at him.

"Good morning, sir," Fritz said as he popped through the office door.

Herr Kemp noticed a commotion when he closed the door quickly and asked, "What was that about?"

"Just having some fun, sir. They are all curious about my visits to your office lately, and I have been teasing them with it."

"Oh, I see," he said with a wave of his hand. "Come in, Fritz. Sit down and tell me about your visit to Koenigsberg on Saturday. Did you see the shop and the farm? What do you think?" Herr Kemp sounded eager to get the news.

"Yes, I had a nice visit with Bernhard and his family." He took the chair in front of the desk. "I did not know they had a new son! They are a fine-looking family."

"They are good kids and doing a good job of raising their own kids. They seem to like living up there. Did he show you what he plans to do and why he needs your help?"

"He made the move sound like a good idea, and I know I can do what he needs. There is a good future there." Fritz was again feeling pleased with the whole idea but tried not to let too much of his excitement show.

"I *thought* you would be able to adapt to his plan easily. What about the farm? How did you like what you saw?"

"It looks like it was a very nice place at one time." Fritz was nodding his head and enjoying the thoughts of improvements he would like to make.

"That was a long time ago. Will you be able to handle the repairs?"

"I will have some help this Saturday when I begin. When I got back from Koenigsberg, I went over to Sigi's, told her about my trip, and asked her to marry me. Now she is excited to go with me and get started on the house too. I think she is looking forward to the move as much as I am!"

"That's great!" Herr Kemp stood up and reached across the desk to shake Fritz's hand. "So, you will have a wife soon. Congratulations!"

Fritz stood up to receive the handshake. "This offer you have made has given me the missing pieces I needed to feel like I can start a family. We both appreciate what you have offered us. It is a dream come true. It is like we are able to begin with a ten-year head start into our future."

"Good. I'm glad to hear that. Sit down, please. There is more to talk about. With the way the economy has been since the war, I have been wondering what to do with the farm. This makes it work out for both of us. What is your plan for doing the repairs?"

"This week, I will be putting together some of the supplies needed to fix the roof and get the walls ready to paint. On Saturday, Sigi will go with me in my dad's truck to help and to look the place over for herself. We want to have the house ready to move into by mid-December when we get married." Fritz was aware of himself, watching and listening for any indication that Herr Kemp might be rethinking the offer. *It is going to make such a wonderful difference in my life that it is easy to think it is too good to be true. My biggest question now is, what is the most polite way to ask for the deal in writing?*

"It's good to hear that you like the plan, because it will mean a nice improvement in my business. I think I have some of the shingles used on that house. They are the same as on my house. You can take them if you like."

"That is very generous of you; it certainly will help. I will be by this week to pick them up. Now all I need for this weekend is some plaster for the walls, and we will have enough to keep us busy for several hours."

"You sound like you are well committed to making this move; that's what I wanted to check on with you. Let me know when the wedding will be and if there is anything else you might need help with. I want very much for this to succeed." Herr Kemp was certain and happy in his manner of speech, which told Fritz that his willingness to help was real.

"Sir, I am sure you know what I mean when I say that this whole opportunity is so wonderful and important to my future that it is still easy to believe that I do not understand something, which could cause it to go wrong and not be real. Would it be possible for Erna to write two copies of a description of what we each agree to do, that we both could sign and have our own copy?

"Sure. That is a good idea! If they are not finished today, then surely tomorrow."

"Thank you, sir. And now I think it is time to start telling others who might like to know about our plan." Fritz pointed over his shoulder to the door where the commotion came from. Herr Kemp began to chuckle in understanding as he motioned for Fritz to go.

Fritz now felt reassured, happy, and confident that this really was happening. He could not help smiling again as he stood up and reached out to shake Herr Kemp's hand before leaving the office. "You know, sir, I think I feel like a different man—a homeowner. Wow!"

As he closed the office door, Fritz turned to Erna. "Hey, Erna, I have some news for you—"

"Good! It's about time!" Erna interrupted, relieved that she no longer had to hold her curiosity in check.

"Maybe you should come out into the shop, so I can tell all of you at the same time." Fritz was heading for the door to the shop and showing her a teasing smile as he looked back.

"This had better be good!" She jumped up, threw an eraser at him, and hurried toward the door. The eraser hit the wall at the same time he opened the door and ducked through.

The commotion got the attention of Jochem and Urs. When Erna popped through the door looking for Fritz, Urs said, "Oh, wow, what have you done now?"

"What news? What has been going on in that office between you and Herr Kemp? You'd better start talking!" She was looking for something else to throw.

"OK, settle down. I can't talk while I'm running."

"Yes, start talking!" Urs was wadding up a piece of paper with a menacing look on his face.

"That's a good idea if you know what's good for you, buster!" Jochem had his hands on his hips, trying to look mean.

"Hey, I did not expect all of this!' Fritz started. "I did not want to say anything until I was sure, so here it is. Last week, Herr Kemp offered me a chance to work with Bernhard to help him expand the business in Koenigsberg. The deal includes a farm that his family no longer wants."

"Do you mean that's where you will stay? For how long and how much?" Jochem wondered how he could afford to live up there on an engraver's salary.

"I will receive a full salary, and after ten years, the farm will be mine!"

"What are you going to do with a farm while you're working a regular job?" Urs asked from his single-young-man-in-a big-city point of view.

"I looked at the farm last Saturday and came home so excited that I went right over to Sigi's and asked her to marry me."

"What? Are you two getting married?" Erna was excited for them and happy for Sigi, who had become her friend over the past five months. "When will this happen?"

"Sigi will go with me this Saturday to start the repairs, so the house will be ready for us by the middle of December. We do not have all the details yet; we will let you know as soon as we do."

"That's wonderful!" Erna started toward him, and he began to back up until she showed him her open hands, with nothing to throw in them, and a melodramatic innocence on her face. When she got to him, she gave him a hug and a kiss on the cheek. "You are two great people. I am happy for you!"

Urs left his station to shake his hand. "Congratulations, my man."

"Make sure you keep us informed about the wedding and if we can help you with the farm. Congratulations." Jochem's expression was one of being happy for his friend as they shook hands.

When Fritz got home after work, he told his dad about the conversation with Herr Kemp and the written agreement and how he felt about the deal being for real. At dinner, the whole family got excited again for him and this opportunity, which would make it possible for him to marry Sigi and for them to begin a life of their own. They made a plan to take care of the weekend uses of the truck during the week so that it would be free for the trip to Koenigsberg on Saturday.

At work on Tuesday, Fritz arranged with Herr Kemp to pick up the roofing materials that evening. As he came through the door, back into the shop, he saw that Val had come with a delivery and was talking excitedly with Urs and Jochem.

"What is this about getting married, and a farm, and moving? What have you been up to this weekend, and why is your good buddy the last to know?" Val walked over to him. "Congratulations, I think," he said with a slap on Fritz's shoulder. "Now, how much of this is true?"

"That is what I had to be sure of before I could tell anybody. That only happened yesterday, and my mind has been spinning since then. I was going to get to you." He had a teasing smile for his friend, which just got him a harder punch on the shoulder. "This has been a busy few days. I will tell you while we unload the stone. Do not worry, you two. I will fill him in on everything."

Urs and Jochem went back to their workstations. "OK, but if you have any questions, Val, just let us know. We almost had to beat it out of him ourselves," Urs said over his shoulder.

Fritz was able to give Val a quick summary of events since Thursday, including the Brownshirt discussion at the Backmans'.

"Wow, you have been busy! What can I do to help?"

"I am glad you asked. I would like you to come with us this Saturday. There is a lot to do, and I want you to know where the farm is for the future. Do you think you could arrange to come?"

"I think so. Mom and Dad will be happy to hear about all of this. I am sure they will help me be able to go."

"Thanks, Val. If I do not hear from you, I will be at your house at eight Saturday morning. We will pick up Sigi and be on our way." Fritz was pleased with the way his Saturday plan was developing.

Saturday morning, Fritz was up early, the first in his family to put footprints in the newly fallen snow.

When a young man is energized by a dream that he believes in, he can accomplish goals that look to others to be impossible or superhuman. With this kind of motivation, he quickly finished the last of the chores that were his responsibility so he could take the truck. When he pulled into Val's driveway, it was obvious that his family was up too, taking care of the early chores. Val's dad came out of the barn to see Fritz and congratulate him on the opportunity that Val described to them. "That sounds like a great thing Herr Kemp has offered you. If I were in your position, I would act on it as quickly as I could."

"Yes, sir. That is exactly how I feel. Thanks for letting Val come with me today. He is someone I know I can rely on and trust."

"Hey, Fritz!" said Val, coming out of the barn behind his father. "You are right on time as usual. Thanks, Dad, for letting me go. I will see you later today." Val almost sounded like he was leaving for a scout outing.

"Say hi to everybody for me, OK?" Fritz waved as they pulled out of the driveway.

"We have a long ride ahead of us today. When we get back, we will have been on the road for probably five hours. Are you ready for that?" Fritz asked his friend.

"Sure, it sounds like fun. And comfy seats!" he said, bouncing on it in an allusion to their motorcycle saddles. "Besides, I want to see your farm."

When they passed the beer hall in town, they saw a car that looked like the one the Brownshirts were driving both times Fritz had seen them before. "See that? I wonder if our buddies are in town. This is the fourth Saturday in October, right?"

"Yes, it is," Val said. "What difference does that make?"

"Sigi's uncle Ben said that on the fourth Saturday of each month, Jarvis carries the payroll for all of the Brownshirts in East Prussia."

"Oh, oh, I think I want to go home." Val moaned at what might be going through his friend's head.

"They must have stayed in town overnight and are now having breakfast before going to their next stop." Fritz was thinking out loud for the benefit of his friend.

"And we are on the way to *our* next stop, which is Sigi's, not a beer hall!" Val reminded Fritz, making a motion to keep on moving.

"Yes, I know, I know."

When they passed the beer hall, Val looked back and said, "Whew, that was close. We have enough to do today."

"Yes, but they are so much fun," Fritz reminded him.

"How about we think of work—not fun—right now? We will all three be happier!"

"OK, but I want to stop here and get three of the pistols and a rifle with some ammunition to take to Koenigsberg." Fritz pulled to the side of the road near where the weapons from their encounters with the Brownshirts were hidden. It only took a few minutes to find their hiding place. "Let's take the time now to check out two of the pistols and the rifle to make sure they're ready to fire."

"I do not like this already. What are these for, just in case a bear jumps out of the woods while we are working on your house?" Val already had one pistol checked and loaded, then started on the rifle while Fritz was still working with a pistol. "There probably are not any more bears around your farm than there are around here, but we have to be ready for them anyway, huh?" He finished with the rifle. "OK, one pistol and one rifle, loaded and ready."

"Good. We need to get on over to Sigi's." Fritz joined Val back at the truck. "We can cover them here in the back with the roofing supplies."

The back of the truck has a canvas top the same height as the cab and same length as the bed. It is supported by wooden ribs, with a flap at the rear that could be tied open or closed, very much like military trucks. This truck was black like most private trucks, not the gray or green of the military.

At Sigi's, they were met as usual by Ahlf, who barked at the unfamiliar truck like the property was being invaded, until he heard the friendly voices of Val and Fritz.

Warin came running out of the house, happy to see his two big buddies. "Hi, Val! Hi, Fritz! Can I go with you guys? I want to see your new house! Can I?" Warin was on the running board as soon as they stopped.

Fritz opened his door and stepped out, with Warin still hanging on through the open window and swinging with it. "Not yet, tiger. It is not ready for visitors. We have a lot of cleaning to do first. I will let you know when you can come." Fritz grabbed him and tickled him until he let go of the door that had swung closed again and threw him over his shoulder like a sack of potatoes. Then he began walking with a little extra jump in his step to cause Warin to bounce more than normal and laugh each time Fritz's shoulder pushed into his tummy.

An inch of newly-fallen snow showed their tracks from the truck to the house and tracks from the early-morning chores that had been done.

On the covered porch, they cleaned their shoes. Klaus opened it from the inside with a big "Hi!"

"Good morning, everybody. How are you all doing?" Val asked as he went in, Fritz behind him.

"Hi, guys. Come in. So today is the big day, the first day of working on your own house!" Herr Backman said to Fritz in a congratulating way.

"Yes, sir. It is still a little hard to believe. I am already looking forward to having you come for a visit when things are settled."

"So am I!" said Herr Backman.

"I am too!" Frau Backman came in from the kitchen, where Trina was finishing up the last of the breakfast cleanup. "We all are excited to see your farm and house. It sounds like it will be a wonderful place for you."

Sigi came in from the bedroom in time to hear what her mom said, adding, "If you are excited, imagine how I feel! I will be able to tell you all about it tonight. I am so excited that I feel nervous. I'm almost shaking."

"I think we should be going so we can get the house ready for everybody to come and see before the stress gets too high around here," Val said with a teeth-gritting, wide-eyed, melodramatic expression of tension on his funnyman face. He turned toward the door with a slightly shaking, stiff, Frankenstein-like walk. Everybody was laughing at him.

Sigi, standing by Fritz and holding his hand, punched Val in the ribs as he walked by, which broke the Frankenstein character back into Val, who again over-reacted with a long "Oooohh," holding his ribs as he struggled to the door.

Trina went to the kitchen and brought the lunch basket Sigi had prepared. "Do not forget this, or these two could get even harder to manage."

This brought a smile from Sigi and an "Oh, is that so?" from Fritz as he started toward Trina with a menacing look on his face.

"Thanks, sis," Sigi said as she pulled Fritz by his elbow toward the door. "Bye, everybody!"

At the end of Sigi's driveway, Fritz turned left toward the road to Koenigsberg. There had been enough traffic to clear the snow from the road where the wheels of the cars had gone. The snow was wet and easily melted. The trees were proudly wearing their light frosting of snow, as if to say, "See how pretty we are in our first winter outfits?" The sky was cloudy with some areas of darker gray-blue, which sent a clear message of more snow being possible at any time.

The cab of the truck was almost not big enough for three adults dressed warmly against the weather. "Maybe in a little while, the engine will get warmed up enough, and the heater will work well enough for us to take off our coats to make more room," Val said hopefully. "Or maybe the jostling of the ride will settle us into one mass that can keep us warm in any weather."

"Oh, Sigi, we saw the car that the Brownshirts drive parked at the beer hall when we came through town," Fritz said in a playfully excited tone, which matched the look on his face. It was as though he was hoping for another encounter with them.

"It is OK with me. If they stayed there all day, I would like it," responded Val, who always preferred to avoid unnecessary trouble.

"Me too," said Sigi. "They cannot cause much trouble among all those people."

"That is right. But we already know what they can do when they come out. I think I have a responsibility to my family and to my country to cause these guys as much trouble as possible. If I can do something to get them disorganized or confused, maybe that will keep them from whatever trouble they were planning, at least until they get things straightened out again."

It is easy to see that Fritz is passionate about this and committed to it, as if it is a special assignment in his life. The thought that Sigi, his pure, sweet, pretty little wife to be, was nearly fouled by these men very quickly made him angry and energized and willing to do almost anything to keep every girl from going through that.

"I think it is wonderful that you feel like that, but you also need to be careful with these men. You could get yourself killed, and then what will your family do?" Sigi said, wondering if she should worry about a husband who thought like Fritz did.

"My family is what this is all about." Fritz nodded his head once for emphasis. "That experience with you girls and the three men shows why it is important to do something. It is true I need to be careful, but if I do nothing, what kind of man will I be? And what kind of life will we have if men like this have their way? There has to be a way to be effective without being too dangerous."

"I am in favor of doing what we can, but I especially like what you said about *without being too dangerous*. There needs to be a balance," said Val, perfectly willing to be reliable but not reckless.

They rode along quietly until Fritz began to slow the truck and look at the side of the road. "On my way back from Koenigsberg, I almost ran into a duffel bag in the road. I stopped to get it out of the way and discovered that it has Russian army clothes in it! I hid it in the woods, and now I want to pick it up and take it with us. It should be right in here." He stopped and went into the woods. In a few minutes, he came out with the duffel bag. "Val, come and see what I have here."

Val and Sigi came around to the back of the truck where Fritz had the flap open and was taking things out of the bag. "I thought there might be something useful in here against the Brownshirts. There are two large winter coats, two scarves, socks, hats, field uniforms—"

"Hey, you guys," Val interrupted, "the Brownshirts just passed us. They looked like Jarvis and Hall."

"We should go." Fritz put the bag and clothes loosely in the truck and closed the flap.

As Fritz stuffed himself into the cab of the truck where Val and Sigi had just settled, Val asked, "Why do I get the feeling that you have some kind of a plan involving those guys?"

"I do not really have a plan, but you know that two men who just came out of a beer hall will sooner or later have to stop and go into the woods to let out some of the beer they had with their breakfast." Fritz started the truck and headed down the road faster than before, hoping to keep the men's car in sight. "That will be a good time to surprise them and see if they have the payroll for this month. If we can get that, it will surely cause problems among all their men in East Prussia. When that news comes from the same two who had an unbelievable story about two girls in the woods and two masked wildmen, it should drop their credibility among the whole group. Some of them will want Jarvis replaced, and maybe there will be a power struggle by those who want his job. That should cause a good deal of confusion and delay in whatever plans they have."

"That sure is a bold idea and does not sound very *un*dangerous," Val was quick to point out.

Fritz said, "There are three things that make it undangerous: first, we will surprise them and have control of them before they know what is happening; second, we will have to wait to do anything more to them until we know who their new leader is; and third, it will probably cripple their strength for months."

"It would be nice to have a break from this stuff … for a very long time!" Sigi said longingly.

Again, they traveled without talking, the only sound being the motor of the truck working harder to keep up the higher speed.

They rounded a curve, and about three kilometers down a straight stretch of road, they all saw at the same time that the car of the Brownshirts had stopped, and the two men, Jarvis and Hall, were going into the woods. "Sometimes these guys are very predictable," Fritz said, smiling and shaking his head.

"I want to catch these guys in the woods and keep them there, so they do not see the truck. As soon as we stop, we need to get a scarf, a hat, and an overcoat from the Russian stuff we were looking at. Any talking we do will be with a heavy Russian accent. They have not been armed before, but until we are sure, we cannot let them see us. Sigi, you will stay in the truck until I say OK. Then you check their car for any guns, ammunition, and money. Move the money into the truck first, then the guns and ammunition, then stay in the truck, OK?"

Fritz pulled sharply in front of the parked car and stopped as near the woods as possible. "Let's go, Val!" Both jumped from the truck, ran around to the back, and in less than ten seconds had changed hats and coats, put a loaded pistol in their pockets, and were tying the scarves over their faces as they ran to the place where the Brownshirts had entered the woods. Val ran by the car to make sure there was nobody else in it.

Fritz crouched by some bushes and signaled for Val to be as quiet as possible. With a hand to his ear, he communicated to Val to listen for voices so they could know where the men were. The noise of getting into position must have alerted the men because they had gone silent. It was a few minutes before their talking started up again. It seemed a little guarded and hushed at first but was loud enough for Val and Fritz to know they were fifteen to twenty meters away. Slowly, the talking became more relaxed and louder … enough to tell they decided nothing unusual is going on. Now they were noisily coming, one behind the other, through the wooded growth, back toward their car, talking in normal tones.

Fritz and Val crouched quietly, watching intently for the first glimpse of them.

As soon as he could see them, Fritz sprang to his feet, with Val following his lead; both were pointing their pistols at the men, which caused them to stop immediately. In his most cordial Russian-laden German, Fritz said, "Good morning, gentlemen. You will raise your hands, turn around, and we will let you live. Do not make any other move until you are told to."

As both men did what they were told, the man in the back asked, "Who are you, and what do you want?"

In a growling command, Fritz loudly responded, "Right now, I want your undivided attention—and no talking until I tell you!"

Val and Fritz moved near where the men were standing. Fritz signaled for Val to stand back about ten feet while he checked the men for weapons and cash. "You in the front, move up to that tree on your right and put both hands on it as high as you can." With a quick little shuffle, he complied.

"You in the back, take three steps up to that tree on your left and put both hands on it as high as you can." He counted off three quick steps.

"Now both of you tip your heads back and look straight up." They both turned their faces up. "Straight up!" Fritz barked at them, which made them jerk their heads back more and caused their hats to fall off. "Keep both hands up high," he growled loudly.

"Oh, now see what you've done," he said mockingly as a smile began to grow on his and Val's faces. "Your hats are on the ground; you are out of uniform." Fritz went to each of them, picked their hat up and laid it lightly on their face. "If your hat falls off again, you will fall, because I will knock you down!"

To make his point, he walked over to the second man. "I do not think your ribs can take much more, can they?" He punched Jarvis hard enough in the ribs to make him groan. "I think I will call you Ribs.

He moved to Hall. "You in front, your nose could use a little work. I think I'll call you Nose." While Fritz talked, he held the hat in place and slowly moved Nose's face down until his head was level and turned slightly toward him, then thumped his hat and the nose behind it solidly with the knuckles of his closed fist. Then he gently pushed Nose's chin up until he was looking straight up again with the hat, now filled with groans, still in place.

"If you should be wondering how I know about your sore spots, I will just tell you that you two are becoming famous in the beer halls around here for the way you are treated when you drive through our neighborhoods. That of course is because we do not like the way you treat our children, as you already know."

Fritz began checking them for weapons. He put his pistol in his pocket and began with Jarvis. Patting his jacket, Fritz found a small pistol. "Ah, a pocket viper! This will fit much better in my pocket than in yours, Herr Ribs."

Fritz finished with Ribs and moved back to Nose. "How about you, Herr Nose? Do you have something that needs to go into my pocket? Yes of course! … Another viper from this pocket, and in this next one, there is a pocketknife. I can probably find a use for it." He was laboring to keep his Russian accent working.

"OK!" Fritz yelled back through the woods.

"Did you two think we were alone? There are a lot of us who don't like you, even in your own country."

Fritz took the pistol from his pocket again. "Before we go any further with the exercise I have in mind, you will kindly put both your hands on your hat and hold it carefully, because you would not want it to fall, would you? Now turn your head down and raise your hat just enough so you can see one meter of ground straight ahead but keep your hands on your hat. We want to move deeper into the woods; we would not want to attract a curious crowd of tourists from those driving by.

"Nose, you will go first, and Ribs, you will follow. Now, start moving slowly back the way you came. Good, you are doing so well that I am proud of you. Just a little farther. OK, stop. Nose, you move ahead to that tree on your left, put one hand on the tree, keep your hat on your face with the other, tip your head back. Now put your hat hand on the tree.

"Ribs, move up to that tree ahead of you there and put one hand on it as high as you can. With the other hand, you will hold your hat on your face and tip your head back like before. Next, you will keep one hand on the tree and, with the other, quickly remove your boots by taking the laces out first.

"Nose, you need to remove your boots and laces—with one hand on your tree at all times.

"Well, boys, we are taking too much time with our little interview here. It is time to pick up the pace. Now you will both follow my directions at the same time. Squat down and pick up your boots and throw them behind you about five feet." Both men slid their tree hand down the trunk while holding their hat in place with the other until they were squatting. They then used their hat hand to feel for their boots and throw them. "Good. Now with one hand on your tree and one hand on your hat, stand up.

"The next thing you need to do is take your pants off; I have a use for them. Keep one hand on your tree and use the other for your pants. Throw them by the boots. OK, now your jackets come off."

A stick broke across Nose's tree, making him jump and cringe like he expected the next one to land on his back. "Remember, Nose, one hand on the tree, even when you have to switch hands.

"Throw your jacket back with the pants and boots.

"Now, gentlemen, you will each use your hat hand to unbutton your shirt and take it off and show my friend what you have there." Fritz turned and smiled at Val, whose eyes suddenly got bigger when the money belts were revealed. Throw your shirts by your boots.

"I will take those money belts. Hands up and hat on while I remove them for you. There we are. That was not hard. No need for you to worry about them; we will give them the best of care. What you need to worry about is holding up your tree with both hands. You have no reason to move at all until we tell you. Cooperation from both of you is expected, because from where my friend is standing, he can take your fingers off one at a time with the pistol he has, if it will help you concentrate.

"You have impressed me, Nose. I thought you were along to ride shotgun, but here you are, carrying a money belt also. Tell me, Nose, how many men do you have in East Prussia? And it better be a number near what I am thinking. Do not be shy. Speak up."

"There are about—"

Jarvis interrupted him, shouting, "Do not say any—"

But he was interrupted by the toe of Fritz's boot landing solidly where his pants used to be.

"You did a good job of keeping your hat on, Ribs; that kick could have been in your ribs." Fritz started cutting the legs off Ribs's pants. "You won't need these pants because I have a much better use for them.

"Talk to me, Nose. How many?"

"About eleven hundred and fifty."

"Good job, Nose. You are within my range. Your nose job can wait.

"Remember, hands high and hats on, gentlemen. My friend has nothing to do but watch you for any movement without my direction."

Fritz cut the pant legs into two strips each. By now, the two men were feeling the cold and beginning to shiver.

"We have come to the final activity of our party before we have to leave you. With your cooperation, this can go quickly. You first, Ribs! Keep your face up, your hands on the tree, and your eyes closed while I put a blind over your eyes." Fritz removed the hat and tied a piece of shirt sleeve on his eyes, which was rolled up from each end to make a lump of shirt for each eye, secured by one of his boot laces. "OK, bring your head level so I can check my work. It looks good. Now lower your hands and put them behind your back so I can tie them." He twisted one of the strips of his pants to work like a rope and tied Jarvis's hands. "Good job here too. Just lean against your tree friend there while I take care of Nose." And then he repeated the blindfolding and hand-tying procedure with Hall.

"For the closing act, I will invite you both to take a seat. I will tell you when and how. Nose, you get to go first." Pulling him by the elbow, Fritz said, "Come right over here and sit down with your feet out in front of you."

He brought Jarvis by the elbow also. "Now, Ribs, you come and sit here with your feet out in front of you." He placed them facing each other. "Yes, that is snow you are sitting in. No, do not think how cold it is. Think of the softness and be thankful. You need to appreciate the cold; if you can feel it, you know you are alive. We do not have time for me to tell you all the reasons I have for putting *you* out of *my* misery right now. Any delay or lack of cooperation on your part could be a welcome relief to me and would solve all your problems in this life. For now, that choice is still in your hands."

Fritz kicked one of Hall's feet farther to the outside. "Nose, move your feet apart. Yes, that is your friend Ribs you bumped into. You will both have your right ankle between your friend's thighs. Ribs, lift your right leg and put it over here. We will tie your right ankle just above your friend's left knee, like this." Fritz cinched down on Nose's ankle and Ribs' knee. "That means your legs will be tied in four places."

As Val started tying the other two knees and ankles together, now that he did not need to hold a gun on them, he said, "That should make it hard for you to get up and run around for a while, which is exactly what we want. Remember, the more you struggle, the more you hurt each other. It would be a shame to start something like that between two friends.

"Just to drive home the point," added Fritz, "I will need the sleeve of your shirts with the red band on it. Thanks so much for providing this knife, Nose! To make sure you keep the noise down, we will put this crooked X in your mouth and secure it with the second bootlace." Fritz finished with Ribs, and Val took care of Nose.

"While you sit here trying to guess what the other is thinking about how to get out of this mess, we will be on our way. Thank you for being so entertaining and so generous." Fritz patted Ribs on the head as he went by.

"If you should plan another party and are wondering who to invite," Val said, feeling relaxed and having fun speaking in his best Russianized

German, "do not give us a second thought. If we want to come, we will find you. It is so much more fun that way.

"If, when you decide to get up and go on about your day, you find that your car is not where you left it, I recommend that you try looking down the road about five kilometers. That is the last place that I will remember seeing it—a curious dilemma for two men who are not wearing pants.

"Gentlemen, adieu."

They picked up the money belts, jackets, and boots and went back to the truck. Talking quietly at the truck, Fritz reminded Val and Sigi that the men could still hear. "Val, you drive the truck. I'll drive the car up the road five or six kilometers and leave it there."

Val handed the money belts to Sigi, who put them inside the truck on the floor. Before they left, Fritz checked the pockets of the jackets again and threw them just inside the woods where the men could find them. They might get sick from the experience, which would help them remember it, but he did not intend to take their lives.

When they stopped again, Fritz and Val quickly checked the men's car for anything that might be useful at some later time. There was a briefcase with a lot of papers in it, which Val put in the back of the truck, but there was nothing more. They got in the truck and left, with the men's car stopped on the side of the road, looking lonelier and lonelier the farther away it got.

Rolling once again toward Koenigsberg, very sure that the men could not overtake them before then, they began to relax. "Whew, I am glad that is over. What did you find in the car, Sigi?" Fritz asked.

"There were more pistols and ammunition but no money. I was getting worried when it took you so long."

"I think it took too long also, but we were just being careful every step of the way."

"Being careful?" Val interrupted. "He was having fun!"

"Oh, you were having fun too, at least there at the end," Fritz chided.

"As long as we are careful, we will be OK." Fritz tried to be encouraging and comforting. "I do not think these guys got a good look at us or the truck. I do not think the Russian accents fooled them much, if at all. They probably wondered why we even bothered. I am sure they do not have anything to go on. Like Sigi said earlier, it would be nice to have a break from this stuff for a long time! Besides, we have a farm to take care of."

Riding together again in the truck, Fritz and Val told her the whole story of Ribs and Nose. The fun and laughing helped pass some of the time of the long trip.

CHAPTER 9

For the next twenty minutes, there was not any talking while they all caught their breath and settled in for the long ride. The snow had not fallen for hours. Even the last traces of it between the tracks of the cars on the road was melting away as the day warmed into late morning.

"Because of our delay with the Brownshirt games," Fritz said, thinking out loud, "we will not have as much time at the farm. We will need to get busy with the roof repair as soon as we get there; that is the first thing that needs to be done, I think. We also have to find a good place to hide the money belts we took from Jarvis and Hall."

"I was wondering what we were going to do with those. There are some things that I can think of to use it for, like a new motorcycle, a new truck for my dad." Val had an exaggerated, longing tone in his voice.

"Sure, I would like to do things like that too, but with eleven hundred and fifty Brownshirts in East Prussia who will be missing their pay this month, there will be a lot of ears listening and eyes watching for somebody who acts like they suddenly have extra money to spend. If any one of us gets careless and draws attention to his actions, or something he says, then we all will be in trouble. The Brownshirt guy who discovers that we are the ones who stole their payroll and harassed their bosses will be a real hero to his friends, and it could be extremely dangerous for us. We need to remember that we are dealing with a bunch of street thugs who are capable of almost anything." Fritz was sure his good buddy already understood this but said it anyway just to reinforce the idea.

"It sounds kind of scary to hear you two talk about what could happen because of the money. We do not want to give it back to those guys and let them continue to get more recruits and become stronger, so I am thinking that we would be safer if we just burned it or threw it away or something."

"I think those are good ideas, Sigi. If we did not have the money, how would we act?" Fritz wanted to make an important point.

"We would act like we did not have the money!" Sigi and Val answered at the same time with almost the same words.

"That is right. If we can think of it as being locked away where we cannot use it, but keep it hidden until we can help someone who has been hurt by those men, then we can do some good with it and frustrate the men again. What do you think of that?"

"There goes our chance to get a break from this stuff." Sigi looked at Val, who was nodding his head.

A car passed them at just the right time to splash dirty water from a puddle in the road all over their windows. Fritz pulled to a stop on the side of the road. Val got out and picked up a handful of clean snow from the edge of the woods and washed the windshield. "I hope this does not happen too many more times; we do not need any more delays," Val said, shaking the snow and water from his hands and getting back into the truck.

"Have you guys wondered how much money is in those money belts?" Sigi looked from Fritz on her left to Val on her right and back again.

"I have." Val's pondering look was directed out the windshield as he comically stroked his chin. "Should we count it?"

"I have too." Fritz was watching his driving. "But I also think that if we do not know how much is there, it will probably be easier for us to ignore the temptation to spend some of it carelessly. If we cannot do that, we would be better off without it."

"We do not have much time to think about what the money might be used for," said Val, shifting the position he was sitting in, "and we want to be careful and do the right thing. So, for now, we should probably hide it away until one of us comes up with a good idea that we can agree on, OK?"

"I think that is a good idea." Sigi raised her hand to show how she would vote.

"I do too! So, the three of us will talk to nobody else about the money, right? Even Trina does not need to know yet. If the time comes when that changes, then we can all get together and tell her, like we did when we told her who the two wild men were. Can we agree on this?"

"I can," said Sigi.

"Me too," said Val.

Fritz put his hand out above Sigi's knees. "Put your hand on mine in a three-way shake, OK?"

"Doing this makes me feel like I'm part of some children's secret neighborhood club," Sigi said as she put her hand on Fritz's.

"That's right." Val put his hand on Sigi's, and together they all shook. "Every agreement or promise, whether for good or for evil, has a point of commitment. That could be a handshake, a nod of the head, the single word *yes*, or a written contract. It could be a business deal or just between two childhood friends. The big question of course is whether this a good thing or a bad thing to agree to. That should be decided before the point of commitment. After that, the good of your partners, maybe even their lives, might be at risk."

"Wow, that is some pretty serious philosophical thinking for a funnyman. I am getting to know more all the time why Fritz says he knows you as someone who can be counted on to come through when times get tough. You will be a good catch for some lucky girl. I have a sister, ya know!" joked Sigi, imitating a country girl and nudging him in the ribs with her elbow. She gave him a playful wink.

They all enjoyed a friendly laugh.

"Oh," Val said in a funny way, as if his ribs had been assaulted. "I would rather have you poke my ribs than Fritz. I have seen what he can do!" Then he added, "I know you have a sister! I have taken some positive notes every time I have been around her in the last few months."

"Oh, I heard that," Fritz said. "Sigi, does Trina know anything about this?" He put a scheming, matchmaking look on his face.

"Not that I have heard about, but I can fix that when we get home!" Sigi gave a decisive nod of her head to show her resolve to tell Trina about what Val said about her.

They went around a curve to the right in the road, and Val exaggerated his weight being pulled by its force, against Sigi, squeezing her against Fritz. "Now who is trying to get who married by the middle of next week? Maybe I should have gotten a children's secret neighborhood club handshake before I said that!"

"I know what you mean. I am sure you know we do not mean any trouble by what we said. We will handle this the way you want us to. I think you could do worse though; I know something about the family." Fritz looked at Sigi and found a warm, loving smile.

"Hey, you two, I saw that. You can just keep these moonstruck looks at each other to a minimum while I am around, eh?"

The late-morning sun was getting higher, and it was getting warmer in the truck. Val decided to take off his coat. He began wrestling with it in the crowded cab, bumping Sigi into Fritz as often as he could, exaggerating his moves against them.

"I mean, they may be great for you two, but they make me feel like a hungry man with his nose up against the restaurant window, watching you have dinner."

By this time, Fritz and Sigi were both chuckling at Val and the obvious frustration he was expressing.

"Hey, Herr 'Man about town' and 'I will show you how to talk to girls' and 'I have lots of dates,' could it be you are interested in having a special girl that you can spend quality time with and maybe develop a future with?" Fritz used a slightly joking tone to lift the pressure of a question that was meant to be taken seriously.

"Is that so impossible? Funnymen are people too!"

"That is right, of course, but you have kept that part of you well hidden." Sigi gave him a nice smile. "I, for one, am glad to hear this from you. I have learned a lot about you lately and have come to see that a good girl would be happy to be a part of your life. I cannot help feeling excited for her. I just hope she learns quickly to appreciate who you really are. If you do have some interest in Trina, I could certainly help her to see you the way I see you now. You do not seem to be good at showing off that side of yourself." She poked him hard in the ribs again.

"Oh, there you go again." Val was holding his ribs again. "You know, if you do that enough times, my ribs will be as sore as if you hit me hard."

Fritz and Sigi laughed a little.

"The only reason you see this part of me is because your *wild man* over there brings it out. Maybe that is why I hang around with him."

Fritz pressed the point. "From what I have seen of Trina in the past few months, she seems to be a very capable girl. You have known her longer than I have, Val. If she is anything like Sigi, she is worth spending some time with."

"For those of you who have suddenly developed such curious minds, I have been thinking the same thing. For those of you whose minds are also inclined to be so active in trying to be helpful, I say thank you very much, but I am sure I can handle things myself," Val said confidently.

It was near eleven thirty when they drove into Heilsberg, which was past the halfway point on their trip. They stopped to get more gas, to check the truck, and refresh themselves for the remaining hour to hour-and-a-half trip to the farm. All during the stop, either Fritz or Val stayed with the truck, just to discourage someone who might be a little curious or looking to cause trouble. The money belts could not be well hidden in the small cab of the truck. Fritz kept reminding Val and Sigi that they needed to be going soon to keep from being too late on their trip back.

After about twenty minutes, they were on their way again. Val was driving now so he could get familiar with the best route to the farm. It was not long before Sigi fell asleep with her head on Fritz's shoulder.

The area south of Koenigsberg was mostly flat and had been farmed for hundreds of years. Where there was a roll in the land, it was easy to see some of the methods people used to get water to the higher places to make them more productive. The fortunate farmers with the flat ground usually used a simple diversion of water from a ditch; others had to dig a well and put in a pump of some kind to bring it up to the surface. With a water table only two to five meters down, almost everyone could get the water they needed.

Fritz became more and more interested in looking at the farms they were passing as they got closer to his. "On one of your visits to the farm, Val, I would like to get your ideas on how to get water to some of the higher places on the back of the property. Today, I am interested in getting the roof repaired, checking the water systems, and making sure the fireplace is useable so we can have some heat … and hiding the money. I am glad you are here, because I think we are going to have a busy few hours before we have to start back."

When they were getting near the turnoff from the highway onto the small road that would take them toward their farm, Fritz woke up Sigi. "Wake up and look at some of your new neighbors; we do not have much farther to go now."

"Oh, yes." She stretched and yawned. "Wow, this is exciting. We are going to be living near here, and I will get to know some of these people. I wonder what *his* name is," she said, pointing at a man walking out of a shed toward his house. "The land is much flatter than where we live now, isn't it?" she added.

"Yes, but it is still uneven enough in some places to make it hard to irrigate easily." Val made a motion like the waves in the ocean.

Sigi showed some concern. "This is a nice area. Some of these houses are large and well kept. It looks like people are probably happy and like living here. I hope the people are as nice as their houses look."

"You might be new at being a wife when we move in here, but you are not new at being a neighbor or talking with older women and being friendly. All we have to do is be happy ourselves and nice to them; we do not have to let other people change how we are if we do not want to." Fritz sounded like a father giving counsel. He concentrated on the road. "I have only been here once. I am hoping I can go right to it." He sounded a little worried but then said, "Yes, here we are. Turn right on that next road."

"Wow." Sigi was starting to get excited. "Is this the road we live on?"

"Yes. In three more kilometers, we will see a small bridge up ahead. It's just past there, on the right."

Nothing was said while they crossed the bridge and turned into the driveway.

Val stopped the truck near the house. "It looks like this was a really nice place a few years ago."

"I think it is beautiful! Come on, come on! I want to see the inside." Sigi pushed Fritz to hurry him up so she could get out. She ran to the front door and went in.

When Val and Fritz came through the door, Sigi was going from room to room, looking them over as quickly as she could.

"I think you have just made yourself some big points with a certain young lady." Val nodded his head and slapped his friend on the back.

They watched her finish her whirlwind tour.

She came running enthusiastically toward them. Val, knowing what was about to happen, quickly stepped away from Fritz.

"Fritz, this is wonderful!" she exclaimed, running right into him and knocking him back a few steps. With Sigi holding him tightly and jumping with excitement, they began to turn as he tried to keep their balance with all the shaking. "I already feel like it is mine. I am so excited I ... ooh!"

Fritz returned her hug, picking her up enough to take her feet off the floor and stop the shaking. They continued to spin with her feet still kicking in the air.

Val and Fritz were laughing and enjoying her excitement.

"I am glad to see this, because it will take a lot of energy to get the house ready in time. Today we only have about three hours to work, so we need to get busy. Sigi, the inside is yours to decide what you want to do with. Val and I need to take care of the roof. All of us need to look for a good place to hide the money. For now, we can have some lunch. Then we will put the money in the lunch box, in the house, where Sigi can see it. We need to see how much we can get done, OK?" Val had already started for the door. Fritz gave Sigi another squeeze and a kiss, put her down, and went out the door behind Val, who had started unloading the truck almost before Sigi's feet were on the floor!

When Fritz caught up with him, Val said, "You have a happy girl in there, my friend!"

"Things have really been going my way. I feel very blessed! I will get the money if you will get the lunch box."

After lunch, Sigi put the money in the lunch box, Val packed the Russian military clothes into the duffel bag, and Fritz went to the barn to get the ladder. He then got up onto the roof. Fortunately, the day was warm enough to melt the snow on that part of the roof.

Val followed him up the ladder. "How does it look? Do we have what we need to fix it?"

"I think so. Some shingles have been missing for two or three years. The tar paper has been damaged for so long that some of the wood is weathered, but it seems to be sound and can be repaired. We will replace the paper, then the shingles, and should be done in an hour or two. It could be much worse!" Fritz was happy that it could be done so quickly.

Sigi got some water from the well for cleaning inside. She went on with knocking down spider-webs and sweeping up rat droppings, grimacing. Even if she did not like doing it, she smiled with the pride of a new owner at each clean area that she added to her new house.

By the time Val and Fritz finished with the roof repairs, they had come up with the idea of wrapping the money and the guns in tar paper and burying them on the property someplace. Sigi agreed, so that was what they did next. On the way back, they decided to take different jobs. Fritz would check the fireplace and cooking area to make sure they were safe for fires, and Val would check the water systems in the house and the water tower outside. Sigi continued with the cleaning.

Fritz checked inside the fireplace as closely as he could and saw no problems. Then he made a fire that was unusually smoky to see if any seeped out between the rocks. The fireplace and the cooking area both passed this test.

The test fires were still burning when a truck came into the driveway in a hurry and stopped in front of the house. Two men got out and were talking loudly and pointing to the roof on their way to the front door. Val heard the truck drive up and joined Fritz in the living room. Fritz opened the door just as the men got to it.

"Hello," the older man said with a wave. "We did not know anybody is here. When we saw the smoke, we thought there might be some trouble."

"Hello! Come on in. My name is Fritz Abbot. I work for Eldrick Kemp in Neidenberg. This is Sigi Backman, and this is Val Adlar. We have been here for a few hours trying to get this place ready to move into. You must live nearby. Is that right?

"Yes, my name is Manfred Archer, and this is my son Tielo. We live on the second farm toward the highway and across the road."

Suddenly, three men came over the fence by the barn and toward the house, attracting everybody's attention.

"And that is Rudolf Hammond. He lives next door to you on this other side," said Herr Archer, motioning out past the barn.

"Werther and Erwin are with him," Tielo said as he watched them.

"Hello! We are all in here! Come in." Fritz motioned to them from the front door.

119

When the Hammonds came through the door, Herr Archer stood defiantly with his hands on his hips, nodding his head. "Glad you could make it all the way from next door." Then with a big, fun-loving smile, he said, "The place could have burned down by now."

"Oh, I know what you mean. What is this anyway, a test fire drill? I do not see a fire," Herr Hammond responded in fun, looking at the three people he did not know.

"I have not even finished our introductions to your critical friend here, because they just got here themselves." Fritz shook an accusing finger at Herr Archer.

"My name is Fritz Abbot." He held out his hand to the newcomer.

"Rudolf Hammond. These are my sons."

"Yes, I was introduced to you through the window when you came over the fence. Which one is Werther?"

The taller one held out his hand. "Hi, neighbor."

"Then you must be Erwin," Fritz said to the shorter of the two, shaking each one's hand.

"Herr Archer, I do not think I shook your hand or Tielo's."

"I should finish my introductions. This is Sigi, who will be my wife in a few weeks, and this is Val, my friend for many years.

"I was just saying to the Archers that we have been here for about two hours, getting the house ready to move into."

"He works for Herr Kemp in Neidenberg," said Herr Archer, already in the know.

Fritz smiled at the neighborhood dynamics. "That is right. He has asked me to come here and work with his son Bernhard in Koenigsberg to help expand the business. My moving onto this farm is part of his plan." He could see they accepted his explanation, so he continued, "I have wondered how I might get to know some of the neighbors. I had no idea that smoke signals would work so well!"

They all had a hearty, friendly laugh with Fritz.

"The smoke was part of my checking out the chimneys. They appear to be in good condition, like the rest of the house, even after being vacant for so long."

"The Kemps were good people," said Herr Hammond. "And good neighbors. Whatever they did was done well. I have always been impressed that this property was built and maintained in the same way while they were here. It has been kept up carefully, except for the last three years or so. I was surprised to see it go like this. I am glad to have someone here now! If you could use a neighbor's help or suggestions, Fritz, I'm right next door."

"Thank you. I will remember that. Maybe this summer when we are settled in, we can invite you and Herr Archer to bring your families, and we will all bring some food, and we can have dinner outside."

"That sounds like a good idea," said Herr Archer, holding out his hand to Fritz. "I am happy to meet you all, and I am glad there was no fire. Like Rudolf said, if there is something you need, maybe I can help. As I said, my place is the second on the right in that direction. We should probably be going, unless there is something we can do for you now."

"Thank you all for your concerned response to our smoke and your offers of help in the future. We are nearly finished with the things we had planned for today. If you are passing by and see a truck or a car here, please feel free to stop and say hello again. If it is not us, and they do not seem to have any true business here, you have my permission to be less than friendly."

They all were chuckling while they went out the door. Sigi, Fritz, and Val went out to watch them go and wave once more to their new neighbors.

"Nice people. I hope the others are like that. I expect to be spending a lot of time in this home. I would like the women who are our neighbors to be friends," said Sigi. She started back in, and Fritz and Val followed. "There is a lot I can do inside. How much more time do I have?"

"About an hour," Fritz responded. "How are the things working that you have been checking, Val?"

"They are all good-quality hardware, but the seals are getting dried out and need to be replaced. That will be easy enough to do. Then they should work well."

"I need to mix some mortar to reset the two loose fireplace stones. Val, if you will mix some plaster to patch the walls, we can be done in less than an hour. How does that sound, Sigi?"

"Good. I think I can be done with the kitchen and dining areas by then. I am anxious to get home and tell Mom and everybody all about our new house!"

CHAPTER 10

When they started for home, it was still light enough to see the road easily. The growing cold had not yet frozen the wet places, which meant driving would not be a big problem. The trees had lost most of the snow that had been on them that morning from the snowfall overnight.

The color of the sky was changing from the gray of most of the day to a bright yellow, then orange, and then red as the sun went down below the edge of the clouds on the horizon. Shining through the heavy, moist air, it spread the colors across the bottom of the dark clouds that formed a ceiling overhead. This caused the earth and everything on it to take on a misty, beautiful, deep pastel glow of the same ruby colors being radiated from the clouds.

There was no talking while all three of them watched the light show spread before them by Mother Nature. When it was finished, the darkness settled in.

"Wow. What a perfect end to a perfect day." Sigi snuggled her hands around Fritz's arm and her head on his shoulder while he drove. "It has been wonderful!"

"It really has been a good day. I am happy with what we have done at the house today. It responded well to our efforts, probably because of the quality that was built into it from the beginning. Like I told Val earlier, I feel blessed by God for the good things that are happening to me." Fritz leaned his head down onto Sigi's.

"There are a lot of things to do in the next few weeks. Fritz has a house to work on, Sigi has a wedding to plan, and I have a little sister to get to know better."

"Good. Glad to hear it—" Sigi and Fritz started talking enthusiastically at the same time.

"We will be glad to help any way we—"

Sigi was interrupted by Val. "Yes, I know. You will be 'as helpful as possible in any way you can.' I thank you for your encouragement, but if I need to call in the reserves on this mission, I am in trouble. If I am in that much trouble, reserves will not help. 'I can take it from here.' Do you remember saying that to me about Sigi? After that, I let you do it your way, right?"

"That is right, and I appreciated it too."

"That is all I am talking about; let me grow this flower in my own way."

"OK, I am sure Sigi will agree, as I do, to try to not interfere. If we slip up somehow, let us know. We want the best thing to happen for both of you. You got us excited by mentioning Trina again. It indicates a real interest, which we are of course happy to hear. I wish you success in your efforts with her. We will be watching with interest but as quietly as we can. If we see something exciting happening, we will go quietly out behind the barn, to do our silent cheering and yelling and jumping up and down, and return as if nothing has happened."

"We know what you mean, Val. We will be careful." Sigi patted Val's arm in friendship and reassurance.

Conversation was soon replaced by the rhythms of travel sounds, the air rushing by outside the windows of the truck, the pulsating motor, and the noise of the tires on the road. They worked together like a mother's lullaby, making passengers who were not even feeling tired eventually become drowsy.

The truck was running well; all three of its passengers were as comfortable as could be expected. It was probably going to be an uneventful, boring ride.

After about twenty minutes of watching the trees and the fence posts and the farms and the animals going by outside their windows, Fritz broke the silence. "Before we all get too sleepy, I want to tell you two what I have been thinking … about how we can use the money we took from the Brownshirts." He had their attention.

Fritz went on, "We already know we have to be careful about looking like we suddenly have a lot of money to spend from some unknown source, …but nobody in this area knows how much money is normal for us. That means the future is wide open!

"I have an idea for a business we can create that can be made to look like we are making a lot of money with it. We can begin small and grow the business like any other, except that we have a fund that will guarantee that we will always make payroll and pay our expenses. We could help a lot of families make some extra income this way."

"It would be nice if we could help people some way; I like that part." Sigi left open the chance to ask her level-headed questions later. "We all know how the value of money can change, by the inflation our country has seen in the past. I hope we can do something with it while it still has a good value. What are your ideas?"

"I have always thought it might be possible to make money by making and selling our masks that we made for riding our motorcycles." Fritz was not sure how his suggestion would be received.

Val had serious doubts. "How can we expect to make money from those when anybody can make one for themselves?"

"They must have given you some benefit when you used them, or you would not keep making and using them. Not everybody would want to wear a scrap from a sweater to keep their face warm." Sigi's mind was starting to catch a vision of what could be done. "If they are carefully made in different sizes, patterns, and colors and designed so they could be worn on the neck in the place of a scarf, or pulled up to protect the nose and ears from cold or dust, they might become popular."

Fritz had been thinking about this while working on the house. "Here are some things to think about when you wonder who might want to buy our nifty little face and neck muffs: not every car and truck has a good heater; within a few hundred kilometers, there are some of the best skiing areas in the world in the countries around us; in the United States, these are such exciting times that they are called the Roaring Twenties. Many people in many countries are investing in the stock of businesses and making great profits, which allows them to come skiing or touring around this part of the world. Our economy is growing and giving some of our people the same hope and enthusiasm for the future as other countries, so that some of this Roaring Twenties feeling is catching on here too."

"OK, my two excitable friends." Val was now in the role of the levelheaded, how-do-we-make-this-work partner. "How do the first ones get made, and how do they get to stores where people can see them and buy them?"

The growing darkness of the evening now made it necessary for Fritz to turn on the lights of the truck. It was more to make it easier to be seen by others on the highway than to see. Needing the lights to see the road was still about half an hour away.

"The first thing to do is get some yarn for Sigi, and maybe her mother and Trina can make the first ones. There will have to be an understanding that because this is an experiment, we will not be able to pay them for their work yet. When I go to work on the house again, I can give them to some store owners in some of the towns along the way to sell at a suggested price or whatever price they like. On my next trip, I will stop again to see what happened and if they want some more. By my third trip, I should know what price they are selling at, and by discounting that price by about 50 percent, I will know what price I can sell them to the store owner at. If we can make them, deliver them, and make a profit at 50 percent of the sale price, then we are in business, right?"

"Yes, I think this is exciting, and I am looking forward to getting started. I also think Mom and Trina would like to help get us started," Sigi said, shaking Fritz's elbow in excitement.

"But what if we do not make a profit? … Ahh yes, I think I know the answer already." Val was nodding his head up and down with a smile of understanding.

"I think you do too." Fritz knew Val's thinking was right with his, as it so quickly had been over the years of their friendship.

"We might not make a profit in the beginning, until we get to understand what our real costs are." Sigi's level-headed thinking was working. "After we learn the costs, we might not make enough profit to stay in business, …except that … the money we now have to invest, …will take a very long time to run out!" She began bouncing in the seat and slapping Fritz's arm when she realized what he had in mind. Her elbow jab at Val's ribs was deflected by a quick move of his arm.

"Ha! Missed! That is one that will not add to the bruise that you have been working on right there. See, you think you can do that any time you want, but I am on to you now. I won that one! My ribs are much happier already; I can feel them tickling."

"Uh oh." Fritz knew what was coming.

Sigi was looking pleasantly at Val and smiling while she listened to his defiant chatter. A second move of her elbow had Val responding with both hands to protect his ribs, just as her closed hand gave him a solid thump on the leg.

"Hey, what was that? Did you see that, Fritz? I think she's trying to start something here!"

"Now, you two settle down right this minute. Do not make me come over there and straighten this out, or one of you will have to ride in the back."

"Oh, yes, Daddy, I will be good." Sigi folded her hands together on her lap.

"Val is a funnyman, but he is a man. There is a limit to how much abuse a man will take, even when it is in fun. When the person who is the object of the joke is not having fun, then it is not fun!"

After a thoughtful pause Val said, "Ya know, Sigi, this guy might make a good dad if he teaches his kids stuff like that."

"I think so too. I am counting on it." Sigi hugged Fritz's arm and shoulder again.

"For friendship and unity!" Fritz held his hand out over Sigi's lap with his palm up. "Give me your hand for a three-way shake." With that, it was understood that all was forgiven and that the three of them had a solid friendship.

"Where are we in our business-planning talk anyway?" Level-headed Sigi was suddenly back!

"We are just getting to the profit part. I think we know what you have in mind, but maybe you should go over it with us just to make sure." Val's clear-thinking side was speaking.

"I will take some money from *my* savings for Sigi to buy the first yarn to start with—oh, whoa! Truck, slow down!" Fritz braked as hard as he could because of a deer that had run out into the road. It became dazed by the headlights and just stood in the road staring at them. Before he could stop, a doe came out of the trees and would have run into the truck if she had not turned at the last second and run along beside the truck for a short distance, until she looked in the window and saw Val going along beside her, looking back.

Fritz was able to stop the truck without going off the pavement into the mud, and with ten feet to spare before hitting the adult buck standing in the road. Two more does, with young ones following them, trotted across the road on the other side of the buck. Finally, the buck turned his head toward the other deer and trotted casually after them.

"Nice stop! But he did not look overly impressed. His look was more like 'You have a lot of nerve delaying us like this; if you cannot do any better than that, then you can stay out of our woods.'" Val watched the buck trot away, then looked around for more deer.

"If he does not like surprises like this, he can get himself some white paint and a paint brush and paint a crosswalk across the road right here where it would be convenient for him and his family. A warning sign, back there a few hundred meters on the side of the road, would be a good idea too!" The large gesturing of Fritz's arms made the cab of the truck feel even smaller than it was.

"It looks like a deer with an attitude gave someone else an attitude too." Sigi smiled up at Fritz.

"Not so much an attitude as a real surprise and scare. Suddenly, I am responsible for the lives of the deer *and* my two best friends, while trying to keep the truck under control and on the road. We could have been stuck until morning if we left the pavement!"

"I am glad you did not hit one of them; you might have killed it." Sigi patted Fritz's arm.

"I am glad too; he could have killed my dad's truck!" This got him a closed-hand thump from Sigi.

It took a few minutes for Fritz to catch his breath before he was ready to drive again. Val offered to drive for a while, but Fritz was sure he wanted to go on; partly because of the trouble it would be to un-pack and re-pack three, warmly dressed, full-sized, people in the over-stuffed cab of their small truck.

"We are having a hard time staying on our business plan conversation, aren't we?" Val said. "We have not gone through Heilsberg yet, so we have plenty of time to talk before we get home."

"Before the deer appeared, I was starting to say I will give Sigi some money to make the first muffs. Val, if you can come up with a way to represent a man's and a woman's head and shoulders, we can put one of our muffs on each of them for display. The man figure will have his up over his nose and ears for maximum protection, and the woman figure will have hers down as a neck warmer. I will take these to stores where I think they can be sold." Fritz paused for a moment, still thinking, and then he continued.

"If we have to sell them at a price too low to make a profit, we can still pay people who work for us from what the Brownshirts *so generously* invested. If, in a few months, we still cannot make a profit, we can close our business without being hurt by a loss. We do not want to have people asking questions about how we keep a business running that does not sell much product. If we do make a profit, then we can help more people earn an extra income." He thought for a moment and then decided it was all he had now. "That might be a simple plan, but I think it is enough to get us started. What do you two think?"

Val had a really puzzled look on his face. "I agree that it is a good, simple plan. My big question is, what do I make these display images out of? Any suggestions?"

"Maybe you can take a flat piece of wood, about three-quarters of an inch thick, and cut out a life-sized side view of a man. You can paint on some details like his eyes, a smile, and a sweater, then put a real muff on him. That would be unusual and probably get people's attention."

A more relaxed look came to Val's face while he listened to Sigi's idea. Then he said, "That could work, but I am not much of an artist."

"It's not important to have perfect detail like a portrait, just enough of an image to show how the muff is used. Trina is good at drawing things; maybe you can ask her to help."

"You are not trying to start something, are you?" Val was not sure if he should be worried by Sigi's suggestion or not.

"No, I am not! Fritz and I have already told you we will leave that up to you. Do not take it personally every time one of us mentions Trina's name. I think she would like to help Fritz and me in any way she can, and I think she would like a chance to make some money of her own. It will give you a chance to know her better, which you already know we would like. If she asks me any questions about you, I will of course answer them in a positive way. My reasons for suggesting her are because she can do the drawing you need, and I am sure she would like to help, not because I am trying to manage your life!"

"OK, OK, I had to check. I will try not to be so suspicious next time."

With a little uncertainty in his voice, Val continued. "This area of artistic design, drawing, and making my part of this project look right is something that makes me nervous; I am sure I will need help with it."

"Whenever something like that concerns any one of us, we need to bring it up so that all three can help with finding a solution. I think we make a good team, one that can usually find an answer when we work together." A happy confidence showed in Fritz's expression. "I like our team, and I am excited about the things we are planning in the future! Now we all have something to concentrate on to help the whole thing happen. If we each just do our best, I am sure the other two will be happy with the results.

"Before we finish talking about this business idea, we should decide what we are going to call our business and our product. Have either of you had any ideas while we were talking?"

"How about All-Weather Face Protectors?" Val had a triumphant smile.

"That's good; it tells what they are for." Fritz sounded positive, but Sigi was quiet.

"I think the name should be more personal, with a real person's name ... or names ... like Val and Fritz's Face Savers." Sigi looked back and forth at the two guys, who both had thoughtful looks on their faces.

As if on a cue from somebody outside beyond the windshield, they both said at the same time, "Naw." Then one mumbled something about corny and the other about wrong names before their voices trailed off into nothing.

"We can call them Sigi's Face and Neck Muffs for now while we take more time to come up with a name we like better," Fritz suggested, "Or Sigi's Nifty Muffs."

"I like that last idea," said Val.

"You two think so much alike that you seem like two versions of the same person sometimes. When that happens, I usually agree with you, because you are right. I will agree this time too ... for now." Sigi felt happy to be with her husband-to-be and his best friend.

CHAPTER 11

O n Sunday, November 15, the day after her first trip to the Koenigsberg farm with Fritz and Val, Sigi was determined to talk to her pastor. She asked Fritz to go to church with her. After the service, they got his attention at the door of the chapel, where he was greeting the last few of the congregation as they were leaving.

"Pastor, we have something we need to ask you. Do you have a few minutes?"

"Of course, Sigi. What is it?"

"You have seen me with Fritz over the past six months."

"Yes," he said with a smile. "He seems like a good young man."

"I think so too. That is why when he asked me to marry him, I said yes."

"Wonderful! You two make such a nice couple. You should be happy together."

"We are very excited. I want to ask you if the chapel will be available for a wedding on the evening of Friday the eleventh of December, just four weeks away?" Sigi looked hopeful.

The pastor thought for a minute and said, "With activities planned here on that day and the next, Friday the eighteenth will be better."

When she told Fritz, he had to swallow hard once, realizing that being married, with all its responsibilities, was fast approaching. With a kiss of reassurance and faith in him from Sigi, he relaxed slightly, and his smile widened because he was reminded of his love for her. With a nod, he agreed that the eighteenth would work well.

The pace of Sigi's life seemed to double after seeing the farm for the first time that second weekend of November. Along with keeping up with her part-time job at the furniture store and her duties around her family's farm, she now had the added responsibilities of planning her wedding and the job of designing and making the first of the muffs.

With her level-headed approach to life and its challenges, she enlisted the help of her mother and Trina to knit the first sixteen face muffs by Saturday. While they sat together knitting, they also came up with a rough plan for the wedding and reception, plus a list of some of the people who would be invited. They were two significant accomplishments.

Trina had also been successfully recruited by Val to help him with the design of a display for the muffs. Together, they made four nice silhouettes that were eighteen inches tall: two of men and two of women. The men were painted black, with basic features of eyes, nose, and mouth outlined simply in white lines. The women were white with features outlined in black. These were each mounted on a piece of wood that allowed them to stand by themselves. The base piece was long enough for a post to be put on it behind the head. The post had pegs in it to hang additional muffs on for people to choose from.

"To save the store people a lot of time explaining what the muffs are, we can write something on the stand." Trina recognized a customer need.

"You are right, but most of the base will be covered by the muffs. We will have to put it on *top* of the post." Val thought about how to make it work.

"I can write on one side, 'Sigi's Year-Round Muffs,' and on the other side, 'Protection from the elements.' Under that, it can say, "Cold, snow, smoke, pollen, dust, and *more!*'" Trina showed confident excitement.

"Those are great ideas. We can make small signs out of a piece of light, thin wood, or metal from a food can that we have straightened, or cardboard, and attach each one to a post top by wedging and gluing it into a groove. I would like to see a light spring with a ribbon, or something up there, so it can wiggle around and get more attention." Val demonstrated a spring wiggle while he talked. "This is going to be fun!"

Val went with Fritz the following Saturday to work on his farm near Koenigsberg. "Before we leave town," Val said, "let's stop at Harold's Clothing and see if we can put a set of displays there. It is one of the largest clothing stores in town and should give us a fair trial of how the public likes our muffs."

"We have to start somewhere; it might as well be there. I want to see what happens."

Val had time to think about their business plans over the week and was now seeing the bigger picture of what could happen. "I already feel nervous and conspicuous about carrying these displays in, and we are not even there yet."

"I do too, but it is part of what we have to do to get the business started."

They were only in the store for twenty minutes. When they came out, they looked happy but did not say anything until they got into the truck. Then Val almost exploded. "Wow, that manager loved our displays and the quality of the muffs, didn't he!"

"He even said they 'fit right in with the trend of these Roaring Twenties to be ultramodern.' My friend, I think we have something here!" Fritz was really excited.

"That was easy!" Val said enthusiastically. "This is fun!"

They were able to place a display set in two stores that day. The displays were well received by the store owners because they cost nothing and could become another source of income, which was always welcome.

The main thing Fritz wanted to accomplish at the farm on that trip was to get the water systems working inside and outside the house. After making repairs to all the mechanisms inside, they went out to look over the well and the water tower. The hand pump at the well was easy to repair, owing to Val's accurate determination of what parts were needed.

The windmill was almost frozen up from lack of use. It took more time than they wanted to spend to get it freed. Then they got the new parts installed, the metal moving parts lubricated properly, and the pump primed. With some coaxing by hand, even with the little wind there was, eventually it began to turn on its own. Finally, after what seemed like much too long, water began to flow into the tank on top of the tower.

"Great! What a relief that is! Now all we have to do is watch for leaks in the tank up here and check our work inside to see if all of our new seals are holding and everything is working as it should." Fritz slapped Val on the back. "You got all the right seals to fix things, my friend! I really do thank you for that."

"Maybe we should unload the paint supplies while we wait for the water to fill the tank." Val did not like to sit around when there was something that needed to be done. "We might even get some of the indoor painting done."

"Good idea. I am sure glad the work was done so well when the house and barn were built that even this tower is still good and solid." Fritz went down the ladder first and over to the truck.

"You and Trina did a really good job on the displays that you made. How did working with her go?"

"It went well. We could talk easily and coordinate our work and ideas in a way that got things done quickly. We are proud of that!" Val's last few steps to the truck were made in a proud kind of strut. "We had fun too."

"I have a series of ideas that I want to tell you about to see what you think, OK?"

"Sure! Why do I get the impression the conversation is about to get heavier?" With his hands full of paint supplies, Val started for the front door, plodding along like his load was almost too heavy to carry.

"You and I have been friends for so long that I will miss having you close by when Sigi and I move in here."

"You are not thinking of me moving in with you, are you?"

"No, no. I do not think any newly married couple should do that. They do not even know how they will get along with each other. To have a third adult in the house would almost guarantee disaster for the new marriage."

"We can put this stuff over by the center wall. I think that would be the best place to start painting." Fritz motioned to the middle of the wall.

Val put his load down where he thought Fritz wanted it. "I would not be comfortable living like that either," he said with a shudder. "What ideas do you want to talk about?"

They paused for a few seconds when they noticed the sound of the windmill change as the wind picked up slightly.

Val listened carefully. "Still sounds OK. We should be able to make an accurate test soon. We can give it about ten minutes, and then we can check the tank. Shall we see how much painting we can do in that time?"

"I am encouraged by the way our displays were accepted in the two stores! One of my ideas has to do with our muff business. What if it is a success? What if we make enough money for you to buy a farm in this area? Would that interest you?"

Fritz was shaking a can of paint to stir it before opening.

Val got out the brushes.

"That is something I have not spent much time thinking about. You really believe this muff thing is going to work, don't you?"

"Like I said, I'm encouraged." Fritz's enthusiasm was growing. "Of course, we will not really know for a month or more. If it does work, it will be something to think about when your apprenticeship is finished in … what is it, another seven months?"

"Let's start our painting on the front section of the center wall. I will start here at the hallway, and you start on the other end. By the time we meet in the middle, it will be time to check the water tank." Fritz opened his can and got started.

The heavy white paint was made for covering things like marks on the wall from years of being lived in by a family with children. The smoky gray from the cooking fire and fireplace had dimmed the last coat of white paint. The brighter difference was obvious next to the unpainted sections. It took about thirty minutes to finish the first section of wall.

"Well, that did not take long." Val stood back with his hands on his hips, surveying their work.

"No, and it is brightening up the room already. I think Sigi will like it!"

"It is time to check the tank outside." Val wiped the excess paint from his brush into the can of paint and laid it on top.

"I think I will start painting the hallway now. Let me know what you find out there." Fritz moved his can of paint around the corner.

Val found that the tank had about twelve inches of water in it. He went back into the house to tell Fritz. "The tank has enough water in it to test everything inside." He stopped at the kitchen sink to turn it on until water flowed from it. "We should let this run for a few minutes till the water runs clear. Same with the other water mechanisms." He went to turn them on. "I think it would be a good idea to run these every time you come here, until you are satisfied that the pipes are clean enough. They are sure putting out some dirty water now."

"I think you are right. I will remember to do that." Fritz was almost halfway down the hallway with his painting. "Do you see any leak problems?"

"No real problems," Val said. "Just a few things to tighten up, and everything should be OK. I can take care of them now."

"Good," said Fritz. "Then we can watch them again before we leave."

Val went out to the truck to get some tools. When he came back, Fritz said, "You asked me if I thought the muff business would work out. We had some strong positive indicators today from the stores we saw. Yes, I think it will work! The way I see it, the more financial backup we have, the better chance it has. I think it is time to see how much backup we really have."

"The sooner we know, the better planning we can do," said Val. "With all the changes going on right now, this is one uncertainty we can nail down today. But let me think about it."

"When you get through tightening things, you can come and help me finish this hallway and the rest of the wall." Fritz was making good progress.

Val stopped on his way to the bathrooms down the hall to listen to what Fritz was saying, then went into the first room to take care of things in there.

Fritz finished the first side of the hallway and called out, "Are you thinking?"

Val came into the hallway on his way to the other room. "What if it is a lot of money? It could be a big temptation to use some of it."

"I know; we talked about how dangerous it could be for us if one of us did that. Remember?"

"Yes. That is a reason to leave it alone." Val disappeared into the second room.

Fritz painted his way to the doorway of the room where Val was and looked in. He was sitting on the toilet, staring across the room.

"I do not need to ask if you are thinking this time, do I?"

Still staring, Val said, "Maybe we *should* count it. I am coming up with some pretty large numbers when I try to figure out how much might be there."

"That is a problem I have too, but my main reason now for counting it is to estimate how the muff business might work for us. I still believe we should use that money only to pay the people and the expenses connected with the business and not for personal wants. We might have to help each other remember that."

Fritz continued, "I also thought that if you can see a secure future, you might think more about getting married yourself and moving into this neighborhood with us. If we continue to work our regular jobs and develop the muff business too, we could do very well! The best way for that to happen is for you to be close enough for us to work together easily."

"For that to happen, I would need to have a job in Koenigsberg like you or be paid from the Brownshirts money. If I could be paid from that money while I worked on the muff business, I would have something to think about!" Val's eyes began to widen.

"Come on, help me with this painting so we can get to the counting. We need to get it over with, because we are just wearing ourselves out worrying and talking about how much it might be."

Val broke his stare and looked at his friend like he just woke up. "Yes, we do not want to be too late getting back to Neidenberg."

The next section of wall took almost thirty minutes with the painting around the doors and the fireplace. Soon they were closing the paint cans and cleaning the brushes so they would be ready to use next time they were needed.

They easily found the spot where they had buried the money and guns the week before. They removed the money belts and lightly covered the guns up again in their hiding place. On the way back to the house, they hoped they would not get any surprise visits from the neighbors while they were busy with the money. Just in case of a surprise, they set up a paint tarp they could quickly cover it with. This made it easier for them to relax while they worked.

Together they counted—and then recounted—for accuracy and to digest the size of the prize they had taken from the Brownshirts that day. The total was 28,750 Reichsmark, which was enough to pay the average working man a nice salary for sixteen years at today's rates! It was a very impressive sum to a couple of young working men. Their excitement grew as they came to understand the value of what they had at their disposal. A feeling of power and of being invincible came with an experience like that, and for a few minutes, they let themselves enjoy the euphoria. While they packed the money back into its belts, they began to talk each other back to reality.

"We need to put this back where we had it hidden and get started for home. I have thought of many things that could be done to this farm with this much money, but that is one of those things that could be dangerous for all of us, so I have to let it go." Fritz was shaking his head. "There is so much I would like to do for my family too."

"I know exactly what you mean; I have thought of my family and some of the things they need. The best thing we can do for them is to make the muff business work and increase our income that way, or at least use it as a cover for slowly pulling money from this stash in a hole on your farm." Val was all smiles and almost laughing. "Now I understand better what you were saying about getting married and moving into this neighborhood with you. I will be thinking of those things in a whole different light now."

"I will tell Sigi what we did here today." Fritz walked toward the door with one of the belts around his waist. "I wondered what it felt like to have this much money on me like this. It feels good, but I will get over it."

Val was right behind him, bouncing a little as he walked, to feel the weight of the two belts he was wearing. "This is fun, but like you said, I'll get over it. That is a shame, but it is the way it has to be. We must pretend we do not know anything about any lost money. I will be OK. I have to be! Well, we need to get this little ceremony over with and be on our way."

The sun was still more than an hour from setting when they finished burying the money, checking the water systems, and securing the windmill. Finally, they got into the truck to head home.

"We did a good day's work on the house in the time we had. We now better understand what we must do for the muff business. I think we did well today! Thanks, my friend." Fritz put out his right hand toward Val.

Val took the hand offered in a clasp of friendship. "My good time, good buddy. My good time."

Fritz turned the truck around, drove down the driveway to the street, and turned left toward the highway back to Neidenberg.

After riding without talking for about twenty minutes while they each thought about the events of the day, Val broke the silence by asking, "So what is the next step in the plan as you see it?"

"With the wedding four weeks away, we need to keep working on growing the muff business, while cleaning up the farm as quickly as possible—*while* Sigi and her family prepare for the wedding, *while* working our regular jobs." He emphasized each point on his list with a nod of his head. "It is going to be a busy time! I am open to any ideas you might have."

This opened a conversation of ideas and plans that lasted all the way to Neidenberg. They decided that before they went home, they should stop at Sigi's, where they could get her and Trina's help in planning for the next week.

Ahlf was always ready with his intruder alert. When Fritz and Val drove into the driveway in the dark, he was determined to make as much noise as he could so that everybody in the house, and maybe some of the neighbors, would know that someone was there. With his tail straight out, hair standing up on his neck and back, standing in the driveway, and barking his most challenging bark, he was making it known that strangers were not going to get by him.

Fritz stopped in front of Ahlf and looked closely at him standing in the brightness of the truck headlights. "I wonder if he gets that attitude from fighting bad guys in the woods with Warin."

Val was slightly surprised at Ahlf too. "I have not seen him like that very many times!"

"Hello, Ahlf! Why all the fuss?" Fritz was trying to let Ahlf recognize his voice and settle down.

"You sure can make a lot of noise when you want to. Can we come in and see your family?" Val was trying to settle him too.

After finally recognizing two friendly voices, Ahlf quieted and began wagging his tail. He came around to Val's side of the truck while Fritz drove closer to the house.

Fritz and Val were getting out of the truck when Herr Backman opened the door of the house to see who was causing all the excitement. "Oh, it's you guys. We know these two, don't we, Ahlf."

"Hello, sir. Sorry for the disturbance. We have just come back from the farm, and we have some ideas for the muff business we would like to talk to the girls about. Are they here?"

"I am here, Fritz. Hi, Val." Sigi popped through the doorway beside her dad, who was holding the door open. She hurried to Fritz, took his hand, and gave him a kiss on the cheek. "How was your trip? How did you guys do at the farm?" She looked from Fritz to Val, expecting either one to answer.

Val looked at Fritz, who motioned back at him to go ahead and answer. "We think we did very well today."

"Please, come in and tell us all about it." Herr Backman motioned them through the door.

Val went through the door first and greeted Frau Backman and Trina in his fun-loving way, with a slight bow and a big smile.

Frau Backman returned the fun with the same bow and a smile.

A smiling Trina returned a full bow as if he were royalty and said, "Herr Adlar, how good of you to come. It is so nice to see you."

He took her hand and, patting it, said, "Not at all, my dear, not at all," as he raised her to the honor of standing in his presence.

By now, even Warin and Klaus were watching and laughing at the fun as Trina carried on with "Please, sir, come into our parlor and sit. We would hear your words." With royal courtesy, she led him by the hand to the main chair in the living area, which he accepted with a royal demeanor and a slight bow, acknowledging her attentions. She bowed again and held it as she backed away from His Highness.

Val watched her with a smile that turned to thoughtful curiosity. He said, "I wonder if she might treat her husband that way." Everybody had a good laugh, and Trina hurried back over to Val, smacked him on the shoulder, and pushed her hand roughly through his hair, leaving it pointing in all directions. He said, "Whew, that sure could have been worse!"

Trina took a seat while Val pushed his hair back into some order and rubbed his shoulder, saying, "Herr Backman, I have noticed that your daughters sometimes like to communicate with their fists. You might want

139

to make a note of that, Fritz." When he noticed a scowl and threatening sounds from both Trina and Sigi and some movement by them in his direction, he quickly raised his hands to both and said, "Oh, no! Wait a minute. No more. I am done." He then loosened his collar around his neck in relief when they stopped their charge. He continued his explanation of the day.

"As I was saying about the house; the windmill, water tower, and all of the water appliances are working. We painted the center wall and the hallway, which made the house brighter and more livable. By the time you need it in a few weeks, it will look nice. We have been talking about the next four weeks and some of the things that need to be done and thought we should talk with Sigi and Trina to get their help with some planning."

The family settled into chairs in the living and the dining areas, except Warin and Lora, who were playing on the floor.

"This is going to be a busy time for all of us. Vater und Mutter Backman, if there is anything I can do to help with the wedding preparations, please let me know."

"Thank you, Fritz, but for now it is early in the process, and we are doing well," said Frau Backman, nodding.

"Val will probably be going with me every weekend to work on the farm."

"I will try." Val smiled.

"I think it will be good if you, Sigi and Trina, could come with us this next Saturday to get the kitchen and dining area, the bedrooms, and the water closets organized the way you want them, so that the things Val and I do will fit with what you want. After that, we can finish getting it ready to live in. I will see if Urs and Jochem can come too and help us get the outside of the house ready to paint and the yard cleaned up.

"Hey, if Trina goes, can I go?" Klaus was looking hopefully at his dad, then at Fritz, and back again.

"Me too! I want to go!" Warin wanted to be part of things also.

"Wait, boys." Fritz put his hands out toward them with a calming motion. "Your dad still needs your help to take care of *this* farm. We do not know if the girls can come yet; that will be up to your dad."

"There is going to be so much for everybody to do in the next few weeks that we will all be working extra hard," Herr Backman said, talking to everybody but looking at his young boys. "If we all do our best on our own place, then we will know if we can go and see Fritz's on Saturday. OK?"

"OK! Yes! We will work hard!" They were really excited! Frau Backman, Sigi, and Trina laughed, enjoying the boys' happiness.

"Speaking of working hard, another thing that needs attention is the muff business." Fritz sounded excited. "The first two stores we stopped at seemed happy to have the display sets. I think we can put many more out in other stores. I would like to know if we can get two more sets with six muffs each, plus six muffs each for the two we placed today. If we can get four sets in stores and keep them supplied with muffs through the end of the year, we will have a good idea of what our business will do in the future."

"I can have two sets of figures done and painted by Saturday, now that I know how they are supposed to look. That way, Trina can help more with the muffs."

"Thanks, Val. We need to show the store owners that we can keep the displays supplied with muffs. We will also know more about how to make production go as smoothly as possible. Sigi, will you keep track of how many muffs each person makes? I think that after the first of the year, we will be able to pay them for their work."

"Sure, and I will try to think of someone, like maybe Ada and her mother, who might be able to help." Enthusiasm showed on her face as the list of possibilities grew in Sigi's mind.

"I am glad to help, but it will be even better when I get paid!" Trina had her hand up and was bouncing in her chair like an excited volunteer.

"It sounds like even with all we want to do in the next few weeks, we might be able to get it done." Fritz smiled at the willingness of people to help.

CHAPTER 12

"Fritz … Fritz …" He did not stir. "Friedrich, come on. Wake up. You do not want to be late for your own wedding!" His mom was pushing on his shoulder to jostle him awake.

With a slightly growling moan, he said, "Oh, OK, I am awake." He managed a smile as he looked at his mom and sat up on the edge of Archie's bed. As his mind cleared, he remembered that this would be the last time his mother would be waking him before he was married and living in his own home.

"It is after three; nap time is over. You only have a couple of hours to get cleaned up to be at the church by six."

Fritz had gotten up at four that morning to load his bed and a few more of his things into the truck. He then went to Sigi's and got her bed and other belongings to take to their new home. After the wedding, the truck would be loaded with more last-minute stuff. Presents from wedding guests would need to be moved there too. With his early trip, he was finally satisfied that the house was ready for them to live in. His nap was a chance to relax and catch up on some of the sleep he missed during these last few weeks of final preparations of the farm.

"Come on, brother, this wedding just will not be the same without you!" Archie joked, coming in to begin getting ready. "I'm glad your motorcycle is still here so I can use it to get to the wedding while you finish getting ready. I want to be there early because I do not want to miss anything. Maybe I can help with the last of the preparations. From the little bit I have seen of Trina, it might be a good idea to see if there are other interesting girls in that part of town."

Fritz was still sitting on the side of the bed when his mother came back in.

"You have made some progress. You *look* like you are awake, but just to be sure, let me see you stand up." Frau Abbot was standing with her hands on her hips and her head slightly tilted as she issued her challenge.

Fritz responded to her by standing up quickly. Putting on a smile, he suddenly broke into a tap-dance imitation. "See? I am up, I am moving, and I am ready to go get married!" His eyes widened as the dancing slowed to a stop. "I hope."

Chuckling, his mom waved a hand at his nonsense, saying, "Good. That will do," as she walked out of the room.

"Your bachelorhood is fast drawing to a close." Archie was beginning to shave at the bowl and mirror in the bedroom. "This is a big-time decision."

"Yes, it is. I figured out a long time ago that once it was made, I could probably expect a lot of what-ifs to pop up. The best thing to do is to have faith in my decision and see it through. Sigi is a fine girl and the only one I have wanted to catch." By the time Fritz finished laying out his clothes, his younger brother was finished shaving, and Fritz took his turn.

Fritz had taken a bath and almost finished dressing when there was a knock on the front door. Brother-in-law Amal opened it and began talking to someone when Kresie yelled, "Fritz, your best man is here!"

Val said hi to everybody and told them he was there as part of his best man duty—and on threat of bodily harm from Sigi—to make sure the groom was on schedule.

Fritz came out of the bedroom. "I am glad you are here, Val. Did you say once that you wore a tuxedo before? Somebody needs to check me over to see if I have all the right pieces in all the right places. Yours looks right; let me check mine with yours. How do you tie this kind of tie?" There was a sound of frustration in his voice.

Herr Abbot, who was sitting close by, already dressed, came and tied his son's tie. "This is for the newest official man in the family, who is about to move on from being a boy."

"Uh … I think that second part is a *maybe*," Val added with a smile as he watched Herr Abbot pull his son's forehead down where he could kiss it.

Frau Abbot adjusted the sash of a soft color Sigi called *blushing peach* that matched her dress. "Just as this sash is intended to connect you to the color trimmings of Sigi's dress, a good man will be careful of his connection to his wife and family in all that he does." She gave him a kiss on the cheek. "And you are a *good* man, my son."

A little more tugging and tucking from Amal and Kresie as she said, "Don't let all this go to your head too much, because you will always be my kid brother."

Finally, everybody was satisfied with how the groom and best man were dressed.

"We will probably need some help just before the ceremony begins, because I feel so stiff that I am sure I will break or loosen something as soon as I move." Fritz looked at Val. "I can see now why some guys call these things *monkey suits.*"

"I think we are ready to go, and it is not even five yet. We will get there in time to be in our places before anybody gets too worried, which will keep us on the good side of the main lady involved." Val smiled and nodded positively. "Sigi is a good friend, and I like to see her happy."

"How did you get here, Val?"

"My dad dropped me off, then went home to get our family. They were almost ready to go when I left."

"You can ride with me in the truck during my last hour and last ride as a bachelor." Fritz had a serious look. Then with a sudden change to a fun-loving, happy smile, he added, "Maybe I can convince you to follow my example so you can feel as happy and excited as I do!"

While everybody laughed, Val thumped him on the shoulder. "No big hurry, good buddy. I plan to take some time yet. But I will ride with you! We should get going!"

They rode quietly for the first few minutes, each alone with his thoughts.

"When I showed up at the church about six months ago to see if you would like to take a ride to Willenberg, I had no idea it would lead to this. What a wonderful set of events came along at just the right time. Now here we are on the way to my wedding to a great girl. You have been the key to the start of things and the main one who has made it possible every step of the way. Very few ever had such a friend as you!" Fritz put out his hand for a shake of love for the boyhood-to-manhood friend riding with him.

"It has been a great ride through the years we have known each other. I thank you for your friendship too, but it is not over yet. We are just getting into the part of our lives where we are beginning to take on passengers. I expect we will need our friendship for a long time." Val understood the love and respect intended as he took Fritz's right hand in his, then patted and gripped their clasp with his left.

"I really do thank you for all your help in getting the house ready in the past few weeks. Between you, Urs, and Jochem, my family, Sigi's family, and some help from the neighbors up there, we have made the place look really good. It will be a fine place for us for a long time!"

"You are fortunate, having such a gift to start off your married life. Maybe if things lined up for me like that, I would get married too. It is easier to see the good things happening to somebody else than to yourself. Maybe I will need the help of a trusted friend to help me with good current sight, rather than seeing opportunities clearly only in hindsight." Val pointed his thumb back over his shoulder and, with a nod of his head, confirmed that he had some experience there. "Meanwhile, I am here to help any way I can. I owe you a few!"

Fritz continued, "Do you remember when I asked if you would be interested in moving to the area where we live if you could make a living there?"

"That was on one of the early trips to your place, wasn't it?"

"Yes."

"Uh-oh. What do you have in mind?" Val was not sure he was ready for what was coming.

"Nothing yet, but I think I am seeing signs that the muff business could be good! If it has to rely on me to pick up the new ones and deliver them to an increasing number of stores, only on Saturday, then growth will be limited. That will mean hiring somebody. That might as well be you!"

They were coming into Neidenberg and were about halfway to the church.

Val tilted his head back with a faraway look on his face. "If what you are suggesting were to really happen, then I would like to live near you, but some important parts of your plan are yet to be proven."

"Yes, but I can hope! I have a ten-year commitment to Herr Kemp and Bernhard, which will be my full-time job. The muff business might *have* to depend on you. For now, we can just continue what we have been doing and adjust to whatever develops."

Val nodded in agreement, and they drove on to the chapel without saying more.

It was almost five thirty when Fritz turned into the parking lot of the church. "I hope Sigi's day has gone well. She has so much going on around her lately, and especially today, that she might be stressed out. If she is, I will try to get her to relax and take a nap on the way to our house, after all the hurrying is over."

"She has a lot of good people around her who are eager to help. She is strong. I think she will be OK." Val wanted to relax and encourage his friend.

They barely came to a stop in the church parking lot when Archie came out the door to meet them. "It's a good thing I came a little early so I could tell Sigi's family and the minister that you are on your way. They have been very busy and careful to have everything ready. The main thing that they worried about all day was if you were going to be back from your trip to the farm today in time for things to go smoothly tonight. They felt better after I got here and told them you were nearly finished getting ready when I left home."

"Have you seen Sigi? How is she doing?"

"She was glad to hear that you will be here soon! Her mom and Trina are helping her get dressed. The reception is all set up as planned, but I am sure the minister wants to see you to cover any last-minute details."

"Thanks, Archie. I am glad you came early!" Fritz slapped him on the shoulder as they went through the large, double glass doors at the front of the building.

The minister was in the recreation room where some final adjustments were being made to the decorations and tables. The serving tables held the small sandwiches, punch, water, and treats that guests could choose from and take to their seats. Each table had a white tablecloth made of paper that was beautifully designed for weddings. In front of each chair around the tables, and folded into a pyramid, was a paper napkin of the same soft, blushing peach as the color accents on Sigi's white dress and Fritz's and Val's tuxedos.

Also on the tables were many different curiosities and pictures related to dating, a wedding day, young children, growing families, and grandma-grandpa years, all to celebrate a future life together.

"This looks great!" Looking around, Fritz could not help but notice a sacred yet festive feeling that had not been in the room when he was there earlier. "This is much better than yesterday when we helped set up the tables and chairs."

Val agreed, noting, "There have been people in here since early this morning taking care of their parts of this rather large production. It seems you two have a lot of friends who want to make this special for you." While making a sweeping motion with his arm, Val noticed the pastor coming toward them.

"Hello, boys. Glad to see you here early enough to go into the chapel and review the ceremony once more. The girls went through their part a short time ago, so they are all set. All you have to do is follow me."

"We should be able to handle this no matter how nervous he gets." Val seemed to be getting fidgety as he pointed to Fritz.

"We start here at the door into the chapel. When the music starts, Val will be just ahead of us. Fritz and I will walk together. We will walk slowly like this."

The young men followed his directions as they walked across the back of the chapel to the center aisle, then up to the front.

"When we get to the front, Val will take about four steps to the right, and Fritz will take one. Soon, our entry music will end, and we will turn around to watch the bride enter. The bride's processional music will begin; that is when Sigi and Trina will come in the chapel door on the other side from where we came in."

By this time, Fritz was getting a little nervous, and Val was getting pale.

The pastor continued, "When they have taken their positions to my right, the music will stop, and the ceremony will begin. Just follow my directions, and we will all get through it."

"It all sounds easy enough when I know we are only practicing, but I wonder how I will do when it is for real." Fritz's smile was a little uneasy.

"After you kiss the bride, the music will start again. You will take her hand and walk back down the aisle and into the recreation room, where you will take your places for a reception line. Do you have any questions?" There was a friendly, happy-to-help look on the pastor's face.

"I think I pretty much know what I am supposed to do." Fritz sounded like he was trying to encourage himself through his nervousness.

"Good. It is time to start getting everyone in place. The best place for you two is at that door where we are to enter the chapel. Wait there for me."

The chapel began filling while the groom and best man practiced with the pastor. Fritz's and Val's families were among those who came in to find seats. They watched the last part of the rehearsal. The boys gave them tight little grins and waves as they walked by on their way to their place by the door.

"It has been a long time since you have had this much attention." Val wanted to lighten the load of his friend.

The pastor asked Frau Adlar to go tell Sigi that it was time to take their places. He went to find Herr Backman and to announce to those milling in the recreation room that it was time to move into the chapel for the wedding.

Standing at the door gave the boys a chance to shake hands with Herr Kemp and his wife and Bernhard and Frieda, who had come from Koenigsberg.

"Wow. There are a lot of people here. Did you know you have so many friends?" Val seemed surprised and happy for his friend as he nudged him with his elbow.

The chapel was nearly full by the time the pastor made it back up to the front. "Come in, come in, everybody, and find a seat." He paused until people were settled and had quieted down.

"Thank you for coming. We are here to celebrate the wedding of Fritz Abbot and Sigi Backman." Then he joked, "For those of you who did not know that but were just driving by, saw the crowd of cars, and thought there must be free food here, you're welcome to stay too!"

"I think we are ready to start." With a nod to the organist, he hurried back to the boys and started the entrance walk with them. Fritz walked beside him, and Val was four steps ahead. When they were in place, he nodded again to the organist, who, after a brief pause, began playing the bride's processional music.

Soon the door opened that Sigi was supposed to come through. Fritz watched closely for the first look at her in her wedding dress. There is Herr Backman walking slowly across the back of the chapel to the center aisle. Trina was a few steps ahead, but where is Sigi? A flash of panic and stress and sickness came with a rush of thoughts. *What if something is wrong? I have got to smile. I thought it was going to be easy to just stand and watch during this part. I feel myself getting pale. Toughen up, Fritz! You do not want to faint!* With a deep breath, he resumed breathing when he realized she was there holding her father's arm and walking beside him. She is small enough that all he could see around her father was a little bit of white veil or white dress pop into view for a split second with some of her steps. He wanted so much to see her that he felt like he was being teased.

Just as quick and complete as was his panic only seconds ago were the joy and the love and the wonder he felt as Sigi and her father turned to walk down the aisle straight toward him, where he could see her well. *What a beautiful lady she is! Is this really happening to me? Is she really coming to me, to be my wife? Does she really want to be with me for the rest of our lives? The way Herr Backman is looking at me, I must have a sappy look on my face. I do not care. Just look at her!*

Herr Backman had a loving smile of happiness for his daughter because of the love he could see on Fritz's face. All Fritz could do was look at her happy, pretty eyes and her warm, loving smile that was just for him, as if her lucent white veil was not even there.

Val had been staring at Trina since she first came in. Suddenly he leaned over and nudged Fritz. "Wow, they are beautiful. Let's have a double wedding!"

Fritz was so surprised that he choked a little and covered it with a cough.

He replied to his funnyman friend, who he realized was probably speaking his true feelings, "There is Trina, and there is her dad. Make your move."

Now it was Val's turn to cough!

The bride and bridesmaid were wearing matching dresses that they made themselves, with the help of family and friends. The top seemed to be suspended from a handmade rose of blushing peach on each shoulder.

The shining white fabric of the dresses gathered beneath them, remaining loose enough in the front and back to flow from side to side in waves, which started two inches below their necks and became smaller and smaller as they extended down toward the sash. From the waves to the collars close around their necks was a sheer white fabric with a ribbon of blushing peach, a gathered, fluffy, white, sheer fringe above that.

The girls and their dad had almost reached their stopping point when Val nudged Fritz again and asked, "Did you mean what you said about make my move?"

Fritz leaned back to his friend. "Sure, there is enough room in our house for you two to start with. The muff business ... or the stash ... can support you." He could see the wheels turning in Val's head and wondered what he might do.

As soon as the girls and their dad stopped, Val stepped around behind Fritz, Herr Backman, Sigi, and Trina until he stood close enough in front of a surprised Trina to whisper in her ear.

Fritz turned to the pastor and said, "A few seconds please."

The pastor was surprised, and Sigi and her dad looked puzzled.

Fritz gave Sigi a quick wink and his happy smile, then watched Trina's face turn from her nice smile to a stare of surprise as Val talked to her in whispers. Soon a smile even bigger than before, now including happy excitement, showed as she turned to him and began whispering back to him with her cheek against his.

Val took her hand in his and patted it to settle her while saying, "OK, OK."

Sigi immediately recognized the extreme excitement of her sister, who had her hand over her mouth.

Val moved over to Herr Backman and said quietly, "Herr Backman, I have asked Trina to marry me, and she said yes. With the approval of you and your wife, we could have a double wedding. Will you give us your blessing?"

Now Sigi had a look of surprise as she put out one hand to her sister in congratulations and the other over her mouth, then turned around to look at Fritz, who shrugged his shoulders with a big smile.

"I bet you think you are the first one to have this idea, don't you?" Herr Backman replied to Val with a smile as he shook his head. "I have heard talk of this a few times in my house over the past weeks. We need to get her mother up here."

The pastor explained to the people, "Please be patient while we discuss some adjustments."

After a short discussion, the pastor said to Herr Backman, "Even with your approval, there is some government paperwork that needs to be done."

"The mayor is here. Maybe we can get his approval today and take care of the papers next week." Val sounded like he had thought this out a little.

The pastor said to the congregation, "Can I ask Frau Backman and Mayor Kuhn to come up here, please?" Then he had a conference with those gathered at the front of the chapel while Val went back to where his parents were sitting to explain the logic behind what he wanted to do.

When Frau Backman and the mayor started back to their seats, Val thanked his parents for their understanding and went up to the front.

The pastor announced, "It seems that the proposed adjustments have received the necessary approvals, and we can continue. It is now my pleasure to welcome you to the double wedding of four of the finest young people I know."

There was an audible, collective gasp from the congregation, then sighs and coos followed by a soft applause.

The pastor continued, "Fritz Abbot will marry Sigi Backman. Come over to this side by your future husband, Sigi. And Val Adlar, come to this side. Val will marry Trina Backman. Stand here on this side of your dad, Trina.

"This handsome gentleman in the middle, whom these young ladies are holding on to, is Herr Backman, their father.

"To all of you in the congregation, I want to say that I have five of the most beautiful people standing in front of me. I believe it is because they all look happy to be here." He took a moment to savor the presence of God in all this beauty and then continued.

"I want to start by saying to all four of you, may you be as kind to each other as you have been to those around you in the time I have known you.

"My first question is to you, Herr Backman. Who comes to give these ladies away? Please answer, 'I do,' sir."

"I do."

"Now offer the hand of each daughter to her future husband. Thank you. Please step back two steps until we are done."

"Fritz, take both of Sigi's hands."

Val and Trina were watching closely, their own excitement growing.

"Fritz Abbot, do you take Sigi Backman to be your lawful wedded wife …"

Fritz looked down into Sigi's sweet, excited, loving face, took a deep breath, and exhaled in a soft *whew* through a smile of love.

"To love, honor, and cherish as long as you both shall live?"

"Yes."

"Sigi Backman, do you take Fritz Abbot to be your lawful wedded husband …"

Sigi could feel her excitement growing as she looked up into Fritz's warm, strong, loving face, all the way down to her fidgeting feet that really felt like dancing!

"To love, honor, and cherish as long as you both shall live?"

"Yes." Her excited voice was somewhere between a scream and a squeak. By this time, everyone could see from her quick little movements and bouncing up and down that below her full-length dress, her fidgeting feet had given in to full-on dancing, in the small area covered by her dress.

"Now, Val and Trina. Val, take both her hands." Val looked nervous, because of the weight of the quick decision he had just made. He had a happy smile because the love for Trina he had felt growing over the past months was no longer a secret.

"Val Adlar, do you take Trina Backman to be your lawful wedded wife …"

Val, looking into Trina's eyes, silently mouthed the words *wife, wow*.

Through a nervous smile of her own, she silently mouthed the word *wow*.

"To love, honor, and cherish as long as you both shall live?"

"Yes."

Fritz and Sigi were now watching.

"Trina Backman." Trina jumped at the sound of her name and looked at the pastor while he continued. "Do you take Val Adlar to be your lawful wedded husband, to love, honor, and cherish as long as you both shall live?"

"Yes!" she said in a high voice that betrayed her stifled excitement.

"By the power vested in me, I now pronounce each couple man and wife. You may now kiss your bride." Still carefully following instructions, Fritz and Val each gave their new wife a kiss.

When everybody in the chapel stood and started cheering and clapping, Fritz sensed the relief that it was finally done, and there were no more instructions to follow. He bent down, grabbed Sigi around the waist, picked her up, and gave her a much bigger kiss to celebrate the huge step they had just taken.

Val thought that looked like a good idea. When he picked up Trina, she squealed in surprise until his kiss stopped her. She then held him around the neck and joined him in the kiss.

The pastor raised his hands to get everybody's attention. "If you will all keep your places while these gentlemen escort their brides into the recreation room, you can all congratulate them there. Will their parents please follow them and form a greeting line?

"I would remind you, good people, that Val and Trina, now finding themselves suddenly married, would probably welcome any financial consideration you can give. I am sure God will bless you. I already thank you."

CHAPTER 13

It was after eight when all the congratulating and well-wishing was done and most of the guests were gone. Fritz and Val thought they might be able to get away, and the girls agreed.

During the reception, Fritz's brothers Archie and Dieter were in charge of putting the gifts on the truck. Fritz and Sigi already had everything they thought they would need to start their life in their new home.

Because Val and Trina had no time to prepare, some things were decided by the four of them in short bits of conversation during the reception. Tonight, they would stop by their homes just long enough to change out of their formal clothes and get a few things. Fritz and Sigi changed before they left the church. Tomorrow, Saturday, Fritz, Val, and Trina planned to make another trip back to Neidenberg to get their beds and other things. But tonight, Sigi and Fritz would use Sigi's bed in the master bedroom, and Val and Trina would use Fritz's, which they would move into the second bedroom. Being newlyweds, two people in a single bed might sound OK, but it was also a very cozy introduction to the sleeping habits of their new spouse!

It took more than an hour to finish what they had to do in Neidenberg and finally get on the road to their home near Koenigsberg.

"OK, everybody, now is the time for all of us to settle in and get as comfortable as possible, because this ride is about two and a half hours long. It is a good thing we are all married, because in this small cab, the couple that is not driving is going to have to be pretty cozy over on that side."

"Being cozy is nice," said Val, happy with Trina on his lap. She was all smiley faced but poked him with her elbow just to remind him to be nice.

"I am looking forward to our turn, but I think that after about thirty minutes, we will need to get out and make sure we can still walk." This time, Fritz got a poke in his ribs.

"Oh, ladies, may I remind you we are in the cab of a truck that was not designed for four people to ride in. For the peace and comfort of all, I think we need a few basic rules. Rule number one—there will be no poking anywhere of any other rider. All in favor, raise your hand." Fritz raised his hand, but Val's hand shot up faster and only stopped because it reached the ceiling of the cab.

Before anybody could say anything else, Val said, "And no thumping of legs either!" and raised his hand again.

Fritz raised his hand and looked at the girls.

Sigi's mouth was open like she was going to say something. She looked at the boys' hands and at Trina, whose hand was not up, and slowly raised her hand. "Well, OK, I suppose it is for the best."

With everybody looking at her, Trina slowly raised her hand. "It sounds like a good idea." Then she quickly put her forehead against Val's and her nose against his and said, "But I will be watching you!"

Sigi and Fritz could not help laughing at the courage of this young wife who had no idea this morning that she would be married tonight.

Val said, "Oh boy."

With her firm look still against his face, she stared another second or two into his eyes and then let a smile grow on her face and quickly kissed him.

His concern was now gone. His "Whew!" told everyone of his relief.

Her happy smile now showing, she put her cheek to his and whispered in his ear, "I love you."

"Oh yes! I can work with that!" Suddenly, his world was bright and sun-shiny, and his future was clear and beautiful as he hugged her closer to him.

"It looks like you two do not have a problem with being cozy right now, but we will see how you feel in another twenty minutes or so." Sigi felt happy for her sister but was still using her level-headed thinking.

Stopping to stretch their legs each time they changed drivers added to the time it took to make the trip. They did not get home until after midnight. Sigi and Trina started a fire in the fireplace to warm the house, while Fritz and Val moved a bed into Val and Trina's room. While the girls prepared the beds, the boys brought the things in from the truck. It soon became obvious that a trip should be made to town the next day to buy food, because the only things in the house were a few jars of fruit the girls had canned with their mother. Tonight, it would be peaches!

Sitting in some dining room chairs that had been given to them, they were warming themselves by the fire and eating their peaches. The conversation soon turned to money and how they were going to manage. There were some troubling questions in Trina's mind.

"I have thought many times tonight how Val and I can get along when we have not talked at all about money and how we will support ourselves. Other than Mom and Dad, you three are the ones I believe in the most in this world. Before the wedding, I had little more than a dim hope that Val and I could have a future together. When he whispered in my ear in the chapel, 'I love you. Will you marry me? Fritz said we can have a double wedding tonight and start our life together living with them,' I felt my dim hope grow into a huge, erupting volcano that could overcome anything. But here we are, in a house that has almost no food in it, using a borrowed bed. I feel like there is something that I do not know—like why are my three best friends so positive about all of this? I have the love for Val that I need, but I do not have the practical answers. From the way you all act, you must have the answers I am looking for. Please help me understand."

Upon hearing the frustration and stress in her voice, the three realized that Trina knew little about the financial strength that they felt.

"We are sorry, Trina. We—"

Val interrupted Fritz and Sigi. "You are right; there are some things that you need to be filled in on. Let me start by showing you the generosity of the guests at the reception." He moved the small kitchen table to where the others were sitting in the dining room chairs that had been moved in close to the fire. Reaching into his pocket, Val pulled out the money he had been given. "I have not counted it yet. Here. You guys can help." He handed some to each of them.

It only took a few minutes for each of them to count and give their total to Trina. "All together, there are two hundred and fifteen marks here, which can buy us some food tomorrow."

Val continued. "For the future, Fritz is sure, and from what I have seen, I believe him, that the muff business can support you and me while he works at his stone-carving job. He will receive a full salary but not have to make any payments on this farm. He invited us here to share their good fortune and to manage the muff business, which we all want to succeed."

Trina was nodding her head while listening and now looked very much relieved. "Great, I feel much better. You see why I have confidence in you guys! Thanks, Val, for understanding." She grabbed a handful of shirt on his shoulder and pulled until he was close enough in his chair for her to lean over and kiss him. His smile showed how much he liked that!

Sigi smiled, happy for her sister.

"That was a very good explanation, Val, but there is more, Trina." Fritz looked at Val and Sigi, who both nodded in agreement. "It is something that the three of us have been very careful about and promised each other that we would keep only to ourselves until we all agreed to tell another person."

"There is more? Wow, what I have heard is enough to answer my questions. Tell me what you mean by *more*."

"Val, you are probably the best one to tell her this story. What do you think, Sigi?"

"Yes, I think so. We are here if you need us, Val." Sigi willingly turned it over to Val. "Just remember, some of us need to go food shopping before the trip back to Neidenberg tomorrow."

"OK, I will give her a shortened version tonight, and we can tell her more tomorrow on our trip."

The fun of the story of Nose and Ribs and their payroll was enjoyed by all four, even in Val's shortened version, which made the time go by quickly. Finally, Sigi said, "OK, everybody, this night keeps getting shorter and shorter. I think we need to get up by seven to get food and have breakfast before starting out tomorrow. I think that as small as the truck is, only Fritz and I need to go shopping. How does that sound to the rest of you?"

"That is a good idea, at least until we have a better plan," Fritz answered.

"We do need to think about how to share responsibilities around here," Trina added.

"If we do not see you when we get home, we will knock on your door so you can get ready for breakfast, OK?" Sigi continued, "You are probably all as tired as I am, so let's go to bed!"

"That about says it all, doesn't it," Val agreed. "See you tomorrow."

A sleepy-eyed Val nudged Trina. "Is that Fritz at the door? We have only been in bed a half an hour or so, haven't we?"

"It must have been more than that, as bright as it is outside."

Fritz knocked again. "Come on, you two! Rise and shine! We have a lot of things to do today." Fritz knocked again.

Val answered, "Thanks. We will be out in a few more minutes."

Fritz went back into the kitchen and began stirring the pancake batter Sigi had put together while he was putting a pot of hot water in the hallway near the bathroom doors for Val and Trina.

"This married life will take some getting used to, but I think I like it already." He came up behind Sigi, put his hands around her waist, gave her a kiss on the cheek, and said, "I like working with you. I liked going to the store with you this morning. It feels right to be married. Having a wife makes me feel whole. I love you."

In about fifteen minutes, Val came out of the hallway. "Thanks for the hot water. It was a welcome surprise."

"Well, it's like this, good buddy. You had the need, and I had the time. If you and I can keep doing things like this for each other when we see the chance, then this time together can go very well. That will make life better for all of us. We are new to this life we have now, so we all need to try hard to make it work." Fritz slapped his friend on the back.

"You got it, my friend." Val held out his hand to shake. "For you two, I can do that!"

Fritz gladly took Val's right hand in his and said, "Let's make this as good for our families as we can!"

"Yes!"

"Families? What families? Is somebody else coming?" Trina came from the hallway. "Is there something else I do not know about?"

"Not right away, but eventually both our families are going to grow. That is who the third bedroom is for!" Fritz was poking fun at her.

"Oh, yeah." She realized what he was talking about and was a little embarrassed as she sat at the table by Val.

Sigi brought some bacon and eggs from the stove. "Breakfast is ready to start eating; don't let it cool too much."

Fritz brought the stack of pancakes to the table. "Sigi and I would like to continue the practice of asking a blessing on our food."

"My family did that too." Val took Trina's hand and bowed his head.

Fritz took Sigi's hand and asked her to offer the blessing.

At her *amen,* Fritz squeezed her hand enough to get her attention, so he could smile a thank you to her. Then he put a couple of pancakes on his plate and said, "Sigi and I talked this morning about how to make this day go as well as possible. Tell me what you two think of these ideas. Sigi can stay here while the three of us go to Neidenberg to get your beds and personal things. That way, you two can make sure you get it all. We will pick up all the muffs that have been made and distribute them on the way back. We can take turns riding Val's motorcycle back so he will have it here. Dad has been borrowing our neighbor's truck when he needs one; when I take his back, I can ride my motorcycle back here. Do either of you have any suggestions?"

"That plan should work, but there is one thing that I would like to see changed, and that is Sigi being here alone all day." Val's concern could be heard in his voice.

"That is the part I do not like either." Trina slowly shook her head as she looked at her plate. "I could make a list of the things I want, and Mom could put them together. If I need something more, I could borrow from Sigi or get it later. That way, I could stay here and work on the house with her."

"I would certainly like for you to be here with her too—if it would be OK for you." Fritz looked intently at Trina, hoping for a positive response.

"It will be fine."

"What do you think, Val?"

"I hate to leave anybody alone on their first full day being married, but I do not have any better ideas."

"Sigi, did you say that you liked the next-door neighbors?" asked Trina. "Maybe if they would come over and check on us every couple of hours, these guys would not worry about us so much. Do you think they might do that?"

"That is a great idea, Trina. I think Frau Hammond would be happy to come with one of her daughters—and probably send her husband over after dark." Sigi was happy with the idea that she would not be alone in a new place all day. "Maybe Fritz and I can go talk to them right after we finish here."

Val finished off his milk. "It might be good for all of us to go over to get a little better acquainted with them."

"That is another great idea! This discussion with all four of us is a good way to solve problems; we need to do this often." Fritz was confident in their plan.

Fritz and Val drove out of their driveway a few minutes after ten that morning in clear, warmer than usual weather, very nice for that time of year. They had a lunch the girls had made, and they each brought some extra layers of clothing for riding the bike if the weather turned colder. The trip went smoothly, and they made good time. Each tried to sleep while the other drove—to catch up on the sleep they had missed the night before. They decided to go to the Backmans' first, because they would be driving a motorcycle when they left Val's family home.

While they loaded Trina's bed and the muffs, her mom was able to gather all the things on her daughter's list. Frau Backman insisted on adding some things to their already large lunch before they left. "Having a double marriage yesterday was a surprise to us, even though we knew of Trina's interest in you, Val. We know that you two are very good young men and you can take care of our girls, and we know they feel the same way. Because they are so young, it also helps to know they are together and can support each other."

"They are young, but the way you have raised them has prepared them very well for their new lives. That is something I was definitely looking for, and I thank you very much!" Fritz put his arm around his mother-in-law.

"I thank you too," said Val. "We have already agreed to do our best for them." Val had the last of Trina's things in his arms that were to go on the truck.

"We want all of you to come back for a visit as often as you can." Herr Backman walked with them to the door and opened it.

"We do not want Ahlf to forget who you are!" Warin was patting his tail-wagging friend outside the door as the older boys came out.

"We will see you next time." Klaus waved from the barn door.

Fritz started the truck, and Val climbed in after putting his load in the back. One more wave to everybody, and they were on their way to the Adlar home to get Val's stuff.

"I had better eat some lunch now if I am going to take the first turn on the motorcycle." Val pulled a sandwich out of the lunch box.

"I can take a sandwich too. Have you thought about what to do about your job?"

"Yes. At the reception, I asked Archie if he would like to have it." Val handed Fritz a sandwich. "He said yes, but he had to check with your dad. In a few minutes, he came back and told me your dad said they could adjust the farm responsibilities so it would be OK. I wrote a letter to Herr Deforest telling him about my marriage and that we would be living near Koenigsberg. I also said I knew Archie well and was sure he would do a good job for him. Archie will take it to him on Monday and be ready to start that day. I think it will work for everybody."

"It sounds to me like the best plan you could have come up with. How long did that take you?"

"About three days." Funnyman Val put a Stan Laurel all-knowing grin on his face, because he knew his friend would be surprised.

"Three days?" Fritz almost choked on his sandwich. "You and I only talked about a double wedding when we saw the girls coming down the aisle!"

"That is right, but what was the first thing I said?" Val still had the grin.

"The first ... let me see ... 'They are beautiful. Maybe we should have'—what? How long have you been thinking about this?" Fritz, in his blustering surprise, could hardly believe what he was hearing.

"Do you remember the first trip you and I made together to your farm?"

"Yes, of course!"

Val went on, "Do you remember saying that it would be good if I could take care of the muff business while you worked your commitment for the farm, but that it would work much better if I lived close to you?" When Fritz nodded his head, Val continued. "That is what started me thinking. Like Trina, I started with only a hope so dim that I did not even want to mention it to you. Each time I went to the farm with you, my hope got a little brighter. Taking the payroll from the Brownshirts made it hard not to say something. After we agreed that the money could not be used safely, I knew I should not say anything, and my hope went back to fairly dim again. Then at the wedding, when you mentioned the muff business again, the stash, and room in your house, along with the 'make your move' earlier, I began to feel that volcano Trina talked about, and I could hardly wait for them to stop walking when they got up to us."

"So, you have been thinking about this for *four* weeks now?"

"Something like that!" Val's grin was still there but more relaxed now.

"You have really kept it well hidden!" Fritz was still so surprised that he did not know whether to move his head up and down or side to side. He had not taken a bite of his sandwich since he heard Val say, "About three days."

"Yes, well, it took a volcano to make me believe it could really happen, but here we are. We have left the starting line, and we are on our way, and I feel great about it." Val showed a happy determination.

"Whoa, I forgot I was holding a sandwich. I had better eat it before I drop it. I was listening to you so intently that I even forgot I was driving a couple of times."

"Don't do that! We have seen enough problems along this road in the past few months. We will be at my place pretty soon."

Kyler came running from back in the property as soon as he saw who was driving into the driveway. Fritz saw him coming. "Hi there, little buddy."

Fritz had not even closed the door to the truck when Kyler ran right into him, hugged him around the leg, and stood on his foot to get an up-and-down ride as he walked.

"How big are your baby chicks?" asked Fritz, who had not been there in a week or so.

"They are much bigger. They are little chickens now! We'll have more chicks soon enough. That's what happens, ya know!" Kyler was showing off his wisdom.

"You are going to be a really good farmer someday."

"I already am. I am just not big enough to do some of the things yet, but I can still do lots of stuff around here!" His ride made him laugh and squeal between words all the way to the front door of the house.

"OK, little man, this is where you get off. I have some work to do to help your brother."

Fritz gave him a hug and then went to see about the bed, while Val gathered his things.

"We will miss Val around here." Herr Adlar handed the last of the bedding to his wife to fold, then picked up one end of the mattress. "He sure is excited about being married and working with you kids in your muff business."

"There are probably more reasons for the way he feels than we know about." Frau Adlar shrugged a little. "I'm glad to see him happy."

Val knew which things he wanted to bring on this trip, and he was able to gather them quickly. They soon finished putting them in the truck. "Bye, Mom, Dad, Kyler."

Fritz watched as they ended up in a group hug, with Kyler standing in the middle like a small man surrounded by three trees. "I will be making deliveries in this area every weekend. I will try to stop in often."

All four of them walked out to the truck talking of the future, while Val got his motorcycle out of the barn and brought it over to where they were for some last good-byes.

Fritz closed the door of the truck, and Val put on his jacket and mask and then started the motorcycle.

"We can still make our muff stops and get home before it gets too dark and cold on the bike. Bye, little buddy. I will see you next time!" Fritz had his arm out the window, playing with Kyler.

The sound of the motorcycle made it too noisy to talk easily. The boys waved once more as they left the driveway.

CHAPTER 14

They had finished the muff deliveries when they stopped in Heilsberg for gas and to stretch their legs. Each one of them had eaten some lunch, so they were not hungry, but they were both tired and just needed a break.

As they thought about this last stretch of road before they got home, they remembered some of the people they had met over the past few weeks whom they stopped to help with car trouble and other things. There were many kinds of needs and many kinds of people. Some made them laugh; some they had seen more than once; some were professionals; and some were tourists. Most were good people who were fun to talk to. Some were concerned about what was going on in the world around them; some did not know; and some were convinced they could do nothing to help. Val and Fritz agreed there was usually something they could learn from everybody.

The sun was almost down, and a light snow was starting to fall. Fritz had put on his extra layers of clothes while they talked and was finishing with his muff, goggles, hat, and gloves. "We better get going, because it will get colder, and we will not be able to go as fast as we usually do. I will follow you, so I can watch what the truck tires are picking up off the road; that way, I can know better when the snow starts to freeze and cover the road with ice. You will need to watch me in the mirror to see if I can keep up."

"When you have had enough and want to change drivers, just turn the light on and off a few times, and I will stop." Val added, "We better not get home with one of us coming down with a cold, or we will be in trouble with two young wives!"

"You are right! I am ready to go when you are."

"OK then, we can go."

The drive went well for the first thirty minutes. It was now dark, and a steady, wet snow was falling and sticking to Fritz's goggles, also adding to the slush on the road. *It is a good thing Val has some wet-weather protection in the clothes he picked up at his parents' home, or this ride would be impossible.* The cold and wet still found ways to soak through in some places. Fritz was glad for the warmth of the engine below him.

After fifteen minutes, he flashed the headlight to signal to Val to pull over and change drivers. A kilometer went by before Val found a place where he thought he could get off the road a little without getting stuck.

Before Val started slowing the truck, Fritz saw the headlights of two cars coming up from behind that were going too fast for the road conditions. *It looks like one is trying to pass the other. If they are going to drive like that, I am going to get as far to the side of the road as I can to keep from being covered by the slush that they are going to splash as they go by. I hope Val sees them!*

The second car tried again to pass. Fritz saw a flash in his mirror and heard a pop. Then the second car fell behind again, and the first got around Fritz and Val. When they went by, the boys recognized the driver as a Jewish friend they met in the gas station in Heilsberg on one of their trips. This time, he had his family with him! When the second car passed, Fritz could see it had four brown-shirted men in it! Suddenly, Fritz realized that the pop he heard was a gunshot! The Brownshirts must have been trying to force his friend to stop!

Val reached his stopping place just after the cars passed. Fritz pulled up beside the truck and said, "That was Efrim Goldschmidt and his family being chased by some Brownshirts."

Val nodded his head knowingly.

Fritz continued, "The Brownshirts were shooting at them! I'm going to watch what happens!" The motorcycle engine revved up for Fritz to take off again.

"I thought you were cold and wanted to change drivers!" Val yelled over the noise.

"Not anymore. Watch for me!"

"Oh boy, here we go again," Val said. "That is what you have to expect from a wildman in a face mask."

The place Val had picked to stop left him with two wheels off the paved road and in the mud; his back tire was spinning when he tried to drive out of it. He got some small branches from the woods and put them in the path of the back tire. *This is taking much too long. Whatever is going to happen will probably be over when I get there!* By rocking the truck back and forth until it got up onto the branches, where it could get some traction, he was finally able to get back on the road.

Fritz could see by the taillights ahead that the second car was unsteady on the road. His mind was working hard. *If these guys are drunk and trying to drive this fast in this weather—and shooting too—this could turn awfully bad very quickly. I cannot do anything on a motorcycle but wait for something to happen. I had better stay back as far as I can and still see them. I do not want to draw anyone's attention away from their driving in this weather.*

The second car tried to pass again but pulled back because of a car coming at them up the road. Being drunk, they were easily angered by the oncoming car, honking at it when it passed. The next time they tried to pass, they lost control and spun out, almost hitting some trees before ending up in the mud and snow at the side of the road.

When Fritz went by, he could see all four of them moving and swearing at the driver, which showed they were not badly hurt. He also knew that it would not take long for the four of them to push their car out of the mud and back onto the road, even angrier and meaner than before.

In less than five kilometers, Fritz found Efrim's car where it had also spun out. The back end of the car was now against some small trees on the right side of the road. He drove the motorcycle into the woods on the left side of the road about two hundred meters before he got to Efrim's car. *This should hide it from the Brownshirts, who will be coming.* He pulled his mask down before he got to the driver's door. He found Efrim and his family in their car in a state of shock and in tears but unhurt.

"Efrim, I am Fritz Abbot. We met three weeks ago in a gas station in Heilsberg. I want to help you.

"I think I remem—are you the ones who are getting a house near Koenigsberg ready to move into?"

"That is right! The Brownshirts have spun out, but they will be coming soon. We need to get you and your family into the woods where you can hide. Come on. We must move quickly. Take my rain jacket, and, Frau Goldschmidt, you can have my other jacket." Fritz grabbed everything he could from the car that would help keep the kids warm and started into the woods carrying the eight-year-old daughter. Efrim followed with the five-year-old daughter, and his wife with the two-year-old son. All three adults were talking quietly to the kids to soothe them and keep them quiet. They had gone about fifty meters into the woods when Fritz stopped and said, "This should be far enough. It is so dark back in the trees like this that they probably will not even look for you. It is important for all of you to be completely quiet. I will go out and try to distract them to the other side of the road."

Fritz had just gotten back out to Efrim's car when he saw some headlights in the distance. When he was sure he could be seen in their headlights, he ran across to the left side of the road, waving his arms like he was telling someone to move back farther. Then he went into the woods and watched.

The Brownshirts stopped by Efrim's car, and all got out with their pistols in their hands. They looked around carefully, and then one of them told another to follow the man that they had seen and pointed across the road. The man crossed the road and stopped at the edge of the woods where Fritz went in, to listen for movement. The other three looked carefully into the woods on their side, then stopped to listen. Not hearing anything, the man giving orders told one man to keep his eyes open while they checked the car. The two at the car put their guns away and turned their attention to the car. One found that it would not start and got angry. The other suddenly started talking excitedly about what he found on the floor of the back seat. The man in the driver's seat turned around to look and excitedly climbed into the front passenger seat on his knees so he could get a better look and reach whatever it was they were looking at.

Seeing their excitement, Fritz thought, *There are some small wooden boxes stacked on the floor that make a bigger area for the kids to lay down on during their long ride. Why are they so interesting?*

Fritz's attention quickly returned to the man coming toward him across the road. He made some rustling noise on purpose as he moved deeper into the woods; this caused the Brownshirt following him to come farther in.

The man in charge got more excited as he counted the boxes. He finished counting and climbed out of the front seat. When he stood up, his wide smile soon changed as though a new thought had come into his head. One hand went up to his chin and mouth, and the other rested on his hip.

Fritz made a noise like a child starting to cry, following quickly with a "Shhh." That immediately brought a gunshot that hit the tree Fritz was hiding behind. *I better be careful,* he thought. *This guy is good!*

The leader called from the other side of the road, "Schumann, are you OK?"

Schumann replied, "Yes. I heard something and shot at it."

"Good! Let us know if you need some help." Still in his thoughtful pose, the leader looked toward Schumann, then back at the boxes, then toward Schumann again, and said to the two men with him, "I should go help Schumann." He drew his gun and crossed the road.

Fritz threw a rock to get the first man to come farther in, past him, not closer.

The leader stopped at the edge of the woods and said, "Schumann, I thought you could use some help. I can't see anything in here. Where are you?"

There is something familiar about this leader, Fritz thought as he watched him come across the road. Hearing the voice this last time left no doubt. *It is Jarvis! I wonder how his ribs are. Won't he be surprised to hear from me!*

"In here," Schumann replied. "Come on in."

The men were about eight meters apart in the darkness when Fritz threw a rock that landed between them. At the same time Jarvis heard the rock hit the ground, he also heard a familiar voice say in a bold Russianized German with a mocking tone, "Hello, Ribs!"

There was a loud, quick gasp from Jarvis; then in anger and fear, he began firing in the direction of the noise and yelling so loudly that he could not hear Schumann yelling at him, "Stop! Stop!"

In desperation, Schumann realized he had no choice but to fire back. Even being surprised, drunk, and now wounded, he was able to get off four shots, one hitting Jarvis in the leg and another in the abdomen.

The sound of shooting and yelling made the man on guard and the one with him crouch down behind their car. They watched across the road for a few seconds. Then the guard yelled, "Jarvis, Schumann, are you OK?"

With his gun in the hand hanging down at his side and holding the wound in the side of his abdomen with the other, a stunned Jarvis realized what he had done, then turned and limped back the way he came.

There was no sound from Schumann.

About the time Jarvis started across the road, Fritz heard a groan from Schumann and some rustling. Obviously hurt badly, Schumann managed to walk through the growth toward the road. When he was near enough the road to see that Jarvis was already across, he yelled to the man on guard, "He's crazy! He shot me! They must want the gold for themselves." Then he collapsed in the newly fallen snow and the half-frozen mud.

When the guard heard this, he shot the fourth man, who was known to be a friend of Jarvis and had to be the other man Schumann was talking about when he said, "they".

Seeing his friend fall, Jarvis shot the guard, who already was aiming at his leader but did not fire until he saw the gun that was still in his leader's hand point his way. The guns fired at almost the same time. Both men were drunk, and both were excited and nervous because of the shootings that had already happened. Still, their military training for the recent war and battle experience through the years of combat made their shots at this close range deadly accurate.

It was now quiet. Just as suddenly as it started, the shooting stopped. Soon, there was an unmistakable feeling that an eerie darkness was now rising away from the scene, as if the spirits of the dead men were leaving.

Fritz listened carefully for any sound of movement from Schumann.

What gold? Is that what is in those little boxes? Why is it in the back seat of that car out here in the dark?

After hearing no sound from any of the men for almost ten minutes, he began moving toward Schuman as quietly as he could until he could reach the gun. Grabbing it and quickly getting clear by two meters, he kept his eye on this man who had seemed to come back to life once already. After watching and listening to all four men for five more minutes, he moved around Schumann and started toward the cars and the men on the ground across the road.

Before crossing, he looked back down the road toward Heilsberg. This time, he could barely see the outline of a truck parked on the side of the road. *Something took him much longer than I expected, but I believe that's Val.*

Carrying Schumann's gun and watching for any movement from the other downed Brownshirts, he went slowly toward them. His first look at the kind of wounds the men had let him know they were all dead. Looking closer at the man shot by the guard, he recognized Hall, whom he had called Nose at their last meeting. *It looks like this wipes out anybody that might recognize us from earlier incidents with the Brownshirts.*

He signaled for Val to come up close.

While Val was coming, Fritz had time to see what was in the Brownshirts' car. He found an extra coat, which he gladly put on.

The truck had barely stopped when Val jumped out with a pistol in his hand and ran anxiously around to the front of the truck, where his friend was still standing at the back end of the men's car. All the way, he was asking loudly, "Are you OK? What do you need me to do?" He looked Fritz over. "I don't see any wounds on you, but it looks like it is over for these four. Is this all of them?"

"I'm not hurt, and there are no more Brownshirts around here right now. See who these two guys are?"

"Would ya look at that." Val was not as surprised as his funnyman overreaction sounded. "This is Herr Ribs, and that looks like Herr Nose. What a shame. Now who will we party with?"

"This scene is going to attract attention, and we need to be gone when it does."

"I am glad you are here. We have a lot to do as quickly as possible. The boxes in this car were taken out of Efrim's car and need to go back into it. His car will not start. I think something was jarred loose when it spun out. It needs to run so we can get his family someplace safe and warm tonight. If you will work on getting it started, I will put the boxes back. When that is done, we can put the family in the car so they can start warming up again. How does that sound to you?"

"Good ideas." Val started toward the front of Efrim's car, then stopped and turned around. "What about these men and their car?"

"It looks like some drunken men killed each other, which is exactly what happened! That way, the authorities who investigate will not be looking for anybody else to blame. That reminds me. I need to put the gun I have back by the man I got it from." Fritz started to cross the road but noticed an unconvinced look on Val's face. "This is a natural scene; it is the truth. We could not have created a better one. I will give you all the details later."

Val thought for a second, *Even with the questions I still have, I know I can trust him to make good decisions, and right now, he knows more about what's going on here than I do.* Then he nodded his approval to Fritz, put his pistol in his pocket, and got busy on the car.

As soon as the boxes were loaded, Fritz went into the woods to the place where he thought he had left Efrim and his family, calling, "Efrim, Efrim, it is safe now. We can go." He walked a little farther and realized he was wearing the coat of a Brownshirt. Remembering the shock he saw on their faces when he first saw them in their stalled car just minutes ago, he put a gentle, encouraging tone in his voice. "I forgot I was wearing this coat. I had to borrow it because you are wearing mine." After he took it off, he heard a little noise. Again he tried, "Efrim, it is clear now. We can go home and get warm."

"Here we are, Frank, over here." Efrim's slightly quivering voice gave away the stress and shock he was feeling.

"Those guys never would have found you. I brought you in here, and I could not find you. You were safe! Is everybody OK?" Mother and children were still in the nest they had made as they huddled together for warmth and security in the things Fritz had brought from the car. He put the Brownshirt coat back on.

"Yes. We stayed warm. The youngest ones went to sleep, but my wife and I are shaking from what was the worst experience of our lives. We know now what it feels like to expect to be killed at any moment or have one of the children killed. What a terrible feeling."

Fritz helped get the children ready to walk to the car while Efrim kept talking.

"We could not get away from that other car. We must get a new car with more power. My wife and I agreed that we will give away that terrible car and everything in it if we can be safe again with all our children." Efrim's voice was getting shriller as he talked, which showed the panic he still felt. "We decided that we need to move from here. It is getting too dangerous for people like us around here. I am not a fighter. I'm a banker like my family has been for hundreds of years."

They started for the car, but Efrim's nervous talking did not even pause.

"If you had not come along to help us, we might have stayed in our car, not knowing what else we could do. I think all of us in my family owe our lives to you for your help. Is there anything we can do for you? Would you like to have our car? We have already decided to get rid of it. Now it will only remind us of this awful experience."

"I do need a car!" Fritz did not mean to interrupt but wanted to break the machine-gun pattern of Efrim's high-pitched chatter.

"Really? Did you hear that, dear? Frank needs a car! That will help us feel like we have repaid you a little bit for saving us and our family when we could do noth—"

Efrim's first glimpse of the cars made him stop in his tracks. "Hey, I thought you said we are safe. That is their car ... and there is somebody sitting in mine. What's going on here?"

"Yes, that is their car, but they can do nothing to any of us now. That is my friend who has been following me, trying to get your car started." Using the most calming voice he knew how, Fritz continued, "The men who chased you were all drunk, and in a moment of confusion, they started shooting and killed each other!"

"I thought I heard shots, like there was a small war going on out here. Did you and your friend fight a war for my family?"

"I did not think of it as a war, and I did not have to do any shooting. This war was won by starting the confusion. They did all the shooting," Fritz reported matter-of-factly. "I do not like the idea of shooting someone, but I dislike even more for them to come bullying their way through the area where we live, disturbing our peace and threatening our lives.

"Did you hear that, dear? This man fought a war of freedom for us and our family without using a gun. The least we can do is give him the car. Do you agree?"

"Yes, of course, of course." She was eager and happy to agree.

"I did what I did to protect my family and others in our country from the kind of men these guys are, not for any reward. I couldn't—" Fritz was interrupted.

"We want to give it away. It will always be the car our whole family was almost murdered in. We will be reminded of that every time we use it. If you will accept it, we want you to have it."

"I can see how that will be a terrible memory to live with."

"If you will bring it to Koenigsberg, I will have it repaired for you."

"This is all amazingly generous of you, but if you are determined to give it away anyway, let my friend and me try first." Fritz helped the eight-year-old into the back seat. "If this is my car now, as you said, I will drive you into Koenigsberg, or wherever you were going, while you get warmed up and rested. How does that sound to you?"

"The car is yours! On our way home to Koenigsberg, I will write up the papers you will need for everything you want to do. Even after your small war, I am sure you will be a better driver than I am, especially tonight! I am still shaking! I would like it very much if you could drive for us."

"I would like to; I need to coordinate plans with my friend. I will be back in a few minutes." Fritz went to the front of the car where Val was working under the hood.

"You may not believe it, my friend, but these people want to give me their car for helping them tonight. I need to drive them to where they are going, and then I will drive it home. I would like you to follow us to the turnoff to our house. If you see any problem with this car, flash your lights until you are sure I have seen you, so we can stop and take care of it. If we are OK, you can turn off and go home, and I will go on with Efrim and his family. I will be home as soon as possible. All right? We can come back on Monday to get your motorcycle. It might get busy around here tomorrow. What do you think?"

"That will work. Where is my bike?" Val asked, closing the hood to the car.

"It's up the road about two hundred meters and on the other side, in the woods a little.

"Good. I will hurry. I think this car is ready to start." Val ran up the road first, looking back at Fritz for directions, and soon found his motorcycle. When he was satisfied with the camouflage he added, he hurried back to the cars.

CHAPTER 15

When Fritz pulled the car out onto the road, he saw Val coming slowly up behind, waiting for them to get up to speed.

"Next stop will be home for all you good people. Please feel free to relax or sleep, and enjoy the ride." Fritz was trying his best to sound like a tour guide to help relax some of the tension of the last hour.

"Are you going to do something about those men back there?" Efrim's wife sounded upset and sorry for them.

"I hate to leave them like that, but with the bottles in their car, it looks like they were drunk and shot each other, which is what really happened. With that looking so obvious, there will be no reason to look for anybody else who might have been involved."

"Oh, I see what you mean."

"How did you feel when they were chasing you and shooting with your whole family in the car?" Fritz tried to ask gently.

"We were scared to death, like I said earlier!" Efrim said excitedly.

"How long did they follow you?"

"We first noticed them about twenty minutes after going through Heilsberg. They did not start shooting until five minutes or so before they spun out." Efrim winced at the memory of his terror.

"Is it possible that someone told them you would be coming this way at about this time, carrying some gold?" Looking in the back seat at Frau Goldschmidt for a second, Fritz added, "They could have been waiting for hours to see you go by."

"We tried to be careful in planning and getting ready for this trip. There must be someone at the bank who called ahead to one of the Brownshirts to tell them about us." Efrim had a look of surprise at this new idea. "I have made this trip many times, carrying gold from my bank in Warsaw to Koenigsberg, where my family is from. I can see the anti-Semitism growing in Poland, and I want to raise my young family where they are safe and free from that. This was to be nearly the last time I made this transfer trip; that is why my family is with me. It was time to move them. I have never been followed like this or felt in danger before."

"Maybe someone arranged this whole incident, because they realized it might be their last good chance to get some of your gold." Fritz could see that Efrim and his wife never suspected that their friends or employees might do such a thing. He continued, "What they did not plan on is that their hastily recruited hit squad would get drunk and greedy and start shooting each other. Whoever investigates this will see from the way the men are lying back there, and the bottles in the car, that is what must have happened. If we even moved the men, it would show that someone else was involved, and the investigation would continue into you and your family. The way it is now, there is no good evidence that you were even there."

The car's heater was beginning to warm everybody up a little, and the kids looked like they would be asleep soon. For the next few minutes, Fritz could see a thoughtful look on Efrim's face.

Efrim's fear and shock showed in his every move and word. "Not only did you come along in time to get us out of danger before the men got to us, and fought a war for us without using a gun, but you also kept us from doing something that would have caused our family problems for a long time to come."

Frau Goldschmidt was getting emotional. "We can never repay you! Giving you the car and the gold in it is not enough for the gratitude that I feel. Efrim will be glad to let you know of some of his connections in banking that will make it possible for you to use the bars in the boxes."

The gold too? Though it had been mentioned earlier, Fritz had not realized what "a gift of the car and its contents" fully meant!

"Did I hear you say that this was to be nearly your last transfer trip like this? Fritz was very curious.

"Yes. I will not risk exposing myself or anybody else to the kind of danger I felt as I was hiding in the woods with my family. I have enough gold to continue in my banking business. I do not want anybody to get hurt trying to get me a little more.

The snow had stopped falling, but the road had a layer of compacted snow and ice that made it necessary for Fritz to drive slower than usual. The moon found an opening in the clouds that let its clear bluish light through. This made it much easier to see and put a sparkle on the ice on the road and the trees. His thoughts turned to his pretty new wife, who would probably stay up waiting for him until he got home.

"You have no idea how much that money will help. I just got married yesterday."

"Yesterday?" Efrim was really surprised.

"You should be home with your new wife at this time of night!" his wife said.

"Yes, of course, Frau Goldschmidt, but we had some delays on this trip before we saw you go by with the Brownshirts following you."

"Oh, I'm sorry! You just made me realize that you have not been introduced to my family. My wife's name is Naomi; our eight-year-old is Elsie; our five-year-old is Meta; and Burke is two. Please call us Efrim and Naomi."

"Thank you, Efrim and Naomi. That makes it easier. You have been calling me Frank, which was understandable in the excitement, but my name is Fritz Abbot."

"I am glad I did not have to remember my own name for somebody!" Efrim shrugged his shoulders with a laugh in his voice.

"My friend driving the truck behind us is named Val Adlar. We have become such good friends over the past three years that we had a double wedding to two great girls who are sisters. We all just moved onto a ten-acre farm a few kilometers ahead that has a house large enough for all of us. He will be turning off soon, and I will go on with you. The girls will be glad to see him, and the neighbor who said she would be checking on them will be relieved. This trip today was to bring the last of the things we thought we would need from Neidenberg, where we lived, to our new place. It will be nice for you to come and meet Sigi, my wife, and Val and his wife, Trina. I think you will like them."

"If they are anything like you, I am sure I will!" Naomi sounded happy about the idea.

"From what you were saying when we came out of the woods, it will need to happen soon. It sounds like you have thought about making a major move. Is that right?" Fritz looked over at Efrim, who was sitting on the passenger side of the front seat. Little Burke was lying on the seat between them, with his head on his dad's lap.

"Yes, we have." Efrim stroked the hair of his sleeping son. "This part of the world seems very unsettled and unsafe now that the Great War has ended. Germany is a nation of proud people who do not like how the war ended, with a suddenly unemployed army that came back to a bad economy. So many of these men who cannot find work are angry and only too happy to keep on fighting for anybody who can pay them. There are those in the world who are willing to supply money to a leader who will follow their instructions and take a country in the direction they want it to go. I know some of them!

"Germany has the manpower, the technology, and the resources to be a great nation again. Unfortunately, we do not have the leadership to take us through the pride and selfishness of all those who are seeking power." Efrim looked angry. "The countries of the world act like they want to see our nation ground into a powder that the wind can blow away forever. Our neighboring countries want to take the best parts for themselves. I think there will be many years of trouble ahead for our country—maybe another war."

From what Fritz had seen, he could not disagree. "You have told me your reasons for moving, but you have not told me where you will go that will be better for raising a family. Where is a good place to live?" Fritz could tell that Efrim had thought a lot about it and might have a good idea.

"The bankers of the world have incredible power over most of the nations of the world and will continue to push one against the other to gain profit or power. But America is so strong compared to its neighbors that there is no threat from them in the near future. That means it will be a peaceful place for its people for a long time. I have been there! I've told Naomi about it, and we have decided we want to live there!"

"When do you plan to go, and where will you live? I do not mean to be too nosey, but I want the same things for my family that you do, and I am looking for the best options I can find."

Fritz's directness and honesty were so refreshing to Efrim after being betrayed so recently by someone close to him that it made him smile, and he relaxed back into his seat.

"We will go as soon as we can make the travel and business arrangements. I know some bankers in New York City, so that is where we will live while I get a feel for the business over there."

Efrim continued, "In 1913, there was a law passed in the US, which created the Federal Reserve. As intended by its creators, this sounds like a government agency, but it is privately owned by bankers. This is a banking system that allows banks to loan out as much as ten times the amount of money they have on deposit. A system like that in the most secure nation in the world is a banker's dream! I am quite certain I can create a bank over there that will have branches all over the country. The gold that is in this car is worth almost two hundred thousand dollars in American money. If you were a banker in the United States, you could make a hundred thousand your first year, a hundred fifty thousand your second year, two hundred twenty-five thousand your third year, and three hundred thirty-five thousand dollars your fourth year. In just four years, you can be worth a million and ten thousand dollars! You can continue to grow at 50 percent per year after that. That is a rough idea what banks can do with money they have on their books.

"The numbers I just gave you do not include what you can make from depositors' money! If you can find a safe way to put your gold bars on display in your bank, you can attract a lot of depositors. They will feel their deposit is secure, because of what they can see."

"It seems impossible that they will let you run a bank that way! That has to be illegal or something!" Fritz could not believe what he was hearing.

"You're right, but the law is over twelve years old now. That shows that it is probably going to stay.

"The concept was discovered by goldsmiths before there were banks. I told you my family has been in this business for hundreds of years. That's why my name is Goldschmidt!" Efrim was smiling.

Fritz laughed. "Oh wow, I never thought of that!"

"Instead of carrying around pockets full of gold, people began leaving it with goldsmiths they could trust and who had ways of keeping it safe." Efrim proudly said, "My family was one of the best! The smith would give them a receipt showing ownership, which they could use to claim their gold at any time. It did not take long to begin passing the receipts around the same way they did gold, because they were much easier to handle. The goldsmith eventually noticed that the receipt holder usually did not come back, sometimes for years. Meanwhile, other people came in to see if they could get a receipt for a few months if they paid him some extra when they brought it back. When the borrower brought in or pledged something of value, the smith agreed, and the lending business was born."

"The idea is simple enough, but it is based on greed and fraud." Still not sure it was right, Fritz was shaking his head.

"All of business is simply two people trading things seen by the one receiving as having value. While I was shivering in the woods with my family, my car and the gold in it had no value to me. All I wanted was for all of us to be safe, somewhere far away from the danger of these men. You came along and provided the way to safety, probably just by surprising or scaring one of those men, but you gave me what I valued and wanted most. Does that sound like a good deal? When we were huddled in the woods with our young children and afraid for our lives, it certainly was to us!"

Continuing, Efrim said, "In the lending business I described, everybody gets something they want. Maybe that is why it has been made legal."

"That makes sense. Is there really a chance I could benefit from the banking business like you said?" Looking back at Naomi, Fritz added, "That is something I know nothing about!"

"I'm sure there is," Naomi answered. "I have full confidence in Efrim's experience, knowledge, and ability in the banking business. If he has any questions, he has many people in the business he can ask. I am glad we now have a new friend who can help us with the nonbusiness side of life!"

For the rest of the ride, they talked of family and politics and banking and the love they have for their homeland and the people there. Fritz received an introduction to banking that left him amazed at the power that it had to manage people's needs, from personal to international affairs, for good or for ill. Efrim and Naomi's respect, confidence, and trust in their young new friend grew. A strong bond was formed.

Fritz could see Val's turnoff coming up, so he rolled down his window and waved to him. He saw him wave back just before he got to the turn.

Now that they were near Koenigsberg, Efrim began giving Fritz brief directions and hand signals for getting to his house. Finally, he said, "One more turn, and we will be there!"

Efrim pulled some papers out of the glove box that he had prepared during the ride and put there. "On this first paper, it says I sold you the car for services rendered. The second says I transferred the gold to you in exchange for service of immeasurable value. Both papers are signed 'With gratitude, Efrim Goldschmidt, and Naomi Goldschmidt.' The third page is a letter of introduction asking that you be given every courtesy and respect that I would be given because of your service to me and my family that cannot be repaid. On the fourth one, I have listed some places you can take the gold, where they can hold it for you in a savings account or put some in a checking account so you can use it. There is also a phone number on this fourth one where I can be reached for a reference or anything else. It is probably a good idea to get these things settled before I go to America. I might be needed to help it go smoothly."

From the back seat, Naomi tapped the back of Efrim's seat, which made him look up quickly and say, "Oh, we need to turn right at this corner. Good. Down about three hundred meters is an iron fence on the right. That's our house."

"Our terrible experience today has been made so much better by this time we have had to get to know you." Naomi's natural sweetness came through with her gratitude. "I really would like to meet your wife."

"I would too. I will always feel like we are in debt to you." Efrim put out his hand toward Fritz. "I have never felt so helpless and in so much danger as I did before you came running up to our car."

Fritz returned his firm, warm shake of friendship.

"Our experience in those woods helped us realize what was truly of value in this life." Naomi was almost getting emotional as she said, "Thank you for giving us more time in life to live with and love our family!"

"I am sure Val and our wives would like to get to know you. I will call you on Tuesday, and maybe we can go someplace for dinner." Nodding his head, Fritz added, "I am sure I will have more questions for you by then about banking and America!"

"Of course, we would like to have you come to *our* house for dinner." Naomi sounded a little excited. "I will plan on that."

Fritz helped them take the sleeping kids from the car up to the door. It opened before they got to it, and a butler came out, saying, "You must have been delayed. It is so good to see you, sir. We were beginning to worry." He took Elsie from Fritz and said, "Will you come in too, sir?"

"Thank you, but I need to get some more things out of the car before I go on home."

Fritz saw his puzzled look and thought, *I will bet he asks Efrim about that one!* as he returned to the car.

As he handed the blankets and some things to the butler, Efrim came to the door and said, "I thought I would walk out with you and take a quick look through the car before you go."

Finished with the car, Efrim shook his young friend's hand again. "Again, I thank you."

"You are very welcome. I will talk to you on Tuesday, my friend. Good night."

"Good night."

It was after ten when Fritz finally pulled into his driveway and stopped near the barn. When he opened the front door to the house, Sigi met him with a big hug and a kiss. "I am so glad you're home."

"This might only be our second night here, but when I came through the door, I felt like I was home. That is a really good feeling!" Fritz finished putting down his coat and grabbed Sigi in a big hug and spun around with her. "I could get to like this!"

"Val has been telling us about your encounter with the Brownshirts. This sounds like the most dangerous of them all!"

Val and Trina came up to him. "I am glad you are home too. From what Val has told us, you had quite an adventure!"

"It is true. This is the first time shots were fired at somebody, but I never fired. And it was so dark that I was not in much danger of being hit. I hope everyone has had some dinner; I am hungry. I did not want to be late for our first dinner in our own home."

Sigi said, "Yes, of course. Come to the table, and I will get you something."

"That reminds me," said Fritz. "We all have a dinner appointment at Efrim's house on Tuesday at six o'clock.

"I see the truck is unloaded. Does that mean the beds are all set up?"

"Yes, everybody has their very own place to sleep!" Sigi answered and looked at the smiles on everybody's faces.

Excitedly, Fritz said, "Oh, before we settle down, I would like to show all of you what I brought home with me. Are you all ready to come outside?" He put a piece of chicken and some potatoes on a plate and started to eat.

A few minutes later, they were all dressed and on their way out to the car.

Fritz said, "Efrim and his wife were really scared after being chased by the Brownshirts and angry that their car could not keep them away from those men. While they were hiding in the woods, they decided they would give it away, *with everything in it,* if they could be safe with their kids again. Well, I helped them be safe again, with Val's help, and so they gave it to me—or I should say they *sold* it to me for 'services rendered,' as the papers he included puts it! This is the car, girls! It has enough room for all of us."

"This is a nice car for us," Sigi said, looking happy.

"It's not very old, is it?" Brushing her hand across the seat, Trina said, "The seats are soft, and nothing looks worn."

"What did you mean 'with everything in it'?" asked Val, curious about what it could be. "The only thing I see is this load of boxes in the back seat. Is that what they meant?"

"Yes." Fritz could see Val's eyes starting to get big as he tried to suppress a smile.

"Is that what I think it is?" Val said excitedly.

"Let's lock up the car in the barn. Then we will take a box into the house and see what is in it."

CHAPTER 16

The car had barely stopped inside the barn when Val opened the door to take one of the wooden boxes out. The girls could not help noticing his growing excitement and looked at each other, wondering what this was about. The big, excited smiles their husbands had made them wonder if they should start to worry now or wait until they knew there was a reason to. Trina leaned over to her sister as they walked back to the house and asked, "What are these guys up to now?"

"I do not know, but the key to this mystery is probably in that little box Val is carrying," Sigi guessed.

Fritz picked up a small pry bar from the barn before he closed the doors.

"Maybe they will tell us all about it when the box is opened." Trina had a look of "Oh no, not again" as she continued, "I hope this will not mean more involvement with the Brownshirts!"

"Me too." Sigi hurried to open the house door, where Val was waiting, holding that heavy little box of whatever it was. Val went in quickly.

Sigi waited for Trina. As she went by, Sigi said, "We need time to be with our new husbands." Trina nodded in agreement.

Fritz took the door to let Sigi go in first. "Now we will see what is in these boxes in the car."

"I hope whatever it is will not mean more trouble that will interrupt starting our lives together." She put a hand on his chest and gave him a quick kiss before she turned and went in.

Val was busy trying to open the strong wooden box with his hands. Almost as soon as Fritz handed him the pry bar, he had it open.

There were gasps from the girls, and the boys took deep breaths. Then there was silence for a few seconds as they looked at the bright, shiny bars of gold!

Val was the first to pick up a bar so he could look at it closer, feel its smoothness, and absorb some of the richness and wealth it represented. "I have only seen gold a few times—and certainly not like this." He rubbed the bar against his cheek to feel the wonder of it.

The others picked up bars and had similar reactions and feelings.

Level-headed Sigi was the first to say something to bring everybody back to reality. "This is wonderful, but it looks like trouble to me. We cannot buy groceries with it, and how do we explain coming into this much money?"

"You are right, sweetheart. For the last two hours or so, since leaving the Brownshirts, I have been thinking about this. With Efrim's help, I have some ideas to tell you all about so we can decide what to do. Because Val has been with me in every incident that brought us to where we are now, I see him as half owner in this gold *and* in the payroll we have.

"I think we really hurt the Brownshirts by keeping this much money out of their hands, which was our original objective. They are going to want answers about where it all went. If the bills in the payroll have identifying marks on them, they can be traced back to us if we use them. The boxes of gold bars will be easy to spot when they are moved, because a bank will need to be involved. I think we should let Efrim deposit the gold in his own account in the bank, just as he planned. That will make it look like those guys chasing him missed or never saw him, and their frustration made them so angry that they ended up on the side of the road."

Val said, "We can also give him the payroll to check for markings, and if they are OK, some of that can go in the same deposit, and we could keep some for our own use."

Trina was catching the possibilities. "It would be great if he could then divide the money into two accounts, one for you and one for Val so that we can be more independent if we want to be."

"That would be great." Sigi was getting hopeful. "Do you think he can do that, Fritz?"

"I am not a banker, so I do not know, but I believe if anybody can, it is Efrim. He plans to go to America and start his own bank." Fritz was already getting accustomed to the idea of having a large amount of money.

"I will tell you some of the reasons Efrim gave me for starting a bank in America and how much money can be made when we have more time. I am sure you will like the idea. For tonight, I think we all need to get some sleep. Tomorrow, we can talk more about any ideas or questions we come up with."

Printed in the United States
by Baker & Taylor Publisher Services